DEVILS
COURTYARD

DEVILS
COURTYARD

JON ST THOMAS

authorHOUSE®

AuthorHouse™
1663 Liberty Drive
Bloomington, IN 47403
www.authorhouse.com
Phone: 1 (800) 839-8640

Published by AuthorHouse 09/03/2015

ISBN: 978-1-5049-3378-0 (sc)
ISBN: 978-1-5049-3377-3 (e)

POISON

Part One

I looked out over the rolling fields and patches of timber, laid out from the caged window of the transport van conveying me from the Rock (Florida State Prison's Main Unit) to the more dreaded East Unit sited a few miles away. All the land, as far as the eye could see, was state property; still, all in all, a pleasant sight for someone who hadn't seen the outside for a spell, having spent the past few weeks in confinement at the Rock undergoing an investigation.

The short journey on an internal access road crossed the New River via a bridge which rumbled under the Van's tires, and I heard someone mention The River Styx. I half listened to the conversations of the prisoners being transported with me, with most of the talk centered on our destination, the East Unit; a mix of speculation, bluster and posturing, mingling with undertones of fear which they attempted to hide. For the East Unit had a fearsome reputation, and was considered to be the end of the line for convicts; a place where prison officials sent all the incorrigible and uncontrollable convicts and those they didn't know what else to do with.

The East unit was said to separate the wheat from the chaff; those who were bad, and those who just thought they were bad. Regardless of which you were, it was certain that you would not come away from the East Unit untouched. I knew most of those on the van with me were wondering how they would measure up in the days and weeks ahead.

Approaching the back vehicle gate giving entry to the East Unit from the access road, I could see the long tan-colored building stretching out before me: well over a quarter mile in length, with wings sprouting out from a central corridor; six wings on the east side and six wings on the west side, with a short wing extending north from the rest. We could see it clearly through the windows of the van.

"That's Q wing -," one of those in the van said, "- it's where they hold death row prisoners whose death warrants have been signed and are about to be executed." Indicating the western side, he continued, "The execution chamber is on this side on the bottom floor, the last three windows on the end." Another spoke up, saying, "The first two wings next to it on this side is 'R' and 'S' wings which house death row prisoners." These were attempts at showing the rest of us how knowledgeable they were about the East Unit, to make us, and perhaps themselves, believe this was not their first trip here.

Gazing out the van windows at the massive structure laid out before us, I thought it had the look of a mythical creature trying to rise out of the earth, holding it, not knowing then how apt the observation would prove to be, as the beast that eats its children.

As the van entered the sally port between the two rows of fences topped with barbed wire, Pony, the prisoner seated next to me who I knew in passing from the Rock, said, "Don't worry Poison, you'll do fine. You already know a lot of people here."

"I imagine so", I replied, continuing to peer out the windows as the driver did the inspection walk around the vehicle, searching for contraband, or perhaps a prisoner who might have attached themselves to the under carriage in an escape bid; crazier things had happened in the past. I could see and hear guard dogs barking madly within the runs on each side of the sally port at the officer, as he did the inspection.

"They have dogs between the fences," I observed, just to say something.

"Yeah, that is one of the security measures to prevent escapes. They train the dog to hate convicts, only getting the meanest dogs. They got an

English bulldog in the run between the recreation field fences who ain't got nothing but truth, tears up car tires as fast as they give them to him," one of the prisoners said.

"They have to switch the dogs around after a time, as either they go crazy like a lot of convicts do, or they make friends with the convicts, making them ineffective. So they have to be taken out to be retrained or gotten rid of," Pony added.

Getting back into the van as the guard in the tower next to the sally port opened the interior gate, the driver began the slow maneuver into the prison property, passing all six wings on the west side, reaching to the end of the wings. There were short gaps in between them, about one hundred feet across. At the end of W-wing, the last wing, there was another large structure running east and west, connected to the rest by the main corridor; the spinal column of the structure.

"That's Maintenance, with the food service above it. The docking area is where all the trucks deliver the supplies to run the prison," Pony said, as he van continued on its slow drive.

On the other side was a huge fenced-in recreation field, and I could see the dogs in the runs there, following the van as far as they could to the end of the runs. The van stopped before a steep ramp, with stairs leading up at its far end next to the building.

The officers let us out of the van and lined us up with our property before escorting us up the ramp, through the double steel doors and into a long wide hallway. Unlike in other prisons, the corridor was its main floor, which would be considered the second floor elsewhere. This corridor continued onward till it ended up with another wing leg coming out the west side, which contained only two floors: Medical on the main corridor and the Education Department below.

To the left was the Food Service Department, staff dining, and staff canteen. The latter two were down at the far end of the corridor, just before reaching the grill gate separating the hallway from the main corridor. To our right was a bank of windows looking out over the area between the building and the Medical/Education wing. Near the gate, there was a staff barber and shoeshine shop side by side.

The set of bars and gates separating the hallway from the main corridor stretched fifteen feet overhead. There was an electronically operated pedestrian gate on either end, and a large vehicle gate which was manually operated with a large key at the center. The control room set directly across the intersection -which was known as Time's Square - was large and fronted with thick bullet proof glass, and its panels controlled all the electronic gates throughout the prison.

As the officer in the control room opened the pedestrian gate on the right side of the hallway, the officer escorting us directed us onto benches to the right, across from the control room and to one side of a large office area. Next to the hallway was the Captain's office. Its door was closed.

Placing our property down, we all took seats on the benches as directed, with the escort officers telling us, "Hold the noise down. Someone will be coming to check you out and process you." They turned in the files and paperwork into the slots in the control room before going back out the gate we had come in for the drive back to the Main Unit.

Seated on the benches, we could hear the loud echoes and clamor coming from the long corridor north of us. The combination of the hum and the loud yells of voices, overlaid with the slamming and turning of the Folger Adam keys in the locks (on steel doors on the wings and on the doors which led to other areas), as well as the opening and shutting of the electronic gates with officers, staff and convicts, passing through Time's Square.

The passing convicts gawked at us, the newly arrived convicts, scanning for homeboys, friends, people they might know, enemies or someone to victimize. I got more than a passing glance from those passing by, but only nodded to them.

We were only seated on the benches for a few minutes before the Captain made his appearance through the office door to the right of us, stepping to the control room to collect a clipboard that the officer inside passed out to him through the slot. The captain was an older man who looked to be in his forties wearing a tan straw Stetson, with an unlit chewed stogie stuck in the corner of his mouth. He stood by the control room looking over the clipboard, which contained the roster of our names and prison numbers, before coming over to where we were seated on the benches and saying, "When I call out your names, answer up".

He called out the ten names and received the response accordingly. He then said, "Welcome to the East Unit boys, my name is Captain Combs. I don't care what brought you to the East Unit. From this point, you start out with a fresh slate. But if you fuck up, you can give your soul to Jesus because your ass will be mine." He paused. "We have a few simple rules here. Respect my officers and do what they tell you to do and you will get along just fine. If you have a problem with an officer and you can't resolve it, you come see me and we will get it straightened out. But whatever you do, don't lie to me, for I can't stand a liar."

The captain, walking down the seated line, scanned our faces, and stopped when he reached me. He blew out his breath, he removed the chewed up stogy from the corner of his mouth and used it as a pointer at me, and asked, "You, what's your name?"

"Keith Marks."

Captain Combs looked it up on the roster in his hand. He stuck the stogy back into the corner of his mouth and took an ink pen from his shirt pocket, and used it to make a change and notation on the roster. Then, looking at me again, he asked, "And what do they call you?"

"Keith"

"No, I mean the name you go by here, your gal name?"

"Oh... Poison, is what they call me."

"Well I am certain whoever gave you that name had a very good reason for doing so..."

The convicts at the Main Unit (the Rock) had given me the name while I was there. When I had come there eight months before, I hadn't had any nickname, nor had I chosen one for myself. I was fresh off the streets and didn't know anyone in the Florida prison system. As young white, petite and with a feminine demeanor, it didn't take a rocket scientist to discern that I might be gay or of that persuasion.

Not that I was a fresh fish, or new cock to the prison systems. I had already spent time in the boys' schools and youth prisons up north, which they called reformatories. I just never acquired a drag queen name; up to that time, they would call me "Little Bit". Even now, I was only 5'6" tall and one hundred and twenty five pounds.

I was at the Rock only a few weeks when a crew tried to take me off in the shower above the kitchen, to run a train on me, using the pretext that the laundry man wanted to see me about the clothing alterations I had asked about. The laundry room was upstairs, next to the showers. As I passed the darkened shower, I was grabbed by someone inside, who put me in a light yoke hold and pulled me into the shower area. The young convict who had deceived me to come up there with him started fumbling with my belt and pants to get them off me. I could sense others waiting within the darkened shower, their forms moving about, laughing and whispering, awaiting their turn at the new whit sissy who didn't have enough sense to hook up with anyone.

Now as I said, I wasn't new to the game or to prison. I had been living in the streets for the most part of my life since I was nine, state raised even before then and in and out of boys' schools and reformatories since I was ten. A small boy turning tricks in the streets for survival and within prison needed an edge. I had been raped in prisons, boys' schools and on the streets, and it had never been a pleasant experience. So, when the whores on the stroll offered to teach me how to use a knife, I had jumped at the chance to learn and I had been well taught by them in the use of knife or straight razor.

I had two knives concealed on me, strapped to my forearms under the long sleeved shirt I was wearing, both with the handles pointing toward my wrists, ready to be drawn. I might have been fresh to this prison - nonetheless I wasn't naive enough to believe the other prisoners wouldn't try me. Therefore, one of the first things I had obtained upon my arrival were the knives and the sheaths to hold them in place.

It was a wonder what a blow-job would get you in a place like the rock, especially if you were as young, feminine, tender and fairly good looking as I was. Often, people would ask me if I was a Native American as I had the blue-black hair, high cheek bones and aquiline nose, with a slight lump in it (from a broken nose which hadn't been set properly, courtesy of a foster parent who believed small children should be seen and not heard). But my eyes were deep blue, almost violet, sometimes appearing stormy gray in certain lights. It's possible I had some Native American or <deepc> tarter from the Russian steppes in my ancestry. However, I was a stray mutt who came with no pedigree.

I had been abandoned as a baby and never knew who my parents were; thus anything was possible, and there were no boundaries. I would reluctantly say "yes" to anyone asking me if I was Indian, just to forestall the further questioning. Most times I could get things in prison without giving up some sex; just some sweet talk and implied future delights. Yet in this case, I paid in trade for the knives and sheaths, ensuring silence about them. He might have talked about the blow job he received from me but not about what he had given me in exchange for it.

Pulling my left knife from its sheath with my right hand, I brought its edge cross the throat of the one in front of me as he was fumbling with my belt and pants. I didn't want to have to fight my way free with the burden of my pants and underwear around my knees. Up to this point I hadn't really resisted, letting them think I was going to be an easy take off, while I got a feel for my surroundings. Thus, the one behind held me only lightly in the yoke.

As the one in front grabbed is throat, yelled and fell away, I stepped to the right and back of the one holding me, and exposing his front, slammed the blade into his groin area. I twisted it while it was inside him to break the vacuum hold and to disable him, as I was going for maximum damage, not knowing how many others I was facing. He yelled out, "The bitch's got a shank," as he released his hold and grabbed himself. This is when the melee within the shower area began.

It was very dark inside the shower area with the only light coming through the doorway. I couldn't really see anything, just shapes, yet I knew everything around me was fair game. I pulled out my other knife and began striking out at anything between me and the doorway, making it there with a few minor scratches, only to be punched in the eye by a fist as I was going through.

The punch jolted and flamed up my anger, and instinctively, I started to head back to get the one who punched me, but caught myself, realizing that they were too many. My survival instincts kicked in, telling me to bail out while I could. So I left them to it and ran out, down the stairs and walking calmly across the common courtyard which separated the cell-blocks from the multipurpose building I had just come from.

Going back to the ten-man cell I was assigned to on D-floor, I stripped out of the clothes I had on, and washed up, checking for wounds as I did so and discovering only the scratches, and what was going to be a beautiful shiner. I put on clean clothes.

The clothes I had been wearing were soaked in blood front and back, very little of which was mine. I rinsed the bloody clothes in the toilet, flushing until all the blood was out of them, then stuck them in a bucket of bleach water to soak.

As I had come into the cell on D-floor, one of my cell partners had asked, "Christ, what happened to you?" seeing all the blood on my clothes and the puffy eye. He had thought I had been stabbed. "Nothing-" I had said, "-just a little misunderstanding" and left at that. He left it alone as well, as it was none of his business, and I did not invite him to get involved.

I had cleaned off the knives, which I had stuck in my waistband as I came off the stairs to cross the courtyard to the cell-blocks, before returning them to their sheaths and placing them on my forearms. At this point, I couldn't know whether there would be any follow up from the affair in the shower, but I intended to be ready for whatever might come my way.

Greg, another one of my cell partners, volunteered to go get some ice for the eye. "Thanks, I would appreciate that," I replied. The adrenaline was still flowing, as well as the tremors I attempted to conceal as the shock set in.

Nothing else happened that day, or any other day, because the shower tally was three dead and three others in critical condition in the hospital outside, and four others with cuts that were stitched up at the prison hospital emergency room. No one brought my name into it, although everyone knew I had been responsible, as it was the talk of the prison. Not brought to the attention of the prison officials, the shower incident was written off by them as feuding among rivals.

I can only say for certain that I caused the death of the one who had me in the yoke hold, as the knife had severed the femoral artery when the blade struck him in the groin. The one whose throat I cut survived, the blade only having just nicked the jugular vein. Two of those in the outside hospital were mine. The others, I could never be certain of, as it was dark in there and I wasn't the only one with a knife; it had been pretty intense and wild for a while in there, before I was able to break free.

I got credit for all the deaths and cuttings, according to some of the remarks meant for me to hear as I was passing by, with no one saying anything to me directly. Remarks like "They say dynamite comes in small packages," in reference to my size, or "I told them fools quiet don't mean scared, it's the quiet ones you got to watch out for."

The one which got me tagged with name "Poison" was, "The bitch should come with a warning label like the skull and crossbones they have on poison bottles, for he is pure poison with a blade." After the remark got around, everyone started calling me "Poison": a kind of backhanded compliment and term of respect for standing up for myself like that.

No one else sought to try me like that. I did have a rainbow black eye which took a few weeks to completely go away. I imagined the other convicts respected the fact that I had heart to stand up for myself even though I was a sissy queen, according to the convict code that you shouldn't have a knife unless you were willing to put it to use if need be. I also believed that the fact that I was a sissy kept others from making any issue out of the shower incident; after all, I had just played out the hand that they dealt.

Having gotten by with that, the next few months I did pretty well, getting settled in and lining up regular customers willing to provide me with things in exchange for sexual favors. I soon had everything I need or wanted.

My trip to the East Unit from the Rock had come about as a result of one my cell partners - Joe. He had brought in a load of knives from the furniture factory to sell, with the officers hot on his trail. Panicking because he knew the guards were coming to the cell, Joe had stuck the knives under my mattress, as I was out of the cell at the time of inspection. When the guards found the knives, they had me called back to the cell to ask me about them.

I knew whose knives they were and the officers knew as well, but it wasn't my place to tell them, and Joe wasn't man enough to own up. Therefore, I went to confinement for investigation, and Joe paid to make the disciplinary report go away. However, I don't think he wanted to face me about him throwing me to the wolves like that, concerned about what I might do to him. So, I became East Unit bound with less than nine months within the chain gang prison system; already being sent to the end of the line.

Captain Combs continued, "How old are you?"

"Eighteen."

"Jesus, you don't look a day over fourteen." Which was true. I had no facial hair and scant body hair. "Well Poison, I am going to send you down to live with the rest of the gals on K-wing. When you get down there, you find yourself a man and settle down. Cause if I hear you're causing problems for my boys, I will bury your ass so far behind gate thirteen that they will have to pump sunlight and air to you, you got me?"

"Yes sir."

"Now for the rest of you, act like men and you'll be treated as men. Do your time. You're going to be here whether you like it or not, so you might as well make the best of it." Handing the roster to the prisoner from the laundry who had just come into Times Square, he said, "Now he will get you squared away with your clothing, bedroll and issue. Just remember what I told you, and you'll get along fine."

Collecting our property, we followed the laundry prisoner from Times Square, through the east pedestrian gate which led to the cell-blocks. The east hallway leading off Times Square was where Classification had their offices, along with the warden and the assistant warden. There was a visiting park for open population, with the security visiting area for prisoners awaiting execution separated from visitors by glass. The rest of death row visitation took place in the staff conference room within the Captain's office.

The prisoner escorting us was named "Radio". He was giving us the rundown and tour of the places we passed by. The first set of double doors to our right as we left Times Square via the electronic gate going north was the Chapel. Glancing through the thick glass windows inset in the steel doors, I could rows of pews leading up to the altar. There were some convicts mingling inside. After the chapel and down the corridor to the left was the library, and two prisoner dining halls. Across the hallway from them was the gym; through the locked doors, also steel, I could hear the squeak of tennis shoes on the wooden floor and the shouts of the players shooting a game of hoops.

Radio, who by this time had let us know whatever we needed from the laundry, we should come see him as it was his main hustle, said, "They show movies in the gym every weekend, but you have to supply your own popcorn or snacks." I peered through the small square of thick glass, seeing a row if steps leading down to the gym floor, with wooden bleachers set in rows along either side of the stairway, incorporated as part of the stairs, descending to the gym floor twelve feet below us. Across the wooden gym floor was a stage with a white screen.

The place gave off an eerie vibe; just looking in through the glass I could tell it was a death trap. I could imagine what went on with the doors locked and most of the lights out, recalling the movies at the Rock where I never got to see many all the way through, as something would always happen, usually fights or stabbings. I did have some good times up in the projection room above the theater area though, and even got private screenings of movies.

Passing through another set of gates, the laundry and the barber shop were set side by side on our right. The prisoner's canteen was across the hall. After a short gap, the cell-block wings began, all marked with a sign above the door, with officers standing in the doorways, monitoring not only the convict traffic in the corridor but also the ones of the wing behind them.

We were in the laundry for half an hour getting our bedrolls, laundry and clothing issued, then tagged along with the issue of supplies: soap, toilet paper, toothbrush, tooth paste and razors. The convicts working in the issue room ogled me, it being obvious I was a gal boy. They made it a point to let me know they were paying special attention to the clothes issued to me, to ensure they fit properly, then telling me, "If you need to have them altered in anyway come see us."

"Yes, and I know what you want from me", I thought to myself. Men can be so obvious at times. I thanked them nicely with a smile and demure look, promising nothing yet leaving the door open. You don't make money by slamming doors; the business will flop. Playing coy and nice cost me nothing, and I never knew what the future would hold.

I knew my first order of business would be to replace my knives, which I was forced to leave behind at the Rock, though I did have a scalpel from the clinic with me. But it's not the same as a good blade; it came in handy to get someone off me but that's about it, unless I got a lucky shot. I preferred the knife's blade.

Once all of us had gotten our laundry issued, Radio handed each of us a slip of paper with our cell housing location on it. His hand lingered on mine with eye contact when he passed me the slip of paper, letting me know he was interested. I knew I would get a lot of that over the course of the next few days and weeks, and I wasn't about to jump into anything without first scoping out they lay of the land.

I had seen too many bad things happen to gals who jumped at the first looking thing that came along: pretty outside doesn't mean pretty inside. With my kind of luck, I'd end up with gorilla love - the kind of man who gets his nose wide open with one shot of sex, while having the attitude that you're all his or it's the graveyards. I certainly didn't need that kind of drama in my life, not when there were so many flowers to be plucked, and money to be made doing it; keeping them at a distance and effectively informing them that it's strictly business. I didn't want any emotional entanglements; brave words, where the heart has a mind of its own.

K-wing was the second wing to the right. There were four open population wings on each side. Then came gate thirteen with five confinement wings; R-wing housed death row while S-wing housed death row overflow and administrative confinement. P-wing was for long term confinement, and N-wing was administrative and disciplinary confinement. Q-wing held a few death row prisoners, with most of the prisoners in it being those who caused problems wherever they went within the prison, or those with fresh charges.

On the right side of the main corridor were J, K, L, and M-wings; then gate thirteen, then N and P-wings. On the left side were W, V, U and T-wings, gate thirteen, then S and R- wings, with Q extended outward at the end of the corridor.

As we passed J and W-wings, the convicts crowded the doorways and the windows of the day-room which looked out onto the corridor, in order to see who had come that day. I got more than my fair share of attention, with blown kisses and ribald comments about sex, even hearing my name called while recognizing more than a few I knew from the Rock.

Each place has its own aura and atmosphere. At the Rock, the tension and violence was a palpable thing that you could sense whenever you stepped out of the cell. In the East Unit, the tension was wound very tight, so that any vibration would set thrumming the miasma of misery, despair, anger, rage, suffering, terror and violence permeating throughout, with the feel of death stalking the hallways waiting to claim another victim.

It was a feeling I had had at only one other place - the Flattop, Florida's old death row which had been built within the Rock's fifty four acre compound over by the hospital. A prison within a prison, and the only one built in Florida with a twenty foot concrete wall around it. At The Flattop, it was an old evil extended past its time, shifting into dust while at the East Unit, it was vibrant and alive. It kept you on edge, and looking over your shoulder to make certain who was behind you. You could feel, and almost taste its presence.

At the K-wing doorway, Radio stopped and stuck his head inside the doorway and yelled, "Got another for you Officer King."

"Send her in," came the reply from within the officer's station inside. It was to the left as you entered the wing, and was really nothing more than a closer with a steel security screen door, where the officer kept supplies for the prisoners and his personal belongings such as lunch, coat, hat etc., to keep them from disappearing. Next to the office was a slanted box with a lid which was bolted to the wall. It held the wing log and for the officer to use for writing purposes.

I was amused that the officer who had charge of a wing full of queens was named King. Officer King was in his forties, overweight with ruddy features and thinning brown hair. I stopped outside the office door, as I saw he was eating a sandwich and chips. "Come over here, I don't bite," he said. I stepped to the doorway, and he said, "My, ain't you a sweet thing… I can see you're going to be a problem… how old are you?"

"Eighteen, and I won't be a problem unless you make me one."

"Feisty little thing ain't you? We'll see how that attitude fares over the next few weeks, with all the bandits that will be coming at you. What name do you go by in here?" He took a bite from the sandwich.

"Poison."

"Oh ho, Poison huh? I'd like to know the story behind that one. I'm sure it's a humdinger. I'm going to tell you like I tell all the rest of the gals, you bring a trick or your lover on the wing, you check in with me first. I like to know who's on my wing. No fucking or sucking in the showers, broom closets or laundry rooms. Use the cells, that's what the beds are for, and for God's sake hang a curtain and have someone watch out for you. I make enough noise when I make my rounds, so you will have time enough to get straight. But I never know when my sergeant might decide to take a walk through and I don't need him seeing shit like that going on my wing… Makes me look bad."

By now, some of the other queens were doing drive-byes to check me out. Two of them stopped in the doorway.

"Now these ladies will let you know whatever else you need to know. What cell did they put you in?"

"First floor, cell seven."

"Oh, next door to Freyda… I'm sure you are going to love that. Duchess, show Poison here where her cell is at, and get away from my door and let me finish my lunch."

Duchess, slender with brown hair, and blue eyes accented with mascara and false eyelashes, said, "Come on dearie, I'll show you where you'll be sleeping at. Oh and this is Cherry by the way."

Cherry was a stocky redhead with brown eyes. She was Duchess' sidekick. Cherry picked up my property, leaving me with the laundry issue and bedroll. Duchess continued speaking, "Poison, that's a hell of a name, who came up with that one?" Not waiting for an answer, he said, "Officer King is really a sweetheart. Just don't get on his bad side, as this is the only wing us girls can live on. This is his wing five days a week. King's off Saturdays and Sundays. Usually then, we get Mr. Green, who is alright but job-scared. If not Green then it's a jackpot choice. One thing with King is, whoever comes on the wing to see you has to pay the toll."

"The toll? What's that?"

"You saw the sandwich and chips King was eating."

"Yeah."

"Well that's a toll. They have to drop something by the office for him letting them on the wing: sandwich from the kitchen, sodas, honey bun, candy bar, chips or whatever from the canteen. It lets him know you appreciate him, and he does look out for us girls. If you have problems with your lover or boyfriend, you keep it off the wing and take it out on the Rec field or gym. He doesn't like a lot of drama on his wing. Likes it nice and quiet, relaxed and smooth. However, if you need something, he'll do his best to see that you get it. You couldn't ask for a better wing officer."

He said all this as we were walking down the stairs to the first floor. Some of the others living on the wing passed by saying "hi" to Duchess, but really were checking me out. Duchess named them off, "Misty, Gerty, Candy, Sassy, Betty, Katz, Dusty, Love -," so many I couldn't keep track of them all. The wing held ninety-seven prisoners, only about thirty of whom were queens. The rest were a selection of bisexual boys, pressure punks, the confused, and the honey-bun tarts (who did it only for canteen); the whole prison was a gamut of alternative lifestyles.

"Now about your neighbor in cell eight, Freyda, I feel for you having to live next door to her. She don't ever shut that trap of hers unless she has a dick in her mouth or eating. Even then, I think she tries to talk around it." Indeed, I could hear a loud voice coming out of the cell next door. Cherry went into cell seven. She hadn't said anything until now, when she said, "We'll let you get settled in, and we'll be back to talk later. If you need anything, give us a holler."

Both of them left, leaving me alone in my new home for at least a minute or so, but as began cleaning up my cell and stowing my property away, the other prisoners kept interrupting me to introduce themselves, some bearing gifts of cleaning supplies or food. They were curious to see the new girl, to evaluate what kind of threat she would pose to their positions among the other queens, while also letting me know how they ranked themselves; the usual sweetness as cover for some nosy conniving bitches, with a few genuine nice ones among the crowd. But otherwise, it was a gaggle of prima donnas, drama queens, queen bees and melt clowns that was all too familiar to me from my years in the streets, boys' schools and reformatories.

All of them were taking up time and space, which was prolonging the time for me to get settled in. Nonetheless, I was learning all sorts of useful information; who to see for lingerie, panties, makeup and perfumes; which among them were in relationship, and what their husbands or boyfriends were like; who had just recently broken up with their lover or was going through difficulties in their relationships. Also, men who to watch out for (this one taken with a grain of salt, as they could be bad apples or just a ploy to keep me away from them). All the usual gossip among Queens, pretending to know everything about everyone and talking about it all among themselves.

I was still in the middle of all the gossip tad bits, when Officer King hollered from the station. "Poison, bring your ass here." I heard him above the chatter of those around me and the loud voice from next door, and said, "Excuse me ladies and gentle people, I have to go see what the officer wants of me," leaving them there to talk among themselves - more than likely about me - as soon as I stepped out of earshot.

I went back upstairs, where I found a convict in whites waiting on the other side of the door of the wing with grocery bags in his arms. Seeing me come up the stairs he asked, "You Poison?"

"That's her", Officer King said.

"Some of the fellas from the Rock sent you a care package to welcome you to the East Unit."

"My mother always told me not to accept anything from strangers," I said. Not that I ever knew my mother. But it sounded like advice a mother would give, especially within the prison environment where there are usually strings attached to it. You don't even want to think about or go there at all if it's possible to avoid them.

"Oh you know these guys. Snake said no strings attached. Joe also sent some money over from the Rock to be put on the books for you. This stuff is just for being stand-up, and to welcome you. There is a note which goes with this, here." He handed me the bags, and took the note from his shirt pocket to hand it over to me, tucking it into the bag nearest to him. "The guys say they know you just got out of confinement at the Rock. This stuff is just to tide you over until you get on your feet. Stop by the canteen after chow, and I'll have dinner and sodas waiting for you. Just ask for Richie."

"Okay, tell them I said thank you and I'll get back with them later," I said, as Richie left the wing. Before turning to go back down to my cell, I asked Officer King, "You want anything in here?" Waving me away he said, "No, go ahead, I'm good. Richie already took care of it. I see you're a popular girl. I don't get many girls who get care packages and ain't been on the wing a good hot hour."

"Thanks for letting me get it," I said, then turning to go back to my cell after seeing him shake his hand as if to say it was nothing. I was a little self-conscious with the two large bags I held in my arms, as I could feel the eyes of the others on me. It made me wonder what kind of problems it might create with some of them later on; jealousy and envy can be very spiteful - even more so with a bitch.

I was surprised to see that everyone had left, and that someone else had replaced them, when returning my cell. "Where is everyone? And who are you?" I asked the person making up my bed from the bedroll I had been provided.

Looking up from making the bed, he said, "Hi, come on in; I'll be finished with this in a second. You need to put that stuff away. I'm Mimi, I ran the rest of the whores off. They were just getting in the way, all they want to do is yap, yap, yap, and not let you get a thing done."

I couldn't argue with that. Stepping into the cell, I made my way past Mimi to the locker, where I began unpacking the bags. The boys hadn't forgotten anything: soap, deodorant, toothpaste, toothbrush, coffee, mirror, hairbrush, lotion, shampoo, baby powder, it was all there. The other bag was packed with goodies: cakes, candies, cookies, sodas, bread, peanut butter, jelly, and even a couple of pints of ice cream with bowls, spoons and cups.

"There," said Mimi behind me, patting the made up bed a couple of times before sitting down on it, "looks like your friends take good care of you... I could see the green floating out of your cell from those other whores when Kingee called you up there to pick up those bags. Jealous-hearted bitches who want all the men for themselves, even the ones they can't have. Which is why I ran them all off. Otherwise, they would have taken inventory of everything, then sniped at you behind your back... How in the world did a pretty thing like you get the name Poison?"

"Long story," I said, looking up from the note Snake had sent with the bags. It said he had sent me a friend and I would know what he meant. I looked at everything, and nothing I had seen could be anything like he said. Then it dawned on me that the bags had been doubled. I had thought it was so, in order to strengthen them to resist the load of the groceries. I decided to investigate the bags a little closer. Picking up the first, I pulled it apart, finding some reefer and rolling paper in the first, and a beautiful little dagger in the second.

"Goody," Mimi said from the bed. "They know a girl needs something to relax with after the ride over here. This ain't like the Rock where you can carry openly or barely concealed. You need to find a spot they won't check if you plan on carrying it around on you."

First I gave him a strange look, as what were in the bags were none of his business, and second, it was bad manners to even mention seeing something like that in prison. "See and don't see" was the convict rule. However, as I soon learned, Mimi was the exception to most rules. He was completely guileless and without a clue as to proper prison manners. He just forged blithely ahead without glancing back.

He was short, with red brown hair which was almost an auburn - neither red nor brown - with blond tints throughout; the kind of hair a woman would kill to have, and not from a bottle. Mimi had hazel eyes which kept shifting colors depending on his mood or the light to blue, green, gold or brown, and had peach-cream skin hinted lightly with freckles, and a splash of them across his snub nose. He had gamine features and looked roughly one hundred and twenty five pounds soaking wet with rocks in his pockets.

You could tell he was Irish stock, probably a fiery Irish with his merry spirit. "Oh don't worry, I won't say anything to anyone," he said, "My lips are sealed but you better eat that ice cream before it melts all over your locker."

"Well then, move over and let me sit down. Least I can do is share this with you since you were kind enough to help out."

Mimi scooted over, and we ended up making ice cream floats, eating them with Oreo cookies while getting to know each other better. Mimi was from South Florida, Palm Beach County, and his family owned car dealerships throughout South Florida by the name of "Cleary Motors". He was the youngest of seven children, his siblings being two boys and four girls, all of whom doted on him.

He had gotten four years for stealing high end imports; I looked at him oddly when he explained this, as you were never supposed to let someone know you were a short-timer. This was in the event that someone with a lot time might try to jam yours to keep you around. But again, that was Mimi. "Dear old dad still thinks - to this day - that I was stealing the Ferraris, Maseratis, Mercedes, Bentleys and Rolls Royces for joy rides, when really I was selling them to exporters and using the money on my own race cars. Racing is an expensive hobby…"

"And I'm the green goblin," I thought. The racing was just an excuse, and I felt like he got a thrill from stealing them.

"You don't talk much do you?" he asked.

"No, you learn more by listening then talking."

"That's okay. I talk enough for both of us."

Getting up and pounding on the wall of cell eight and hollering, "Shut up that noise you old sea hag," he then turned to me saying, "Watch, she'll be over here in a minute. Whatever you do, don't start a conversation, or we will never get rid of her."

"Why'd you pound the wall for?"

"You'll see, just watch."

Just then, Freyda stepped around the corner of the door into the cell. "Who in the hell are you calling a sea hag? You fucking sawed off midget who escaped from a carnival side show."

"You, you old ding bat Freyda, I want you to meet my friend Poison."

Freda was in his thirties, tall, with brown hair and eyes, with pleasant features and thick sear on the front left side of his neck. "Hi Poison." Then words just poured out of his mouth so fast I couldn't keep u with them, so I just waved at him.

Mimi said, "Alright Freyda, you two have met, now shut up and go away."

"Who are to tell me to shut up? You don't tell me to shut up…," and so on she continued.

"I just did, now scat-shoo! Go the hell away," Mimi said waving her hands in a shooting motion.

"Well I never…" Grumbling to himself, Freyda turned and left, going back next door where the loud droning rumble continued…

"What was that about?" I asked Mimi.

"I just wanted you to see her, so you don't make the mistake of striking up a conversation. That girl don't ever shut up. She'll be the first thing you hear in the morning when you wake up, and the last thing you'll hear at night before you go to sleep. You see the scar on her neck?"

"Yeah, what about it?"

"One of her former lovers cut her throat right up by the officer's station upstairs. It only nicked the jugular but it was squirting out pretty good. She was yapping the whole time. Captain Combs had to tell her to shut up and keep the pressure on the wound, or she would've bled to death before they got her to the clinic. We have some real live wires around here."

"Which reminds me, I wonder what happened to Duchess and Cherry? They said they would be back," I said.

"Those two are probably in the cell running a train on Joe, Duchess' old man. Or I shouldn't be saying that, as I don't know what they do in the cell together. Some kind of threesome. You have to overlook Duchess sometimes, as she actually believes she runs the wing, that God died and left her in charge."

"She seemed nice."

"Yeah, she'd like for you to think butter wouldn't melt in her mouth but really, at heart she's just a skanky bitch. Cherry's alright whenever you can get her away from Duchess, which isn't often, as Duchess keeps her on a tight leash. I'd trust Duchess about as far as I could throw her.

Mimi continued, "See you don't have much in the way of clothes. Come up to my house and we will get you fitted out properly. I can't have my girlfriend looking like she fell off the back of a truck."

"Where do you live at?"

"The penthouse, of course. Third floor, last cell. This side, come on I'll show you. Don't bother locking up, we don't have thieves on this wing. They get gone as soon as they get here, as King doesn't like people steeling from the girls. He thinks it's his job to protect us."

Leaving my cell, I pulled the door closed without locking it, and followed Mimi upstairs to his cell, which would have fit in nicely in a whore house: dark red beach towel bed-spread, stuffed animals, and what looked like a warehouse of lingerie and cosmetics, everything a girl could dream of.

Mimi said, "We're about the same size, your butt's a little bigger but it's not a problem," while pulling out assorted clothing from his locker and boxes under his bed for me to try on. We smoked a joint that Snake had sent with the bags of groceries before I started trying on the clothing.

"Whatever fits you can have... I have lots more! Now on to make up. Your color is darker than mine so let's see... I have some of this which is wrong for me and right for you." There was an assortment of eyeliner, mascara and eye shadow. "You don't need false eyelashes, yours are naturally long and I have just the perfume for you," Mimi said, pulling out a bottle of "Poison" perfume - "Poison for Poison" - and some lip gloss of different shades.

"What will I owe you for all this?" I asked, learning long ago on the streets that there was no such thing as a free lunch.

"You don't owe me anything, we're friends. Friends share with each other."

I dint know how to respond. My street instincts sent warning signals, while my scarred heart didn't know what to make of it. The way I had grown up, it was all about survival; doing what you had to do to make it to the next day. The closest I'd ever been to a friend were the street whores and hustlers, who taught me the tricks of the trade. You always knew that if someone did anything for you, you had to see what was in it for them. Yes, I had partners on the street who helped each other, yet we were aware that tomorrow was another day.

I didn't want to say any of this to Mimi, as no one ever did anything out of altruism for me. If I needed shoes, I would turn tricks for the money if I couldn't get a chicken hawk to buy them for me. Most times, rather than spend money I could use for food, I would walk into a store and find a pair of shoes I liked, put them on, and walk or run out with them the first chance I got.

But neither had I survived this long by looking at a gift horse in the mouth too long before accepting or rejecting it. Therefore I said, "Thank you," while holding private reservations. After all, what did a street urchin and this obviously privileged person have in common?

Yet we did become best of friends. Mimi became a brother/sister I never had. She could make me laugh, a rare trait indeed at that time. Underneath it all, we did have a lot in common. With his generous attitude and irrepressible joy for life, he would fall in and out of love with alarming regularity, the relationships never lasting more than a few weeks to a couple of months. Then, he'd always come crying to me. We'd talk, smoke a few joints and eat ice cream floats and Oreo cookies.

In the process of doing so, we traded life stories. As I suspected, Mimi came from a wealthy family that, as I was to learn, had let him be sent to prison to teach him a lesson; a tough love approach. Nonetheless, his dad made certain it never got too rough for him. I don't know who he paid off but Mimi had an invisible shield around him; none of his ex-lovers or boyfriend ever gave him a problem during or after break up, which in itself was unusual within the prison environment, although Mimi dealt with young attractive men. There should have been some flak from some of them when the relationship between them soured. This was simply based on the fact that he looked out for her boyfriends and lovers with gifts and money as long as the relationship lasted.

Soon I was to learn that daddy's money went a long way to ensure nothing happened to their youngest child while he was in prison. Surprisingly, Mimi was lost unaware of all this. Only eyes as cynical as mine would make the connections after a couple of incidents where former lovers that appeared to be threats disappeared or simply walked away, which meant someone had had a little heart to heart talk with them about the facts of life, thus causing them to make wide detours around Mimi.

Mimi never betrayed me by letting lose any of the secrets I related to her during our talks and soul baring, unlike the others who couldn't wait to trade a juicy tidbit of gossip about someone. However, all that was in the weeks and months to come. My immediate concern was what to do with the conflicting emotions and suspicions about what Mimi was up to, and what was expected of me in return. The hustler's creed was "Get all you can get while the getting is good," which conflicted with not wanting to take advantage of what appeared t be a genuine offer of friendship without strings attached.

I knew how it felt to be used and taken advantage of. While I might do it to many people, I wouldn't ever want to do it to a friend. Therefore, on the fragile thread and basis of hope, I decided to adopt a "wait and see" approach, as I knew time would reveal all things.

As it did. Mimi knew instinctively we would click. She brought laughter into my life, while I provided a stability her life had lacked, completing each other; she was strong where I was weak, and vice-versa.

We spent the rest of the first day in her cell and mine, with breaks for counts, chow and the canteen, where we both got dinner and ate in my cell. Our relationship was tentative as we were feeling each other. We smoked more reefers, and as I said, he could make me laugh, as she had an acerbic tongue and wit which could strip paint off walls.

As we were headed for chow and the canteen, Mimi pointed out a stocky black haired boy living on the wing with us. Poking me in the side she said, "You see him?"

"Him who? There are several dozen of 'hims' up here."

"Him," pointing at the boy discreetly, "the one with the bruises."

"What about him?"

"We call him Grubworm. The boy's got some serious problems"

"Yeah and we don't?"

"Not like his. Grubworm likes to be tied up, whipped with belts or beaten. In short, it's how he gets his jollies. Of course there's sex involved, but my God, what kind of warped mind could you have to get off on stuff like that?"

"You might want to consider that it might not be all his doing."

"See, you take all the fun out of it, I'd rather think he's perverted, not what got him that way."

"I'd rather think about how perverted whomever they were to do that to him. He didn't reach that point on his own."

I never did get to know Grubworm, as he was called something very sick and twisted, whom my intuition said it was best to stay away from. Officer King wouldn't permit him to conduct his sessions on the wing, especially when he was on duty, so Grub had to wait for King's days off (Saturdays and Sundays). He would get his fixes of restraints, whippings, beating and sex on other wings.

After we had smoked joints and eaten the meals from the canteen, Mimi filled me in on her latest flame and lover - Brett- living down on T-wing, west side of the hall, last wing before gate thirteen. According to Mimi, "He's a dreamboat, just worth dying for."

I had seen many men. I had been with many; I just hadn't ever run across any I thought were worth dying for. Mimi's whole attitude towards relationships was totally foreign to me. Love was an interesting concept, except not something for the likes of a guttersnipe like me. Within my life, love was something others used to manipulate and abuse me until my heart was embittered and estranged from attachments; I felt its lack and the need of it, not knowing really what it was I was missing, for it had never been a part of my life. You can't really miss what you never had, but oh can it leave a large empty space within your soul.

After lock down for the night, with Mimi in her own cell, I contemplated the day's events. Even with the lights out and most of the prisoners locked within their cells, the prison had sense of malignant waiting. I reflected upon the strange turn of events that had brought Mimi to my cell, and speculated as to exactly what she was up to; I would have to play it by ear and see what came of it. I didn't think it could hurt me and I had nothing to lose by it. I had never had a real friend and it would be strange to find one in such a place.

When the doors were unlocked the next morning at six by the officer via control panel at the front of the tier of cells, I was already awake. It would be an hour or so before they would be calling the wing for breakfast. Freyda was already up next door, talking to someone or maybe himself.

While making myself a cup of coffee, I debated whether to smoke a joint, or wait until after breakfast.

Mimi had told me before lock-in the night before that, "I don't do breakfast, I sleep in." As for me, whether to go or not to go was not an option; I had to go in order to start learning the prison routines of what I would be dealing with, as different shifts of officers had a tendency to run their shifts in a different fashion than the one before. Thus, you had to learn the quirks, and ins and outs of what they expected of you before you would know what to do to avoid problems with them.

It would take me a few weeks to get the rhythms and patterns of all three shifts of officers and prisoners down pat. Hustling was in my blood; it was how I survived. Nonetheless, whether hustling or not, survival alone demanded that I know my environment, and how to maneuver within it.

After breakfast was completed, the morning count was conducted at shift change, the prisoners being locked once again in their respective cells until count was cleared. When we were released from the cells after it cleared, there was work call. I didn't have a job assignment as yet, so I wasn't concerned with it. Mimi had told me that he was assigned to work as a houseman for the wing, and clean up. However, Mimi paid one of the housemen to do his work for him. The officer didn't care who did what as long as it got done.

At 8.30 AM, when they called for morning recreation for those unassigned a job or those off duty, as instructed in Snake's note, I went out when the wing was called. However, I didn't make it to the recreation field until ten-thirty, as I was met at the west door by Snake, who was standing at the top of the ramp by the stairs which descended on the north side. Snake pulled me from the line saying, "Poison, this way," leading me down the stairs and heading for the maintenance area where he worked as one of the electric shop crew.

The crew in the electric shop provided me with fried egg and cheese sandwiches and french fries from the kitchen upstairs and mug of real perked coffee, not instant, before smoking a couple of joints and shooting the shit about what was happening over at the Rock and what was going on over here; things I would need to know to get by. Snake told me, "Once you get settled in, we will set you up with something to make money with, besides your moneymaker. I know you are sitting on a gold mine, but you might want to have something on the side so you don't have to work that thing so hard." We laughed, as Snake had been one of my regular customers at the Rock and probably would be again.

Then, feeling it was a little like a betrayal of what and how much I didn't know. I asked Snake, "What can you tell me about Mimi?"

"That dirty bitch? She goes from man to man, never with one more than a few weeks."

"I mean as a person."

"She is alright, I guess. Never got close to her personally, but I know she's got a lot of juice or clout somewhere. As the word is, just let her go her way and not cause her any problems, or you would end up with more problems than you need. The bitch herself is too clueless to cause problems for anyone and her family has more money than God, from what I heard. Best I can say, she is an airhead, but a convict in spite of it, she's no snitch if that's what you're asking."

"No, I was just wondering, that's all. She seems to have attached herself to me. Nothing sexual mind you, so, you can get the leer off your mug."

"Damn, and here I was thinking of the two of you in bed together doing the wild thing," he said laughing.

"No, it's nothing like that at all, more like girlfriends. And I was wondering what her personality is like from another perspective."

"She's a sweet person but like I said, a complete airhead. If she has two brain cells to rub together, she'd be a genius. You had better get out to the Rec field so, you don't get in trouble."

Snake got his tool belt and a couple of light bulbs from the shop, slinging the tool belt over his shoulder, and we headed for the recreation field. At the gate leading into the recreation field, Snake told the officer, "We have to check the lights at the Rec office." The office told us to go ahead, while adding us to his count. We parted ways on the Rec field with Snake saying, "If you need anything, just send me word and I'll see what I can do. I'll be there to see you once you get settled in, take care."

"Thanks for everything and I look forward to seeing you again", I said with a smile.

Snake had given me some more reefer. I smoked a joint of it as I checked out the Rec field, walking the pathway convicts had made around its inside perimeter, which was over a mile around. During my walk, I observed the dogs in their sectioned runs in between the inner and outer perimeter fences. The English bulldog that Pony had mentioned was there, chewing on the latest tire. He didn't growl or snap at the fences like the other dogs in the runs did, or run up and down the fence line growling and following you. I also saw some of the convicts making friends with one, the challenge being to remove the choke chain from around its neck and replace it with a bandanna, a process which usually took a few weeks or months of sweet talk and feeding it treats.

I greeted and talked for a few minutes with some convicts I knew from the Rock. I could I imagine the number of knives which were buried out here or stashed around the Rec field; I would have to stash one out here myself if I didn't want to carry one all the time. And I would have to come for the fresh air and sunshine, if nothing else. Staying in the building all the time could be wearing on the nerves; the constant noise and tension was something you couldn't get away from inside, and at least outside you had a sense of space around you to relax a little.

As we returned to the wings front the Rec field, I had to step around a puddle of blood and blood trail to get back into the wing. I figured someone must have gotten stabbed while we were out at Rec; a pretty good hit, judging from the amount of blood on the floor, which also explained the ambulance that had come in and gone a few minutes before we came off the field.

I was washing up in the sink when Mimi showed up in my cell doorway. "Knock knock," he said, as he eased by me to get into the cell.

"When did you decide to get up?" I asked.

"I've been up since they cleared the morning count, Brett came over to visit."

"So that's why you have that fresh fucked look," I said, causing Mimi to blush and burst into laughter. "Can you really tell just by looking?"

"Your skins got that glow to it."

"Anyways, they're fixing to count. I just came down to tell you that I have some things to tell you. Girl, you just don't know. I'll be by after count. We can go to chow together."

When Mimi returned to my cell after count, he tossed me a large bag of weed and a pack of rolling papers, telling me, "Roll us a fat one. Never could get the hang of rolling," and flouncing down on my bed, "Girl, you should hear what the whores in the wing are saying about you."

"Well it can wait until we smoke this joint."

"Then hurry up and get it lit, you've got to hear this," he exclaimed, bursting with the news and eager to tell me, and to satisfy his own curiosity about what he had heard.

After smoking the joint, Mimi said, "The word is on the wing that you're in prison for killing your lover on the street with poison. That's why they call you Poison. You're like a black widow, all your lovers die. And they say you killed a bunch of people at the Rock which is why they sent you to this unit. They also say, you're doing life. Is any of this true?"

I laughed, wondering if I shouldn't be outraged by the larceny the jealous-hearted bitches had dumped on me. I said, "Only a small part of any of it is true."

"What part? Come on, you gotta tell me. I cross my heart and hope to die, I won't tell another living soul."

"Well I'm not in prison for killing my lover with poison or any other means. I don't have a life sentence. I've never had lovers, just tricks and johns, who are still living as far as I know."

"So what about the people they say you killed at the Rock? They said it was like five or so... and what are you in prison for? If you don't mind me asking..."

Impulsively, I told him, "I'm in prison for larceny. I got a three year bit with two to go. If I hear about it, I will know where it came from."

"You can trust me. Believe me, no one will hear it. Now, what about these people they say you killed over at the Rock?"

I ran it down to him about what had happened in the shower, and how I had gotten tagged with the nickname "Poison".

"You really killed them?" he asked, looking at me with wide eyes.

"No, the knife killed them, I just happened to be on the other end of it."

"I could never do that, I mean kill someone. Don't you get nightmares about?"

"Not about that. You don't know what you are capable of until you are in that position," I said, while thinking Mimi was right, he wasn't capable of killing anyone.

"No, no, I mean I just couldn't do it. I admire you for being able to stand up for yourself like that. But I could never do it. I gives me Goosebumps even to think about it."

"Then you need to stop your foolishness, as this is no place for you," I thought to myself, while realizing at the same time that most people underestimated Mimi's intelligence. They would talk around him or tell him things, thinking he's harmless. But he just acted ditzy; he lacked street knowledge as well as a criminal heart nor mind, but he wasn't dumb by a wide margin. He could repeat the whole conversation verbatim, while not realizing exactly what was going on.

Within the prison, as on the streets, there were always three stories to everything, the first being for public consumption, the second being the one participants tell among themselves and each other, and the third being the true story hidden behind the facades of the other two. A good convict and street hustler learns to read in between the lines and pick up pieces of the real story.

Thus Mimi, in relaying these things people would say around him to me, was a source of information. He didn't realize this, as I could pick out the salient points to know where to look for the rest.

After our return from chow, we smoked a couple of joints. Mimi told me the story of how he acquired his nickname. He said it originated within his family. "When I was just a toddler and saw anything I wanted, I would point at it and say me-me, meaning give it to me! So they started calling me "me-me", which naturally became Mimi when they saw which way the skirt was blowing." Mimi's family accepted his sexual orientation, not necessarily wholeheartedly approving of it, but it was Mimi's life.

I related things about myself I had never told another person: about my upbringing, how I had never known my parents, being abandoned as a baby and state raised. The only difference between the places the state kept me in and the streets had been the three hots, a cot and a place to bathe. Other than that, it was the same old, same old. You survived the best way you could, with what you had at hand; no one was about to give you anything or have your back, and the only one you could depend on was yourself, for God always seemed to be looking the other way.

This was over the period of weeks and months ahead, as my wary heat learned I could trust Mimi. Among ourselves, Mimi started calling me "Orphan Annie", and I called her "Richie Rich Bitch".

Mimi never had to worry about money while I had to chase the dime in order for me to have anything in prison, just like on the streets; you lived on what the land provided you or you did without. I was always reluctant to accept any of Mimi's largesse; I was too used to being independent, never wanting to be dependent n anyone or anything, for you never knew what tomorrow would bring. Plus, other people had a way of using it to manipulate you, or throw it up on your face in case you developed an attitude. But Mimi was different. He had never been without, always having so much. It never occurred to him to use it to buy friendship, to manipulate someone. Material things did not have that meaning for him.

Still, I came to value Mimi's friendship, and didn't want anyone to think the only reason we were friends was for what I could get from him. What he had meant nothing to me, for I could get it on my own. What I valued more than anything else was the bond and trust of friendship which had developed between us. It was nothing sexual; we just admired each other, though we agreed it wouldn't do to let something like sex spoil our friendship as we could get it somewhere else.

During one of our tête-de-têtes, he asked me, "You ever had sex with a woman?"

"Before I answer your question, I want to be certain you understand that I was a male prostitute. I became one just so to survive while living on the streets. When you're doing that, you will do whatever it takes to put food in your belly and to provide yourself a place to sleep. The whores on the stroll - male or female - taught me a lot more than how to use a knife. They also taught me the tricks of the trade, from sucking a pole to sucking a hole. When a John wanted a threesome whatever the combination, as long as the money was good, I did it. So the answer is yes! I did have sex with a woman, whether I wanted to or enjoyed, that's another question I have asked myself because it was strictly business. I read somewhere that it's ninety percent mental and ten percent physical."

"I mean aside from that, would you want to?"

"No. I like men. I like being feminine. I appreciate women's bodies… I'd want one myself. As to the questions about sexuality, I have never given it much thought. Growing up, I always thought girls had the better deal: pretty clothes, dolls and things. I always felt more female than male. Boy stuff didn't interest me while growing up. I was teased, more than I care to think, for being a sissy boy who acted like a girl and who would rather play with dolls than baseball."

"Me too." Mimi said.

"And this was way before I had any awareness of my sexuality or sexual preferences. Then, within the orphanages, foster homes, boys' schools and reformatories where others forced their attentions upon me, I didn't think of it being sex at all. While out on the street, it was just a way of survival when there was no other means. Therefore, it wasn't a matter for me to like or dislike. It just was what it was. Now, if I had to say anything, t would say like the way I am. I like men. I like the attention, and being this way somehow completes me. I don't think about it as being gay, homosexual, transsexual or anything else. It's just me being me."

"Well, I tried it with a girl, and I didn't like it at all. I couldn't see what all the fuss was about."

I started laughing.

"What are you laughing for?"

"You, of the thousand and one, two week affairs with all these young studs can't see what all the fuss is about?"

"I'm not that bad, I just haven't found the right one yet. Besides, that's different."

"No, it's not. You are just geared differently. It could have been other way as well for you. You're like me in that you feel you were born this way and you are only doing what feels natural and right for you. You couldn't be happy any other way."

"Yeah, you're right, I wouldn't."

"So be yourself, you can't live your life trying to please other people, to fulfill their expectations about what they think you ought to be. You do that, then they're living your life for you. You'll never be happy."

A few weeks later, during one of our smoke and talk sessions, Mimi asked, "You ever had sex with a black man? I am only asking because the bitches on the wing say you're a coal burner."

"When you sell sex like I do, you're not worried about the color of the skin. Only color of their money and whether they are clean. Their money is just as green as any others."

"I've always been curious and wanted to try it with one but I'm too scared. They say all them have huge dicks..."

"No, that's not true. You will run across some which are large but majority are like any other man, with short ones, fat ones, skinny ones, long ones, bent, crooked or straight, cut or uncut. However, you might want to scope out his merchandise before trying it, or you could end up with someone like King Sol (a prisoner whose penis almost touches his knees, even when not aroused) also in here, you would have to be extra careful, as racism and exploitation is a two-way street. There would be plenty who would think nothing about setting you up to run a train on you."

"Oh, I would never try it in here. Too many haters on both sides of the fence. And a lot of whites don't mess with you if they think you are doing it with a black guy. That being said, I may give it a shot once I get out. Just to see what it's like."

"Better be careful. They do say, once you try black you don't go back."

"You actually believe that?"

"Nope, just some more male chauvinist bullshit, as I said, unless your taste happens to run that way. They're just like every other male, it's just a matter of taste, also known as jungle fever when it's interracial, which works both ways"

The girls on the wing would never say any of those things about me to my face, or I would have put them in their places. They were supposed to stay out of my business and mind theirs, but were jealous backbiters with cat claws. Whenever they came to me, they were always sweetness and light as they were a little afraid of me, or at least my blade. While talking to me concerning Mimi, they would refer to him as "your little friend" with the italic marks around it. Snide bitches are what they were. Mimi mostly put them in their places in the wing. I would either be engaged in hustling and making money or in my cell reading, and I really did not have time for their foolishness, nor did I play those kinds of games. Mimi thrived on it whereas I was mostly a loner, with the exception of Mimi, who would barge in on me whenever he took a mind to.

Like I said, when not engaged in hustling on the wing or acting as a look out for Mimi's trysts with the current lover, or bullshitting with him, or doing nails, shaving legs, trying on different styles of makeup and clothing, I'd be in my cell reading. That is, if the Rec yard wasn't open. Most weekends during the day, Mimi would get visits from his family, if he wasn't in confinement. His family would fly up to the Jacksonville or some municipal airport close to the prison, and during the visits, Mimi would always tell them about his best friend - Poison, and how we looked out for each other.

I would send him care packages of cigarettes he could use to trade for peanut butter and snacks while he was in confinement, and pay the kitchen workers to fix him special trays to be delivered to him during chow time. At first I was using my money to do these things for him, but once his family saw I that I was really his friend and not just using him, they started sending money to my account, and nothing I could say would persuade them not to, as Mimi had also told them I had no money or family to look out for me.

I left the money they sent in the prison account, and only used it to ensure Mimi got everything she needed while in confinement. And he would do the same for me whenever I ended up in the hole, usually for being in unauthorized areas as I made my pounds, and taking what chances I had to, in order to hustle and make money.

In doing so, it provided me with a closer look at the seamy underbelly of the prison, learning who was really in charge and overseeing all the prison black market activities. Most of the big time hustlers would like for you to believe they were totally independent and beholden to no one. However, Whitehead on the black side and Mike on the white side always had a piece of whatever action the hustlers had on.

Whitehead worked as the gym clerk, and was native to area around the prison. He was a six-foot-six tall and two hundred and ninety pound muscle-bound freak, whom prison officials utilized as their enforcer. Mike was the maintenance supervisor's clerk, and was more laid back. Both worked with the knowledge of the prison officials, who I am certain got their cut of the pie. Such payoffs were a part of doing business, to ensure the operations ran as smooth as possible without being disrupted by busts, shakedowns or robberies. They would also get advance notice when shakedowns by the officers were going to occur. It was all about making money; whatever their costs were, they just passed them down the line to their customers; business as usual whether in outside or inside.

While on my rounds, I would generally end up in the library, as a lot of business took place in the back rooms and among the shelves; also because I was an avid reader, always on the lookout for a good book to read. When out on the streets, the library had been my place of refuge, somewhere I would be left alone and undisturbed, escaping the realities of the world I live in. It was nice to dream by vicariously living the lives of the novels' characters. Besides, the libraries were warm in the winter and cool in the summers, and the bathrooms were always open and there was no one trying to run you off.

It was at the prison's library where I first encountered Stonewall, a clerk in the Law Library section. He expressed interest in me as a person, yet I could sense a sexual undertone. But nothing came of that, as we became friendly to each other, ending up with him teaching me how to do research on legal issues.

I never did find out whether Stonewall was his real name or nickname. He did however know a lot about me, saying, "I had to know who and what I was dealing with." He was a light skinned black with freckles, taller than me at five-nine feet, with a medium build, always wearing half-sized reading glasses which he would look over when addressing you, or have them perched on the top of his head. Stone had gotten off death row due to some Supreme Court ruling.

I also knew he was the head of one of the black factions in the prison who were always at odds with each other, with him being next in line to replace Whitehead, should circumstance change to favor him. For the present, Whitehead had a lock because his connections among the guards at the prison, who he had grown up with or did dirty work for inside the prison.

This is not to say the unit beast didn't get regular does of blood and death from among the prisoners, even with all the hustling going on. The major players stayed pretty much above the fray, but the rank and file of regular convicts was a gore fest. Not a week went by without a stabbing or killing; it was nothing unusual to have to step around blood, or a body lying in the main corridor of those who couldn't quite make it to the clinic on their own, or died before they could make it very far, leaving blood trails trying to get up the long corridor. There was no telling of how long it would take the medical team to get them in the hallway, and those stabbed and leaking had to try and get there before they bled out.

You would think that with such a violent atmosphere and the constant tension, the convicts would be more wary and respectful towards one another. However, it seemed the opposite was true. The malignancy of the place filled them with blood lust and plain stupidity, in thinking they could do whatever they wanted to and to whomsoever they pleased, for they feared no evil, believing themselves as the meanest and worst motherfuckers to ever hit the East Unit. And they often would find out the hard way that they weren't as mean as they thought themselves. Even if your fight or knife game were excellent, you'd still go to sleep or shit or shower. Your back can't always be in a corner. No matter how good you are, there are always moments when you are vulnerable to someone who might be waiting for such a moment of opportunity.

There were times when the unit would go for a week or a month - sometimes two months - of relative peace. Then everything would just start popping off in a chain reaction. Was it really worth your life to skip line, thinking the people behind wouldn't resent it, seeing it as disrespect and plant a blade in your back while you were standing there? Almost everyone had knives, and were willing to use them to prove a point, or just to release some tensions.

Within the first few months at the unit, only Pony and myself of the ten in our group avoided entanglements. One got stabbed, and one got killed; three got turned out and came over to K-wing, and two ended up with murder charges. I avoided problems by staying mostly out of everyone's way while doing my own thing. I think some of Mimi's protection juice helped, as we were always together.

As I had thought, the gym was a death trap. If you weren't the first wing to go to the movie night to grab all the high seats, putting your backs to the wall or had a friend who could save you a spot there, you had to sit down in the bleachers. You could tell the homeboys and factions as they sat together, watching each other's backs, or at least making it harder to target one particular individual from among them. There were always more knives there than you'd find at a cutlery shop. I only went to the gym on movie nights if there was a movie playing that I really wanted to see, or had some business to take care of. Otherwise I stayed on the wing in my cell reading if Mimi wasn't around.

During one of the stays in confinement, I was called next door to Sugar Bear. He was a burly black with a round face; I could see where they got the Bear part from, but couldn't quite see it connected to Sugar. Unless it had to do with that Bear on cereal boxes - which is not to say Bear wasn't a nice guy. He was pleasant enough and we got along well. Once he saw I wasn't into the racial bullshit, we got on friendly terms, meaning he wouldn't try to exploit or hurt me and might speak up on my behalf to prevent others from doing so.

Mimi had asked me what my plans were for when I got out, asking, "What do you want to do with your life?"

"I always thought I would like to be an animal doctor, or a fancy chef."

"Can you be a vet with a record?"

"Not with a felony record. I could possibly be a vet tech, but not if it required licensing."

"Well the, what about cooking? You could get a job at a restaurant."

"Most family restaurants want cooks with experience. I'm not speaking of McDonald's or other fast food places, or a breakfast cook at IHOP, Denny's or Waffle House. If I were to go into it, I'd like to try it at Cordon Bleu level, working in five star restaurants and hotels. To get to that level of the profession, you have to attend a school for culinary arts to master the basics and technical aspects there are four types of cooks: fast food, institutional which covers schools, prisons and hospitals, the majority of family type dinning out restaurants and finally Cordon Bleu. The Cordon Bleu schools cost money, and at least two years, one year of schooling and another under a top flight chef, with perhaps more schooling later. A lot of training which I could never afford. I don't have the money to eat in one, much less go to school and learn to be a chef in one."

"So you would like to be an "Oh La La" chef with the fancy hat and strut your French stuff?"

"Yea, it's something I always wanted to try. I think I would be good at it since being a vet could never happen. Neither will the other. It's just a dream you fantasize to about, knowing it will never be."

Mimi said he didn't know why they had sent him over to the East Unit in the first place, as he hadn't done any real wrong. My take on it was his family had probably spoken with some bureaucrat in the prison system's central office in Tallahassee about ensuring Mimi's safety while he was in prison. The clueless official most likely thought that maximum security prison meant maximum protection as well, and shipped Mimi to the East Unit.

I was going to live in Tampa immediately after release. However, I had no intentions of remaining in Florida for long; I couldn't really recall why I had come here in the first place. Probably a spur of the moment which seemed like a good idea at the time; for the sun, the beaches. They said the hustling was good with lots of rich tricks, which was all true. However, they failed to mention that Florida would send you to prison for things which wouldn't get you arrested for, or even at worst get you a citation and fine in other states. The iconic joke among the convicts in Florida was that Florida's welcome sign at the state line should read, "Welcome to Florida. Come down on vacation, go home on probation, and return on violation to visit its scenic prison system, far from the beaches."

The days, weeks and months passed on; not quickly, but they did pass on. It then seemed suddenly that I was a short-timer. Mimi would have to serve another four months after I had left. We both knew our time together was growing short, even as we bonded closer without friendship; her, the rich kid, and me, the street urchin were as close as sisters or brothers, if you had to say it that way. The trust we had in each other grew with our friendship, and therefore in a large way, my rapidly approaching release date was somewhat bittersweet.

Certainly I would be going free, yet I would be leaving behind the one real and true friend I had made in life up to this point. The brambles around my street urchin heart had been brushed aside by the brash irresponsible spirit of Mimi. He felt the same, knowing he would miss me terribly when I was gone. It was a subject we avoided for the most part, except for teasing about how short I was getting, all of which changed the week before my scheduled release. Mimi came flouncing into my cell and did her usual pirouette onto my bed.

"Well it's settled," she said, tossing some brochures onto the bed between us.

"What's settled?"

"You're going-away present."

"I'm being released. I don't require a going-away present, your friendship is enough."

"I know all that Poison. Nonetheless, I couldn't stand being in here knowing you were out there turning tricks to survive, or stealing out of stores. So I took care of it."

"I'm almost afraid to ask... what did you take care of?"

"You're enrolled at The Culinary Art School of Fine Cuisine in Tampa. Classes start three weeks after your release, which should give you plenty of time to get settled in. Here are the brochures about the school," handing then to me after picking them up off the bed.

"Settled in? Mimi, I am not even certain where I am going to stay in Tampa. And I still need to eat, so I'll have to get a job and a place to stay, which is going to take time. I can't attend school while holding down a full time job as well. Plus I have to find a job first.

"Don't worry your pretty head about a thing because Ms. Mimi's been on her job. Daddy has leased a three bedroom apartment four blocks from the school. The lease is paid for eighteen months. Utilities included, and a weekly stipend for food and incidentals through an attorney friend of his Tampa, so everything is taken care of."

"You didn't have to do all that. I could have gotten along out there," I said, not really knowing what else to say, overwhelmed by all of it, and not just a little put out. I was used to doing it for myself. Little miss independent.

"I know all that, however, I couldn't have you out there running the streets, with me not knowing how to find you. You're my best friend. Friends look out for each other. And Daddy says they'll pick you up in Tampa when they come to visit me, so we will get to see each other."

I dint know whether to laugh, get mad or cry. The little hussy had just completely taken over my life and arranged it to suit herself, yet I couldn't object as it took care of all my worries; I had an opportunity to do what I desired.

I had accumulated some monies on the books, from hustling and what Mimi's family had sent, but I knew just how fast I would blow through it out there, starting from scratch in a fresh place. The following week, I was released and started classes on schedule at the Culinary School of Fine Cuisine.

THREE YEARS LATER

Mimi's accident started it all, or at least I should say, brought its closure, bringing me back to Florida, when I had done so much to leave - while under an investigative cloud that I hadn't even been aware of, two years before.

The Culinary Arts School was a dream come true, albeit a lot of hard work involved. The first six months at the school, I hardly had time for anything else other than bi-weekly visits to see Mimi until he got released, topping by a Tampa on the way home to visit. After his release, we cruised the gay clubs together, and we would go back regularly, dressed to the nines. Mimi continued to flirt from love to love while I kept a sugar daddy or two on the line; you can take the hustler out of the street, but not the street out of the hustler.

After the first six months of classes, I was finally catching on as to what world class cuisine was all about; it required I do a lot of work, and study to catch up with those student who were more knowledgeable about culinary arts. Everything we did at the school, and I mean everything, you had to make from scratch: no packaged mixes. All the sauces, soups, gravies, condiments, powdered sugar, cake, bread and pasta flours; all the cuts and preparations of meats, fish, poultry, pork, lamb, beef, venison ; the spices and wines, deciding which one's go with which foods. Nonetheless I must say I took it like a duck to water.

At the end of six months, I had already taken a side job with one of the major convention hotels out on the causeway, working as a sous chef under the administrative head chef. Not top of the line, but a good start for beginner like myself. I took the job at the urging of Chef Paul, our teacher at the school, for the experience and to earn some extra money.

Plus, I had other little hustles going with the other students at the school and the waitresses, waiters, bellboys, maids and delivery personnel at the hotel. There was always a way to make a dollar or two. I even rented out one of the bedrooms in the apartment to another queen called Rachel, the other bedroom being reserved for Mimi when he visited.

Rachel worked the drag shows at the gay clubs, making fairly decent money. She was always trying to get me in the scene with him. I liked dressing up, true enough, but not overdoing it; besides, I had enough going on without the drag queen routine. Don't get me wrong, I usually dressed as a woman when not in school or at work.

We all -students and chefs- had to wear these tacky black and white checkered pants. They made me feel like an advertisement of a cab company, and there was only so much you could do with them in order to make them halfway presentable, or at least that is what I'd tell myself. The pants were so ghastly that I kept an apron. The white chef's jacket was cute, although I always brought a change of street clothes with me, changing into the pants at school or at work and going back into them before leaving; I wouldn't be caught dead on the streets wearing a pair of pants like those.

Aside from the dreadful pants, I loved school and work. Everyone knew I was gay, and would join in the women's gabfests where they accepted me as one of them. But the school and hotel didn't want me broadcasting it by being too cute, which made me reluctant to begin the hormones that Rachel kept urging me to take. Oh I wanted to, but decided to wait a little before starting them. I wanted to get school out of the way first.

It came to be a few months before graduation rolled around, I still hadn't decided on what aspect of culinary arts I would specialize in, as I loved it all. I was leaning towards baking breads, pastries and doing desserts, yet there was so much more I wanted to learn before going for a specialty, if that is truly what I wanted to do. Two events took place as graduation neared. Chef Paul, the head chef and teacher at the school, whom we called God behind his back, summoned me to his office at the school.

"Come in Keith and have seat." I took a seat across from his desk, which was piled with paperwork, just a teeny bit uneasy wondering what this was about, while searching my mind for possibilities. I thought I had been pretty careful in my dealings, and drew a blank.

"You've been doing quite well in class. Near the top of the students presently enrolled," he started.

"Thank you," I said.

"When I have a student whom I believe really has a talent and love for the culinary arts, who, if they applied themselves as you have, could be a top flight chef, what I do in such a case, is see if perhaps I can find for them a position in the appropriate milieu to give their talent full expression. You with me so far?"

"Yes, sir," flattered somewhat but still dubious about where this was going.

"Well, in your case, I took it upon myself to contact a chef I've known and worked with for many years, and who has worked in some of the finest five star hotels and restaurants on the content and in the states who is now the administrative and chief chef of his own restaurant in Los Angeles. Chef M. is always looking for top talent that he can help along. We discussed you, and he is willing to offer you a position in his kitchens to further your education and training within the culinary arts. Have you decided if you're going to specialize in any one field yet?"

"No sir, I want to first get a good working knowledge of all aspects of the culinary arts."

"Good, good. I'm glad to hear you say that, for as intense as our classes here have been, we have only begun to touch the surface of the arts of fine cuisine. There's so much you still need to learn to really end up as a top flight chef."

I had pretty much figured that out already, but it was nice to have it confirmed.

He continued, "There's not many who would be willing to teach you many of the finer elements of cuisine for gourmet palates. At least not with you just beginning your career. There are some really fine advanced culinary arts schools around; however, they want you to have working knowledge and experience within the trade environment before they will consider accepting you. And I truly believe that would be a waste of your time and talent, in working in the trades just to acquire enough practical experience to be considered by them. But here you have the opportunity to cut off the process with the chance to learn from one of the best in the business."

"You did say Los Angeles? That's in California, right? I'd have to move out there?"

"Yes, Chef M. is quiet willing to help you relocate if money is the problem. Your salary would be commensurate with your abilities, increasing as you progress and develop. Would moving to California present a problem for you?"

"No sir, I hadn't made up my mind as to where to go next. But I was considering Las Vegas or out west somewhere. I haven't considered where the best place for me would be."

"Opportunities like this don't come along often. You should take the advantage of it. I can envision you as being one of the top talents in the field within a few years, and I would like to believe I had something to do with it."

"Well this kind of sudden, and I would like time to mull it over. I'm inclined to go for it, however, I don't want to be hasty either, and jump at the first thing that pops up."

"This is hardly something that just pops up! But I understand you will need some time to think it over. We still have a few weeks of classes. You should come to a decision."

"I appreciate you going out of your way to present me with this opportunity."

"Why, thank you. However, I consider it more in the line of not seeing talent go to waste. The culinary field always needs fresh talent of those who share a love of fine cuisine and its operation. Just see me some time before graduation day with your decision so I may confirm to Chef M. Oh, and Keith, let's keep this between ourselves. I don't want any of the other students to feel as if they have been slighted."

"You got it Chef Paul, and thanks again."

I got up from the chair and returned to the kitchen. The opportunity was really a godsend for me, not only for the chance to develop my skills in the trade, but also because I had been contemplating a score at the hotel where had I worked.

As a street hustler, you develop the ability to discern patterns developing where others only see random arrangement, so the opportunity existed for an astute hustler to come up with a score. Since I had started working at the hotel, I had noticed two Latin gentlemen (and I use the term gentlemen loosely with respect to one of them) were frequent guests of the hotel; attending the dinner buffet and ordering room service.

The hotel hosted a lot of conventions of doctors, lawyers, sales people and business men to whom we would serve meals to in the convention rooms, as they listened to the speeches of their lecturers or discussed sales and business among themselves.

The elder of the two Latin gentlemen had some class, and was always polite. His name was Jorge, while his partner - the short greasy pig who called me a "maricon" the first time he laid eyes on me - was called Enrique. Enrique was crude, loud and gross, although he was a good tipper, throwing money around; he thought it gave him the right to be rude and insulting. He definitely had no class or taste, with his flashy clothes and jewelry. Street knew street when they saw it, and whatever country and city he came from in South America. I knew where he got his start.

Jorge always dressed well and conservatively. I just couldn't connect the two together. They always had adjoining penthouses on the top floor of the hotel when they stayed there, which was every two months for up to three weeks. I knew because I checked the room service tabs for the preceding year, which told me their tastes in food and room locations, as well as the frequency of orders.

I was doing a lot of the head chef's administrative paperwork at the hotel: inventories, ordering, menu and menu planning. The chef (Chef Steven) said it was to further my education, but I believed it was more in the line of scut work that he pushed off to me. Yes, I would need to know all of it if I planned on being the top chef or having my own restaurant. Nonetheless, some of those details should never be left in the hands of underlings or novices.

I had charge of late shift room service on weekends, which also covered early breakfasts. I was also in charge of the buffets, the pastries and convention meals, plus ensuring everything ran smoothly in the kitchen and dining places. Chef Steven would come check up on me, usually with another list of things for me to do.

I would take the purchase orders for the coming week's kitchen supplies to the manager's office for the hotel manager to sign off on. And yes, there was plenty of wiggle room, so I could make some money here which wouldn't be noticed; I helped myself as I could without being greedy. I was out and about the hotel at all hours, and I couldn't help but notice Enrique and Jorge's movements. At first I didn't pay much attention to them.

With Enrique being such an obnoxious bastard, I tried to avoid him as much as possible, while still having to deal with him when they ordered room service at the request of the hotel manager. They would often order enough food and serving for a group of people, although they would be the only ones I would see inside the suite. Enrique was very demanding, and there had problems when the bell hops or room service waiters had delivered the meals to the penthouse. I imagine it made him feel important for the chef to deliver the meals personally. He tipped well, but might as well have had "asshole" tattooed on his forehead for all the good it did I never forgot the faggot remarks, nor his attitude whenever he encountered me.

I was never in the suites long, as the doors were always closed when I came in with the serving cart, but I noticed that Enrique, Jorge and their visitors always had large wheeled baggage with them. I never claimed to be the brightest bulb in the bunch, yet something struck me as odd about the whole set-up, and soon my street sense was tingling. Something was going on, which smelled like money. I didn't know what or how yet, but the street told me it was there.

Where there was money, there was always a means of having some of it stick to my fingers, so I started tracking their movements, trying to figure out what they were doing. I didn't have much free time to spend on it, so, it took me a little while to uncover what they were up to. Once I did so, I felt like a complete dumbass for not setting it sooner, as it was too obvious.

Enrique was using the hotel as cover for moving major drugs and monies, with Jorge as his accountant or manager. I was certain that Enrique at best was mid-level in the hierarchy of the organization he was with. They didn't keep the drugs on the hotel premises going off to make their deals, but the money now, would be a different story. Thinking about all those rolling suitcases, and checking a little further, I found out the maids were only permitted into the suites when Jorge or Enrique were present, and even then only at certain times to change the linens and clean only certain areas.

The more I thought about it, the more sense it made, with all the conventions the hotel hosted year round. There was always a constant flow of traffic in and out of the hotel, mostly baggage or wheeled suitcases: lecturers, product salesmen, conventioneers, hotel guests. The money couriers mingling among them wouldn't attract any attention at all.

It was pretty astute of them to use the hotel as a cover for their activities. The question I was yet to answer was how to go about acquiring some of the money I was certain was in those suitcases. It was being moved, which meant it had to be on the premises. If I had to guess, I would have said within the penthouse suite Enrique was in.

Further observation provided the best times to venture out, to investigate my guess. The two of them would be out for hours at a time. Thus, when they left I knew I would have plenty of time to snoop around the suites, the only problem being I didn't have a key or means of accessing the penthouse; a conundrum which only stumped me momentarily, for I remembered seeing a master pass key hanging in the manager's office.

Every hotel has master pass key to access all rooms and suites in the event of an emergency. This hotel's keys were hanging in plain sight inside the manager's office, and it was nothing for me to get him distracted long enough for me to make a wax impression of the key (the kitchen had plenty of wax), which I then took to Jerry, a shady locksmith I knew. He had a shop on Florida Avenue and I had him make a key from the impression, and presto, I had my own master key.

Waiting for the right time when both of them would be out of the hotel for a few hours and things were slow in the kitchen, I made up a room service cart order for the floor below the penthouses. Loading up the serving cart with the food, I took it off to make the delivery, while trying to look as normal and inconspicuous as possible. By now I was a familiar sight around the hotel, and no one paid me any attention.

I was nervous as I checked out the door and lock of Enrique's suite for any hairs or tape being used as a detection device. Not finding any, I let myself into the suite, pushing the serving cart ahead of me. Once inside, I began my search in the master's bedroom suite.

When I opened the doors of the walk-in closet, the smell immediately hit me like a solid blow. In case you didn't know, money stinks! Not the new crisp bills issued by the Federal Reserve, but the bills which have been in circulation awhile inside people's pockets, wallets, hands and purses. Get a bunch of it together, and it has a sour acrid smell, a really rank, sweaty-oily odor.

The money was stacked along the walls, and covered the floor of the closet to about waist height leaving only a narrow walkway down the middle of the rows. There was so much money here that I couldn't even begin to guess how much money in there; millions and millions. Having never seen so much of it, it scared and excited me at the same time.

Walking into the closet, I started checking out the banded stacks, noticing they were all hundred dollar bill denomination, Ben's face staring at me. There was five thousand to each band, fifty one hundred dollar bills. I was too stunned by the sight and smell of the money to do something right away, so I went back out into the suite to search for the rest. Enrique had a block of what I took to be cocaine in the refrigerator. I imagined it was for a customer sample, so they would know what kind of product they were getting.

Leaving that for the moment, I went next into Jorge's suite through the connecting door between them, and inside the master bedroom's closet I found the same setup, with the addition of money counting machines, bands to go around the stacks as they were counted and digital weight bathroom scales.

I deduced that they counted it there and stored it until the couriers could move it, probably to a safe house somewhere. I didn't have a clue what they did with it; the amount was staggering, far beyond anything within my experience, only having seen a few thousand dollars before this. The problem I now had was how much could I safely take without it being noticed right away. I wasn't certain how much had already been counted in Jorge's room.

Bringing the serving cart into his room, I lifted the skirting on the cart and stacked the money with new bands on them from the closet onto the cart's lower shelves, locking Jorge's suite door behind me on my way out. I completed loading the cart from the rows in Enrique's closet, making certain as I had next door to get the money with new bands, and leave the rows of money so there wouldn't even be a gap.

Going to the refrigerator, I got a zip-lock baggy and dumped some of the cocaine into it. The stuff was so compacted and hard that I had to break chunks off, making sure I didn't leave any small pieces behind inside the refrigerator. Before leaving the suite, I checked and made certain I left no evidence of my presence there, doing so even though I wanted to do nothing more than get out of there as fast as possible.

As I left the suite, I was trembling and sweating so bad, with my heart racing so fast I thought I might have a heart attack; both scared - no, terrified - and excited at the same time, while wondering if I was doing the right thing, worried they would notice the money missing right away.

I hoped not, as I didn't have the faintest inkling about what to do with the money I had taken. It was just too much, in that it blogged the imagination. "It must be a couple hundred thousand dollars on the cart," I thought, then wondering if perhaps I had gotten too greedy and taken too much or that perhaps I shouldn't have taken the cocaine, with the latter two thoughts shuttling back and forth in my mind while waiting on the elevator and on the trip back to the kitchen. If anyone had said "boo" to me, I would have died on the spot.

In the kitchen, in the dish-washing area, I got a large black trash bag and filled it with the money off the cart. Then taking the bag, I stashed it in the back of the walking meat freezer, locking it. The head chef and I were the only ones with a key to it, as meat ha a way of walking off - we had whole sizes of beef, pork and lamb in there.

Finished with that, I went back to work, distracted and hyper the rest of my shift. I got a gym bag out of the hotel's collection of items, left behind and never claimed for, and packed the money into it inside the meat locker. Then I placed the bag inside the trash bag, carrying it out back and putting it in the dumpster. Since it was now the end of my shift, I got out my shoulder bag and changed into street clothes, then went back outside to the dumpster, taking the gym bag out and putting it inside my shoulder bag, leaving the trash bag in the dumpster.

Normally after work, I would go for a walk on the beach before heading home - not today. I just wanted to put some distance between me and the hotel. I hadn't gone through the hotel lobby, as I didn't want to risk the possibility of encountering Enrique and Jorge; not that they would have known what was in the bag but my nerves couldn't stand the thought of such a meeting. Neither was the shoulder bag light weight, although I had to tote it like it was. Such were the paranoid thoughts that ran through my mind.

I walked around the side of the hotel to the front Porteneu where the guests were dropped off and picked up, and where Fred the doorman had his post. Seeing me, he asked, "Not going for a walk on the beach tonight?"

"Nah, too tired (really too wired), I'll just catch a cab and go home. Could you get me a cab? I need to catch up on my sleep"

"Sure thing", he said, stepping out and motioning for one of the cabs posted out front of the hotel. The causeway was a prime cabby area with plenty of tourist and those attending the conventions who needed to be taken places around the city.

When the cab pulled in under the Porteneu, I climbed in while telling Fred, "Thanks, and see you tonight."

"I'll be here," he replied. I gave freed a wave as the cab pulled off. I could feel some of the tension bleed off as the cabby drove away. I gave him my address then tried to settle back and relax, something that wasn't about to happen, for the money in the bag had a siren effect. I kept touching it to ensure it was really there.

What I wanted to do was take the money and run, to tell the cabby to take me to the airport, and catch the first flight out to wherever it was going. I had keep telling myself it would be a dumb move on my part to do anything like that, as it would be the first they would expect and look out for when they discovered some amount money was missing.

Therefore, I kept telling myself to play it cool and smooth, while not having any idea of what to do with so much money. I didn't even know yet how much I had taken; all I knew was that I loaded the cart with what I could. I didn't count, as I was more worried about making certain what I had taken from the closet wouldn't be noticeable, and about evening everything out.

When the cab arrived at the apartment, I paid the fare and a couple of dollars as a tip. I fumbled with the apartment keys when I reached the door, as I didn't want to set the bag down. Once inside, with the door locked, drying off and dressing, I took the bag into my bedroom. There, I debated whether to leave the door open or closed. I was curious to know if Rachel was home yet, not wanting anyone to see the cash. Compromising, I left the door cracked so I could hear if anyone was coming into the apartment.

I took the gym bag out of my shoulder bag, and unzipping it, upended it on the bed. The money tumbled out, with some stacks spilling out onto the floor from the pile on the bed. The baggy of rock tumbled out as well, and I tossed it on top of the dresser to deal with it later. I replaced the money which had fallen to the floor on the bed with the rest, then began counting it, then stopped before starting over.

One thing working in the school and hotel had taught me was that when counting money, you will have to count it two or three times - so you might as well make it easy on yourself by sorting and arranging it where it could easily be counted. Thus, I started stacking the banded bundles, five to a stack, before I finally began counting. I counted four times, the last two with pen and paper to be sure the count was accurate, as I couldn't believe how much I had gotten. It hadn't even made any dent in the rows of money within the closets, just the top layer, yet I had sixty-five stacks with five bundles to a stack for a total of three hundred and twenty five bundles. Twenty five thousand in each bundle times three hundred and twenty-five totaled to one million six hundred and twenty five thousand dollars.

The amount was staggering and frightening. There must have been over a hundred million dollars in those closes, but even so, this much would have to be missed. Perhaps not right away, but such an amount had to be missed sooner or later when the totals didn't match up; and then the proverbial shit would hit the fan. I had thought I'd gotten maybe three hundred thousand at most, yet the counts didn't lie.

I needed to relax and calm down, so I could think things through; I didn't want to do anything rash that might attract attention on me. I rolled a fat joint out of my stash and smoked it, then went to the kitchen, made coffee and something to eat. Then I washed the dishes and later on cleaned myself up before beginning to evaluate the problem.

I had left the money where I had counted it - on the bed. The money itself was the problem. There was just too much of it, and I couldn't think of what I was going to do with it. I couldn't just leave it lying around, and began to wonder where I could stash it. I couldn't spend it, at least not right away, and not much at a time when I could. Nor could I open an account with it at the bank, as too many questions for which I didn't have answers would be asked.

It then occurred to me that the problem wasn't only the money but also me. I had no experience in handling large sums of money; I doubted I had ever had over six thousand dollars at any one time and that only recently. But, then it struck me! I might not know what to do with the money, but I did know someone who would, and the amount wouldn't mean anything to him - Mimi!

Going to the phone, I dialed Mimi's number in West Palm Beach. As I listened to it ring, I was saying, "Come on, come on, and pick up the phone." After the fifth ring, I heard someone fumbling to pick up the phone on the other end. Then Mimi's voice, thick with sleep, came in the line, "- ello? I don't know who this is but it better be important waking me up at this ungodly hour."

"Mimi its Poison."

"Oh, hi Poison, but couldn't you have waited for a more civilized hour to call?"

"You shouldn't have stayed out whoring all night. Look Mimi, I need to see you."

"Can't you tell me over the phone?"

"It's not the kind of problem that I can discuss on the phone."

"Girlfriend, what have you gotten yourself into now?"

"The sooner you get up here, the sooner you will know, trust me on this; I wouldn't be calling if I didn't need you."

"I know that... as soon as I'm up I will drive over there. Be there this afternoon. You've gotten me really curious about what you've been up to."

"Good. If you make it here before three, then pick me up at school. I'll be in class."

"I don't know what you've gotten yourself into this time, but it must be a humdinger for you to call."

"Certainly is, and I need your advice and help."

"Okay, girlfriend, I'm on my way. Hold the fort down until I get there. You want me to bring help?"

"No, I don't believe we need to go that far. You'll see what I mean when you get her."

"Well then, I guess I'll find out when I get there."

"Drive safe, ciao!"

"You bet, Love," she said and we hung up the phones.

I smoked another joint, then repacked the money into my shoulder carry-all bag, which I used to carry text books, cookbooks and my changes of clothing. It was leather with a shoulder strap, so the weight wouldn't drag my arm down. I placed the bag under the bed, and lay down to get some rest before I had to get up to school.

I was exhausted; more from nerves than anything else. I didn't think I would sleep but I must have been a lot more tired than I imagined, for I fell asleep while pondering my next move. I only had six weeks of classes left before graduation. I figured to give my notice to the hotel in about a month. The next thing I knew was that the wake up alarm radio went off, and it was time for me to get up and get ready for school.

I smoked a joint, put on a pot of coffee and took a shower before fixing breakfast, then cleaning up afterwards; something that the school instilled in all its students. Chef Paul said, "You make mess, you clean it up. Safety first always. The mess you leave could cause someone else to get hurt or delay what they needed to do by having to clean up your mess first. Simple curtsy and safety, both important issues in any kitchen."

It was a common sense rule of thumb, like always keeping to right going through the swinging doors from the kitchen to the dining room, so you wouldn't run into a server, waitress or busboy with a lot of dishes - little common sense rules that make a restaurant kitchen run smoothly.

Our schedule at school wasn't all that difficult anymore. We were doing mostly book work, as by now we pretty much had all the fundamentals in hand, with the students prepping and preparing a meal every day to be served for lunch to whomever paid the nominal fee to eat in the school's dining room. We always fed all the students from the dental college and beautician's cosmetology schools next door to us, as well as the doctors and nurses from the hospital down the streets, and the university students whose campus was nearby; all of whom knew a good bargain of quality food at a low price.

After the meal was served and the dining hall closed, we would clean up the serving line and kitchen, tag and store all the leftovers in the coolers, then either have classes or projects to work on. I was still hung over from the emotional overload, yet it wouldn't do to miss class. I could always leave early if need be.

Pulling the bag from under bed, I headed out, checking Rachel's room and seeing he had been in and out, locking the apartment door behind me. The school provided lockers to store our personal belongings in while in class (you had to provide your own lock), and I stowed the bag inside while getting out a clean uniform. Nobody would think twice about the bag, as everyone knew I carried my books and clothes in it.

The morning passed slowly. I kept glancing up looking for Mimi, though knowing he couldn't be there until afternoon. Nor were my thoughts ever far from the bag or its contents. I wasn't even thinking about spending any of it; I just wanted it out of my hands and somewhere safe.

Mimi showed up around two. He must have broken every posted speed limit on the highway to get here so quickly; which he could do, as he had installed in his cars all the state of the art radar detectors for speed traps, as well as police band scanners to avoid run-ins with the Highway Patrol and the County Sheriffs on patrol. Mimi had also taken driving courses for race car drivers and defensive driving courses for security purposes.

Mimi gave me a wave, and I held up one finger meaning give me a minute. Going to the office, I told Chef Paul, "I'm through with my work. I need to leave early to take care of some business."

"Go ahead," came the reply.

I grabbed the bag and changed clothes in the bathroom, stuffing the uniform on top of the money in the bag before going out to the dining room, where he greeted me saying, "Hey girlfriend, I got here as fast as I could."

"I see that," I replied, smiling, "thanks for coming. Let's go."

"Can't a girl get something to eat first? I'm famished."

"I'll fix you something at the house. Everything is already put up back there."

"Well then, let's go. I need to put something in my stomach."

I had the bag over one shoulder, and was and carrying the textbook in my arms. Mimi reached for the shoulder bag saying, "Here let me carry that for you."

"No I got it," I said, trying to keep others from discerning how heavy it was. But Mimi felt the weight when he tried to lift it from my shoulder. "God what you got in there? Bricks?"

"Shh," I warned, "you'll see. Come on, let's get out of here," leading Mimi out of the school and into the parking lot, where Mimi's Porsche was being admired by a group of students from the dental college next door. They stepped away as Mimi and I approached.

I got in the passenger side, putting the bag on the floor between my legs. As Mimi got in the driver's side, I told him, "Don't show off."

"Don't worry I got your covered," he replied, picking up on my tension. He started up the car and drove sedately away, to the watching students' disappointment. On the short drive to the apartment, we didn't say anything. Parking at the complex, we went to my apartment, unlocking the door and going inside. Once inside Mimi asked, "Okay now, what's this all about?"

I held up my hand, putting my finger before my mouth in a shushing way, and said, "Wait a minute I need to check on something," putting the bag down on the couch.

"Well hurry up am starved".

I checked Rachel's room; it seemed like she'd been there and left; she must have had a real live one on the line to be away this much. "Thank God for small favors," I thought, seeing the coast was clear, then told Mimi, "Okay it's safe to talk. You check out the bag on the couch while I fix you something to eat. How does egg omelet and toast sound?"

"Like a winner, just get cooking, and what's this thing with the bag anyhow?" He went over to the couch, "I mean, what's the big deal? It's just a bag with your school books in it." Picking it up, he said, "Jesus, you got rocks with the books?" setting it back down on the couch and pulling the zipper tab. It opened to reveal the chef's uniform. Pulling the uniform out to reveal the banded stacks of money, she asked after a moment, "Girlfriend, tell me this isn't what I think it is."

Looking up from the kitchen, where I was slicing mushrooms and dicing tomatoes, onions and green peppers for the omelets before grating a couple of potatoes for hash browns, I said, "What do you think it is?"

"It's got to be counterfeit right? Girl you are going to the feds if you try to spend any of this."

"No, it's as real as it gets, all good ole US currency, "I said, whisking and blending the egg mixture and spices.

As the hash browns and other ingredients browned in the skillets, turned the vegetable mix by tossing, another skill acquired in the school. Taking another skillet, I set it on the front burner, moving the hash browns to the back burner. I put some butter and balsamic vinegar to heat in the skillet, and once the butter had melted and frothed in the pan with the vinegar, I poured in some of the egg mixture, then popped four slices of bread in the toaster before turning to the hash browns and vegetables again.

"Where in the world did you get all this money?" Mimi asked, "There's got to be over a million dollars here."

"How do you know that?" I asked, bewildered, scooping the mushrooms and other vegetables into a bowl. I set it aside and put a couple of rashes of bacon to cook. Meanwhile, I set a pot of coffee started and left it as I spooned the vegetable mixture into the omelet, along with some cottage cheese and shredded cheddar sour cream before folding the omelet over it. I waited a few seconds, then flipped it over. Pulling some plates from the cabinets, I flipped the omelet unto the plate when it finished cooking and started another while turning the bacon over. Also, I stirred and flipped the hash browns then put some more bread in the toaster.

"Because of the weight, silly. The top is all hundreds, that's all I can see, and a million dollars in hundreds only weighs about twenty-five pounds. There's more than twenty five pounds here. It's all hundreds isn't it?"

"Yes, it is. But how do you know that is what weighs?"

"Because each bill has a specific weight. That's how banks, federal government and drug dealers count large sums of money. It's easier to weigh it than count it bill by bill," which explained the digital scale I saw in Jorge's suit.

"Then how much would a million dollars in ones weigh?"

"Over a long ton… now stop with all the questions and tell me where you got it! Did you have to kill anyone? And who is going to be looking for it, and you?"

"Come on and eat first and I will tell you all about it," I replied, flipping the other omelet from the pan onto the plate before dividing up the hash browns and bacon between the two plates, then setting them on the table. The butter and jelly was already out, and I grabbed the pot of coffee and some fresh jalapeno peppers and brought them to the table, pouring each of us a mug of coffee.

"If I wasn't so hungry, I swear I would strangle you," Mimi said, sitting down and digging into the food. "Damn, this is good, I guess you are learning something after all."

"This is nothing special, just something whipped together," I said, sitting down to eat. "I don't know what it is, but I'm never hungry at work, in the kitchen at school or the hotel, but as soon as I stop, I'm starved. I guess because you taste and nibble all day."

After we finished eating, we cleaned up (I washed and he dried), I told Mimi, "Come on into the bedroom and I'll tell you the whole story."

"Just tell me first."

"No... come on," I said, picking up the bag and carrying it into the bedroom, careful not to let any of it spill out of the opened bag.

"I got some good sense bud if you want some?" I asked, setting the bag on the floor by the bed.

"Yes please," he replied, flouncing onto the bed, which is why I hadn't set the bag there knowing he would do so. We smoked the joint as he fidgeted, wanting to know about the money. When we finished he said, "All right... give... tell mama all about it."

So I related the story of how I had come into the possession of the money. He gasped and said, "Honey, if those Colombians, Cubans or whatever, find out you got their money, they'll cut you up into little pieces and feed you to the crabs in the bay,"

"Yeah... well let's hope they never find out, since I don't feel like being food for crabs."

"How much did you get?"

"According to my count, and I counted it four times to be certain, one point six-two-five million. Three-twenty-five stacks of five thousand, in hundreds".

Mimi got up from the bed, and pawed through the bundles of money before leaving it and walking around the bedroom, where he spotted the baggy of rock. I had tossed it onto the dresser top the night before, and had completely forgotten about it.

"Oh ho, what's this?" he asked, picking up the baggy and examining its contents. "Girl, where did you get this?"

"Same place as the money. They had a block of it in the fridge, I just broke that off."

Sticking his finger into the bag after unzipping it, he scraped some off onto a fingernail and finger, which he put into his mouth, rubbing his gums. "Girlfriend, I would say you ripped off some major cocaine cowboys, if this is representative of their product. This is primo… hundred percent pure, straight off a key."

"A key?"

"A kilo, two-point-two pounds. It's how it's packaged. A bale can be anywhere from thirty to sixty keys in it."

"Oh I thought it was about a pound of it in the fridge."

"That's because it was compressed, which is why it's as hard as it is".

"How do you know it's pure? I thought cocaine was white. This is a creamy color, almost a pale yellow with pink streaks."

"Yeah they call it 'butter' because of that. You got a mirror and a razor blade? I'll show you."

After getting what he asked, I watched him break off a small piece from the chunks in the bag, dividing it into fine lines. Taking a bill from the top dresser, he rolled it into a tube, saying, "I'll show you how to snort it," inhaling one line of powder into each nostril, before handing the bill to me.

"Now your turn," he said, "just inhale through the bill and follow the line like I showed you." I tried once, not getting the line at all.

"No, inhale as you go along the line of powder. Get it all," he instructed. I did as he said with the other nostril, and felt a pure rush like a train came roaring into and through my body and head. We actually had to wait for it all to pass before continuing our conversation; I couldn't even feel the effects of the reefer we had smoked.

Locking the zip-lock baggy over, Mimi said, "You must have close to five ounces here, or more."

"Then we'll split it, you take half."

"I'm not going to argue with that. Now, what did you have me come all the way up here for? Just to tell me all this?"

"No I called because you know about money. I got this, and I don't know what to do with it. I can't keep it under my bed, or tote it around with me everywhere I go. I'm at sea about what I should be doing with it. I'm not used to money like this, and I thought you would know what to do with it."

"Then you did the right thing. The first thing we need to do is get this to a safe place."

"A safe place like where?"

"Like a bank, into an account with your name on it."

"Wont the bank have something to say about opening an account with this much cash? Not to mention the authorities".

"Just depends on the bank, and I'm not talking in the state anyways. What are you doing this weekend? Can you get away?"

"I can call in sick at the hotel and make up for it later."

"Well then do that. I'll borrow daddy's plane and pilot and we'll take a trip over to the islands where our family has some business interests and we know the people. We'll get you an account set-up, then start wiring money around to use it legitimately."

"What will I do with it until then?"

"I'll take it with me, and throw it in daddy's safe at the house until then, he said, which is what I had been hoping he would say, as having that much money around scared me. It was just too much.

Going to the bag, he pulled out five stacks of hundreds, saying, "This is the odd twenty-five thousand you keep in case you got to get in the wind. It'll give you some running room. The rest I'll take with me. Just don't get stupid and greedy and try to go back for more - those boys will slice and dice you. I happen to be partial to crab, and I wouldn't ever be able to eat it again if something happened to you."

"You don't have to worry about that, "I assured him. You couldn't melt me and pour me back into that suite after some more. I get the willies even think about it."

We talked some more and did some more cocaine. Then I got a large zip-lock baggy from the kitchen and we split the coke up. Then Mimi said, "I'll pick you up for the airport bright and early Saturday morning. I'll call you before we leave from down there. Bring some swimming trunks, we'll stay all day." We hugged as he was leaving, and I said, "Drive safe, and be careful".

"You don't have to tell me that, this is a whole lot of time I got right here," he said, indicating the bag. "I'll look like a grandma on her way to church on Sunday morning, going back. If I had known this was coming, I would have driven a loaner or a plane, but it's no biggy, I'll manage".

"Sorry about that, there's no way I could tell you all this over the phone."

"Don't worry about it, I got you covered. We're sisters right?"

"Right as rain." He drove off with a wave of his hand out the car window, and I returned to the apartment.

I still had to prepare for work at the hotel. Getting rid of the money had taken a huge load off my mind, but still, I wasn't looking forward to work, not knowing whether the coke and money had been missed by Jorge and Enrique.

I had to play it out as if I had done nothing wrong, so as to not to draw attention to myself; there are many times when a rabbit has ended up in the cook-pot because they broke from the cover, when if they had stayed put where they were, the hunter would have passed right by.

Most people would believe me to be crazy for letting Mimi drive off with all the money like that, as he could as very well keep it and tell me to fuck off. I didn't believe he would that, while truthfully I wouldn't really have minded if he had. Of course, it would have meant the end of our friendship, which I would mourn more than the loss of the money. If it had been a few thousand, then it might have been different, but the amount of money in the bag was just too much for me to get a handle on.

At the hotel that evening, Jorge and Enrique dined at the buffet and acted normally. I had a room service call to their suite later in the evening, and sweated bullets and almost died while going in the suite, knowing they were waiting on me. I had a baby Fairburn blade in a spring sheath strapped to my forearm, and a throwing blade at the back of my neck, the blade extending along my spine in its sheath. Nonetheless, I recalled the adage about bringing a knife to a gun fight.

I prayed the whole time going into the penthouse, and while inside, I prayed, "Lord, you get me through this, I will never do anything like this again." I was a hustler, but, I wasn't cut out to be a criminal. I felt reborn leaving the penthouse after delivering the serving cart inside, like I had cheated death, although nothing unusual at all happened in the suite while I was there. Still, I was trembling with adrenaline rushing in my veins, and held tight by the grip of fear as the door of the suite closed behind me. I waited for the elevator and returned to the kitchen.

Saturday, I got the call from Mimi at four-thirty in the morning, telling me, "Our ETA at the municipal airport is six-thirty. Be at the airport, as we have a long day ahead of us, with little time to waste if we want to hit the beach."

"Don't worry, I'll be there, waiting."

"Any problems on your end?"

"No, it's still as if nothing happened."

"Good, let's hope it stays that way, and don't forget the trunks."

"Trunks?"

"Swimming trunks, silly. Unless, you want to go au naturel?"

"Yeah right, I'll see you at the airport. Ciao."

"Ciao back at you," he said, and we hung up.

I smoked a joint, showered, made a pot of coffee and ate before catching a cab to the municipal airport on Ralcher Road.

The corporate jet Mimi arrived in was sleek, able to carry eight to ten passengers with a lounge and sleeping quarters. There were just the two of us and the pilot. They were a little early, and we were back in the air by six-forty-five; the flight would take an hour or so. Mimi chatted with the pilot up front for a while, before coming to join me in the passenger section. "Daddy leases this for corporate business, and it's not used all that much," he told me, "Tom (the pilot) is glad to get the flight time."

Not having seen the money anywhere I asked, "Where's the bag?"

"You mean the one with the money?"

"What else!"

"It's already over there. Daddy had to go over there on business anyway, so he took it over with him on the yacht. It's already at the bank, waiting on us."

"If it's already at there in bank then why are we going?"

"To swim!" Mimi said, laughing, "No, just joking, because there's a lot of paperwork you will have to take care of at the bank. Plus, the bank is very particular about it not being done by proxy. They like to know the people they are doing business with. For protection, you have to provide passwords for the accounts to access them, as most of your transactions will by wire or phone unless you want to run over there every time you want to get some money or make a transaction. Don't worry girlfriend, Mimi's got you covered."

"Your father didn't think it's strange? The bag of money?"

"Daddy did what I asked him to. If he had wanted to know, he would've asked. Our family has been in Florida for a long time - he has seen more than his share of strange things." We talked for a while, and dozed the rest of the flight.

At the island airport, customs examined the paperwork, walked through the plane and left. At the bank, Mimi introduced me to the bank's general manager, a Mr. McKenzie, who was short, slender, light skinned black and more than a little gay. It wasn't hard to tell we shared the bond of being sisters under the skin. "Mac... I want you to meet my best friend, Poison," Mimi said, "he's your new depositor".

"Poison is a very unusual name for a person to have, what were your parents thinking?" McKenzie asked.

Mimi laughed, "Poison is not his birth name; it's a nickname some people gave him."

"Do tell. I must say it isn't every day one gets to meet someone with a *nom de guerre* as that. We welcome you as a client of the bank, Mr. Poison, and hope our business together will be mutually satisfying."

If I didn't know better, I'd have sworn this guy was making a pass at me. I said, "I hope so too..."

"Come into my office and we'll get your accounts squared away and in order." We followed him into his office, where I spent the next hour signing forms and documents, with Mimi alongside telling me what I was signing for. "I had Mac set up five accounts under five different corporate names," Mimi explained, "with all of them being subsidiaries of PKM Ltd."

"PKM?"

"Your initials."

"Oh…" I said, getting it. The P had stumped me for a second; P for poison.

"The corporations are set up over here, so anyone looking to find out anything about them or you will come up blank. Four of the accounts have three hundred and fifty thousand in each of them. The other hundred is your mad money account. The rest are for investments. Two of the accounts will be tied up in certificates of deposit with various banks, one account will be a portfolio of investments in Blue Chip Stocks and the fourth will be with a financial firm".

"Financial firm?"

"Stocks and bonds. You just can't let your money sit, you have to make it work for you to make more. Otherwise, before you know it, it'll be all gone."

"A million dollars?" I asked, surprised. It seemed like a million dollars would last a life time - at least it should.

"Trust me, you could blow through millions fast and easy. A million is nothing in today's world. Once you got into the habit of spending on this and that, it would soon be gone. There's one hard rule: don't touch investments or principal, live off your interest."

"Sound advice Mr. Poison," Mac interjected, "One I would take to heart. As a banker I give the same advice to all our customers. Those who listen usually do well. Those who don't soon learn the proverb, 'a fool and his money are soon parted' is a verity. The bank will make every effort to assist you in managing your funds and serving your needs. However, we can't prevent you from acting foolishly. After all, it's your money to do with as you wish."

"I see," I said, feeling a little overwhelmed. I hadn't known money carried such responsibilities. As a hustler, it was either feast or famine when you had it; when you didn't have it, you looked for ways to get it, or went hungry. It certainly did make sense though, a steady income was better than no income. Last week I had been virtually a pepper on the grind trying to make something happen for me. This week, I was a millionaire whose only worry was to stay alive long enough to enjoy it.

Once all the papers and documents were signed and notarized, Mac took us into the safety deposit box vault and gave me a key to one of the boxes, saying, "You'll want to keep your copy of the documents in the box, so they don't fall into the wrong hands. You will be the only one with access to the box. Mimi had the foresight to rent it from your funds."

"Okay," I said, placing the documents inside the box and locking it back, with Mac using the banks key on the second lock before escorting us back to the lobby. "That concludes our business for today," he said with a smile. "I'm going to have a little get together later at my place, and you both are invited to attend. It will be just a few friends."

Mimi answered, "Next time Mac, we really appreciate the offer but we just came over to get this done and go for a swim. Poison has to be at work, and has a lot of studying to do as her finals are coming up."

"Do tell, what are you studying, Mr. Poison?"

"Culinary Arts."

"He wants to be one of the oh-la-la chefs," Mimi said.

"I see. We have many fine dining establishments on the island. Perhaps you might have a position on their staff one day."

"That's always a possibility," I said, "though I still have a lot to learn."

"Well, you're young yet, so you have the time. Maybe on your next visit I could show around the island and you can see for yourself."

"I will most definitely do that...," I said, thinking "this guy was coming on to me", "I am certain we share many of the same interests."

"Until next time then."

"I'll look forward to it". We said our goodbyes and left the bank and Mac behind.

We caught a cab for the beach, and on the way there I asked Mimi, "I didn't want to say anything while we were at the bank but the amount didn't add up. I came up with one-point-six and not one-point-five".

"The bank charges a five percent service and handling fee for such large cash deposits," he replied, "the rest went for the corporate paperwork, and the safety deposit box rental. You didn't think they would do this for free, did you?

"I didn't know. As I told you before, when it comes to money, I am lost at sea. And didn't you get the impression Mac was coming on to me?"

"Most definitely girl, just don't take it personal okay? He does it all the time. Mac is the most outrageous flirt you will ever meet."

"I see, do tell...," I mimicked, causing us both to burst into laughter.

The beach was beautiful, and the swim refreshing; I didn't know signing papers could be such work. After getting a bite at a small restaurant just off the beach, we headed back to the airport for the flight back to Tampa.

Mimi and I talked most of the way back, with Mimi giving me advice on how to manage the money, followed then by chit-chat about clothes, future plans and his current flame. He told me, "You have to come to the ranch for a few days to visit before you head off to California. The family has been wondering when you will come and you know what they say, "All work without play makes Poison a very dull girl.""

"I was just planning on a visit anyways," I said, since I was going to give the hotel notice prior to graduation, settling all my affairs in Tampa, so that after graduation, I could send out my stuff to California with a shipping company before following it out in a few days' time.

I was planning on flying out to see if I could find an apartment close by Chef M.'s restaurant, or the one I would be working in. I had told Rachel about the planned move, and Rachel would take over the apartment lease while renting out the other two bedrooms to queens at the Club.

"Yes, please do that. We don't know when we'll be able see each other again."

"We'll still talk by phone."

"Yes, but that is not the same thing as seeing each other and you know it."

"We'll figure something out then."

"That we will."

We parted with hugs at the municipal airport in Tampa, Mimi telling me, "I'll hold you to the promise of coming down to the ranch for a visit. The family really wants to see you also."

"Count on it love." She left, and I caught a cab back to my apartment.

At the apartment, I fired up a joint and got a soda from the fridge, then sat back and contemplated everything that had happened that day, taking it easy as I wouldn't have to work at the hotel until tomorrow, for the buffet and room service

A few things occurred in the next couple of weeks for which I hadn't taken into account. I still got butterflies every time I saw Enrique and Jorge, especially when taking the room service, which was still a death defying feat from which I was glad to escape alive each time, although there was never any hint of anything amiss with them.

Rumor started floating around the hotel about a sneak thief who was hitting some of the guest rooms. There was some mention that whoever was doing it had to be using a passkey. I did not make the connection then. I didn't really even give it much thought as the penthouses weren't mentioned, and because the passkey I had made was safely down a sewer drain, where temptation couldn't get it back. Not that there much chance of me tempting fate again.

Then, when I came in to work the following week, the hotel management summoned me to the front office. The head honcho, Mr. Williams, was seated behind the desk with Mr. Peters, the general manager seated to one side.

"Come in and sit down Mr. Marks," Williams said as I entered. I took the seat across from him, while wondering what this was all about.

"I'm sure by now you have heard the rumors about someone slipping into the guest rooms and stealing valuables. Well, regrettably, the rumor is true," Peters began.

"I've heard the rumors, but what does that have to do with me? I'm not going in the guest rooms and stealing valuables," I said, while mentally crossing fingers.

"Nor are we accusing you of it either. Most of the thefts occurred while you were off duty, and at school," Williams said, meaning it had occurred to them, if I went so far or cheek all that out. He continued, "However, it has come to our attention you were recently released from prison."

"I was released a year ago," I said, agitated.

"Hear me out. Because of the unfortunate timing of these incidents, the manager of the hotel feels it would be in the best interest of the hotel and its guests to ask you to resign your position with the hotel service".

"But I haven't done anything wrong."

"We're not saying you have. However, we have the hotel's reputation to be considered. We don't want to fire you, because that would look bad on your resume. As you said, you haven't done anything wrong - you've been a good employee. The hotel management will provide you with a letter of recommendation for any future employer, and we will give you the full severance package. But, we must insist on your resignation."

I sat down and mulled that for a moment. I had planned on giving notice anyways, though I didn't like what they were doing. I could understand their reasons for doing so: it wasn't just the fact that I had criminal record and access to the master key, or a belief that I had to have some involvement with the thefts. What really concerned them was appearance, and the hotel's reputation. If it got out that the hotel was employing criminal fresh out of prison with a wave of thefts going on at the hotel, it would damage the company image.

"If I agree to resign under these conditions, when would it become effective?" I asked.

"Immediately, we have the paperwork for you to sign right here," said Peters, pushing it across the desk.

I signed the papers, while noting that the severance check and paycheck for the wages I had earned working to date had already been made out, and only required a signature. I passed the completed paperwork back to him, and he signed off on the letter of recommendation and the checks before turning them over to me and remarking, "We regret the unfortunate circumstances which brought this about this about, as you were a real asset as an employee here at the hotel and we wish you the best of luck with your next employer."

"Thank you," I said, which is about all you can say to a pat on the back after a kick in the balls. Even had I wanted to be outraged I couldn't. After all, it meant I wouldn't see any more of Enrique and Jorge.

"I'm certain you will understand if Mr. Peters escorts you from the premises," Mr. Williams said.

"Of course." They were now giving me the bum's rush now they had gotten what they wanted.

And wouldn't you know it, as we were crossing the lobby of the hotel to go out, there were Enrique and Jorge at the front desk with their luggage, checking out. I stuck the checks and letter of recommendation into the shoulder bag I had gotten to replace the other. I said goodbye to Fred the doorman under the Porteneu who, by his sad face, already knew what taken place. But he couldn't say anything with Mr. Peters present.

I left the hotel grounds, and walked across the causeway to the beach area to think over this turn of events. It had occurred to me while I was at the manager's office that it was just too much coincidence for those thefts to suddenly happen shortly after I had made the pass key made. Being one of those who didn't believe in such a thing as coincidence, I put two and two together and came up with Jerry, the shady locksmith I had gotten to make me the key. This meant it would certainly be worth my while to pay Jerry a visit, so I took a cab to Florida Avenue.

The way Jerry acted as I walked in the front of the door of the shop was like he wanted to run out the back, letting me know I was spot-on about my suspicions as to what he had done.

By way of greeting, I asked, "What was your cut?"

"Cut? What are you talking about?" he asked nervously, looking around everywhere, seeing nothing but me.

"You know what I'm talking about. What was your cut with the people you gave a copy of the master key to?"

"You want some money?"

"No, I just want to know what your cut was."

"Fifteen percent… why do you want to know?

"Because I wanted to know if you had gotten enough to take a vacation."

"A vacation? For what?"

"Because if those mutts get caught, guess whose name is going to get tossed into the hat ring of a let's make a deal round?"

"These are solid people, they don't do no talking."

"That depends on who's doing the asking, and the methods employed, and we're not talking about the po-po".

"What are we talking about?"

"What I'm talking about is some very nasty people might take interest in learning from your friends where they obtained the key from."

"How does that concern you?"

"It concerns me Jerry, because it will lead them to you."

"I wouldn't give you up. You needn't about that."

"Oh I think the first time they clamp a pair of vice-grip pliers onto one of your testicles, you'll sing like a canary."

"Vice grips…testicles? But you don't have to worry, the crew has skyed."

"Yeah, well they will be back for another shot at the honey pot. And you better hope it's the police who nab them first. You've heard the term 'swimming with fishes'? If the wrong bunch gets to them, you'll be dining with crabs - only as the main entrée- and I don't want to be joining you there at the crab fest."

"Jesus, you really think so?" he asked, showing a sick look on his face knowing I was right. Now he knew the crew would be back another go for the honey pot, saying, "Oh man, what have you gotten me into?"

"No, you mean what I have gotten myself into. I paid you well to make one copy, you took it upon yourself to make another and put it out there. What comes of that is on you. My concern is ensuring you're not around if they come looking for you. So it's best if you took your show on the road for a month or so."

"Man, I can't leave my business."

"Depends on how much you love your life. Consider it a vacation - the business will be here when you come back."

"Well, I do need to go see my mother. She's been bugging me to visit for a while now. I just couldn't find the time to do so."

"Trust me, now is the time to go see her. Make her happy, and possibly save your life".

"You really believe it's that serious?"

"Do you really want to take that risk? At least this will give everything a chance to blow over. If the po-po ain't here waiting for you to come back, then you should be free and clear."

"I told you, the crew is solid."

"For your sake, let's hope so."

I left him looking worried, and I knew he'd be gone before the day was over. Catching a cab back to the apartment, I called Mimi up and relayed the latest news, ending with, "which means I'll be free this weekend."

"You want me to come pick you up?"

"Nah, I'll just catch a flight down there. You can pick me up at the airport."

"No, I will pick you up at the municipal airport up there, say Friday after class. Catch a cab to the airport, I'll be waiting."

"Going to borrow Daddy's plane again?"

"Something better, you'll see. Gets you out of the area as well, in case those two or their friends come looking for you."

"Somehow or another, I don't think that will happen."

Not that I knew; I hadn't caught any vibes of the two during that period; Enrique wouldn't be able to conceal his anger about being ripped off. Either they hadn't missed the money, or had written it off as an error. I couldn't envision the former, as they were too organized.

"Anyway, I do think the cat burglars will be back for another shot at the hotel. According to the rumors, they got a half to three quarters of a million dollars in cash, jewelry, travelers check and electronics. I don't see them passing on an opportunity to score like that again".

"All the more reason you should be down here. You got any of the other left?"

"Other?"

"Butter!"

"Butter?" Then it hit me - the coke. "Yeah, I got most of it. After you left, I tossed it in the freezer and forgot about it."

"Bring it along. I'm about out."

"Not a problem, I'll just call you the Hoover Girl."

Mimi laughed, "Whatever, see you Friday, ciao!"

"Ciao back at you."

This would be my first time visiting the Cleary Ranch. Mimi usually came down to Tampa, as I had been so busy with work and school to get there.

During class on Friday, Chef Paul, who had heard about what had happened, told me, "It's their loss. A damn shame, but there's little you can do about it, except go with the flow. At least they gave you a glowing letter of recommendation. Have you given any thought to the matter we discussed in my office?"

"Yes and the answer is yes! So you can tell Chef M. to expect me."

"Good, you're making the right decision. I expect to hear good things about you."

I left class early to go back to the apartment, to pick up the bag I had packed with everything I would need for the weekend. I didn't forget the coke, as well as an ounce of weed, although Mimi would have plenty of it. I didn't mind giving up the rest of the coke either. I would do some with Mimi, but it just wasn't my kind of thing.

I called a cab which carried me out to the airport where Mimi waited in the lounge. Seeing me, he said, "Hey sis! Let's go. The plane is out there."

"I didn't see the plane," I said, expecting to see the Learjet.

"It's the twin engine Beechcraft parked over there, come on".

I followed him to the small plane, where Mimi did a walk around, pulling some small chocks on lines from under the wheels before opening the door to the aircraft and throwing the chocks in.

"Come on, get in. Time's wasting," he said.

"Where's the pilot? We can't go anywhere without a pilot."

"I'm the pilot, thank you."

'You know how to fly this thing? I didn't know you could fly."

"Now you know. I soloed when I was fourteen."

'Which doesn't answer my question, can you fly this thing?"

"I flew it up here; I'm rated for multi-engine aircraft. Now stop with the questions and climb aboard."

"The plane isn't hot, is it?" I asked, still uneasy.

"Stop with all the questions and get in. the plane is ours. Nothing to worry about."

"So you say," I muttered under my breath as I climbed aboard.

Mimi went through a checklist before starting the engine, telling me, "Take the co-pilot's seat and put on the headset so we can talk. The plane is noisy up here in the cockpit when we're in the air."

"Oh I see," I said, putting the headset on.

Mimi put some maps into a case and called the control tower for clearance, and after a minute or two, hung up and said, "I already filed the flight plan and were cleared." He taxied the plane out to the runway, then took the plane up smoothly, with me holding my breath until we were in the air.

"Oh stop worrying," he said, "I'm a good pilot, I will get you there safe and sound."

"You never told me you could fly a plane,"

"It never came up and I had no reason to. Never thought about it, tell you the truth. There are a couple of thermoses in the back with coffee in them, and some donuts. Could you get me a cup of coffee? I don't want to get up from the controls and give you a heart attack up here, since you don't know about the autopilot."

"No problem," I said, as I wanted him to stay there. I certainly couldn't fly this thing.

After I had gotten some coffee and donuts, I asked him over the headset, "You have a car waiting on us at the airport?"

"We're not going to the airport, we're going to the ranch, which has a landing strip for our plane and a hanger."

"Jesus, how big is this place with its own runway?"

Nearing the end of our flight, we flew over a large acreage of citrus groves and planted fields, spotting the runway which was set in a large cleared area with a cluster of Quonset huts including the hanger. "That's the family ranch over there," Mimi said, indicating the large palatial two story home sprawling out amid other buildings, with barns and paddocks set further out. "We keep a few horses, all my sisters, nieces, nephews and mother likes to ride. Daddy has some, thoroughbreds at our place up in Ocala."

"Who owns all those orange groves and fields? It looks like they have your place surrounded."

"Those are ours also. Everything you see is ours."

"You really are Ms. Richie Rich Bitch."

"Yes, but you're no longer an Annie, you have family and a stake now. We'll have to find you a new name."

"Nah, I think I'll stick with Annie."

Mimi landed the plane smoothly. He had me open the hanger doors as he taxied the plane inside, before shutting it down, telling me, "Dave will refuel it and take care of it as we would need it later for the flight back." We used one of the nearby golf carts to carry us to the main house.

"So this is how the other half lives…," I said. I had known his family had money, however it was one thing to know something in abstract, and quite another when confronted with its reality.

"Oh come on, we're not that rich," he laughed.

"From where I am standing, it sure looks that way," I replied, getting out of the golf cart by the long barn-like garage. The house was still a way off.

"Are we going to walk to the house?"

"No, we're not staying here, nobody's here. All the family is at the beach house in West Palm Beach. We just stopped here to pick up a ride, come on now." He led me into the garage where his car was among some others. We to the beach house, which was somewhat a misnomer as the property was huge. It had access to the beach, but also a dock and mooring for their boats. The house itself was large enough to accommodate the whole family and extra, but it also had guesthouses, which is where Mimi and I stayed that weekend.

The whole family greeted me warmly with hugs. We had a blast that weekend, with Mimi teaching me how to water ski: full of sun and fun. We flew back to Tampa on Sunday, where we hit the gay clubs. Mimi slept over that night and flew back home on Monday.

It turned out that Chef M. had called Chef Paul and told him to let me know that he had leased an apartment for me which was close to his establishments, and that he would be waiting on me when I came after graduation.

Mimi and I repeated the routine the following weekends, with him picking me up after class on Fridays, staying at the beach house and flying back on Sundays to do the clubs. He was there when I graduated with honors from the Culinary Arts School, where Chef Paul presented me with the chef's hat and jacket given to the top student of the class. It came as a total surprise for me, as I did not expect it.

The following weekend I was in California, in the new apartment, getting ready for work with Chef M. at his restaurants. I believed then that with the exception of Mimi and the Clearys, I was through with Florida. I was never more wrong.

Chef M. had three restaurants in the Los Angeles area. The one I spent the most time in at the beginning was "El Almin", which only served brunch from ten in the morning to one in the afternoon, and dinner from six in the evening to eleven at night; mostly by reservation, with very few walk-ins. However, Chef M. would rotate me among his three establishments in order to broaden my training and experience. Of the other two restaurants, the one in Hollywood Boulevard was full dining, lunch and dinner. The doors would open at 10:00 am and close at 12:00 am, while the one on

Sunset was an exclusive bistro for gourmands whose menu was written on a write-erase board each day.

I had gotten my driver's license for my twenty-first birthday at Mimi's instance, saying that he never heard of anyone my age not knowing how to drive. I never took him up on the offer of a car as I didn't need one in Florida; I could always catch a ride with someone or a bus or cab.

California however, was totally different; you required a car to get from place to place, and you were lost if you didn't have one. Therefore, I bought one from a co-worker at the restaurant on Hollywood Boulevard. It was an old model car in good running condition, but I didn't buy it for its looks. It had to be in good condition, otherwise it wouldn't be allowed on the road in California, with its strict vehicle inspections.

Two things I didn't like about Los Angeles were the smog, and rush hour traffic. Most times I would miss rush hour traffic, as I would be doing prep work at one of the restaurants as Chef M. insisted I learn everything from setting a table as a server to bussing and washing dishes, saying, "A good chef should be able to do every Job in the restaurant or kitchen and fill in where needed. This is a fine dining establishment, not a school of prima donnas."

The smog was something else. When sky was clear with a breeze, it was beautiful, but there were days when the smog settled like a haze over the city, leaving an oily taste in the back of your throat and burning your eyes. I always kept Visine and throat spray handy whenever I had to be outside on those kinds of days.

The first few months at Chef M.'s establishments were hectic, with getting all the routines down and learning so much, which had to be remembered and assimilated on off duty hours. I would spend hours in the apartment's chef's kitchen, which Chef M. had ensured was present before leasing it, studying and trying out new recipes.

AS Chef M. told me, "Never be afraid to try something new. It's all a matter of perspective and taste. A chef has to be both creative and innovative to stay ahead of the game in creating and developing their own style. Cooking at this level is an art-form, and should be appreciated as such. Presentation is as important as preparation, or even more so, because it is what the customer sees before they even taste."

Therefore, I didn't have much time for a social life during this period. Mimi would fly down every couple of months or so to drag me from my "dungeon" as he referred to the kitchen, with him and my neighbors being the beneficiaries of some of my creations. "This is so delicious! You keep this up and I'll be as big as a house," he used to say. We visited gay clubs and cruised, as we had no intention of returning home alone.

The money I was earning in salary was ending up in my regular bank account in California. I hadn't touched the accounts in the Islands, and I had no time to think about them. I had only spent a few hundred of the twenty-five thousand Mimi had given me from the bag as my getaway money. The rest resided in a shoe box in the back of my closet. Come to think about it, I wasn't spending much money at all.

I would receive regular monthly statements on the accounts in the Islands, the earning from which were reinvested. The banks statements were delivered to a post office box I had taken out under the PKM Ltd. corporate name. I was too busy at the time to give any of it any consideration. The money was doing fine, growing steadily and increasing as I wasn't spending any of the earned interest or dividends. Usually I would just glance at the statements before tossing them in a drawer, thinking I would get back to them sometime.

Through the contacts I had maintained in Florida, I learned that the hotel had experienced a few more thefts. It turned out that the first crew was a lot smarter than I had given them credit for, as they had figured the same way as I had, that going back for a second shot at the honey pot would be too risky. Therefore, what they had one was to go to Jerry to have several copies of the master key made from the one they had then put them out on the street for a price, where they were snapped up by thieves who each believed they were getting the only copy.

When security caught a third thief with another copy of the pass key, the hotel management had had all the locks changed out. The new master key had been placed in the hotel's vault, with the managers being the only ones with access to them.

All of this had muddied the waters up nicely, as now it would be almost impossible to trace the original copy back to Jerry or me; so much for Enrique and Jorge; crab would remain a main entrée for Mimi's dining. I had gotten away scot free with their money - how fate must have laughed at me.

The fifteen to eighteen hour days, six days a week, were taking their toll. Chef M. finally told me, "You need to take a few days off, give yourself a break. You're coming along nicely, you're a quick study and you really have a feel and talent for this. I don't want you to burn out, so take a few days off. Go visit some friends and relax. All work and no play, and your artistic edge begins to suffer, as does the quality of your production and product."

I called Mimi to tell him I would be coming to Florida to spend a few days. However, when Mimi answered the phone, the first thing she said was, "Funny you should call. I was just fixing to call you."

"I'll be there shortly, and you can tell me in person," I replied.

"I would hold off on that just now, if I were you."

"Why?"

"Because Daddy's attorney friend in Tampa called. The police were there to inquire as to your whereabouts. There's a warrant out for your arrest in Tampa."

"Arrest? For what?" I knew it couldn't be about the money. They wouldn't go to the police about someone stealing from them, that would be something they would handle themselves.

"I don't have all the details as of yet. Something about fraud and grand larceny at the hotel."

"It has to be a mistake!"

"I know, but let me do some checking and get back to you on it. Maybe we can get it all straightened out. I'll call you back as soon as I get all the details." He hung up.

The upshot of all this was that my trip to Florida entailed turning myself in with an attorney and bondsman on a prearrangement, on nine counts charging me with fraud and grand larceny. I went through the formality of being booked into a jail, then released on bond, all within a couple of hours. Mimi's family put up a surety bond for me to guarantee my presence at any future court dates while having retained one of the better criminal defense attorneys - Benny Lazzra- who was well connected within the court house and political circles of Hillsborough County.

I was outraged from reading the indictment and information concerning the charges, as I knew I had been set up as a patsy and fall guy for the head chef, Chef Stevens, who had resigned and disappeared before the fiscal yearend audit. The scut work I thought he had me doing had really been him setting me up to be his fall guy, stealing right from under my nose all the time, padding inventories and invoices for products which are never delivered, or diverted elsewhere.

All the paperwork he had made me sign for or deliver to the general manager had me with a bull's-eye squarely on my back when the shit hit the fan. What steamed me the most was that I hadn't had a clue that it had been going on; snookered like a sucker. It only amounted to something like fifty six thousand dollars, but still I was street and he was a square John. This wasn't supposed to happen to me, not by him anyways; if anyone got over on anyone, it should have been me on him.

The attorney, Benny, told me, "I wouldn't worry about it too much. We will put an investigation on him and see what he comes up with, go back to California, and let me work on it. I will delay the case for as long as possible to give the hotel management time to cool off. Right now they want your blood. We got to give it time to settle down and change their minds."

It wasn't hard to figure out why the hotel was out for blood, because not only did they believe I stole their money, they now also believed I had something to do with the thefts at the hotel. Both of us were outraged for different reasons. After talking to Mimi, I caught the flight back to Los Angeles, where I explained what happened to Chef M., telling him, "I am innocent of those charges."

He held up his hand in a stop motion, saying, "You don't have to convince me of that. I know you didn't have the know-how to pull something like that off. Maybe now, yes but not six to nine months ago when all this took place. It would have required knowledge and experience you didn't have at the time. Besides, this is not Chef Stevens' first trip to the cookie jar."

"You mean he's done it before?"

"Yes, at least twice. Once in New Jersey and again in Maryland I believe…"

"Didn't the hotel in Tampa know about it when they hired him?"

"Probably not. Most of the hotels try to avoid bad publicity like the plague. So they allowed him to resign, swallowed the loss and forgot about it. I don't know why the hotel in Tampa is making such an issue of it." I did, but it was best to let that sleeping dog lie.

Chef M. Continued, "Chef Steven could easily have had everything I have now, except he loves to play poker. He has a gambling problem, and he does poorly at the tables - hardly ever wins. I imagine when this gets out; he will have a difficult time finding another position within the trade."

"Why is that? He's done it before and nothing happened."

"Yes, but he never involved a novice before, and letting them take the blame for his egregious conduct is totally unacceptable, and the trade will take a dim view of it."

I spent the next seventeen months perfecting my craft while deciding to specialize as a pastry chef, doing desserts, pastries and breads. I loved the rest of it, yet my heart was in those, and I was well on my way to making a name for myself within the trade for my desserts and breads, especially among the customers.

One of my hits was the double chocolate devil's food cake topped with whipped cream and strawberries, with the whipped cream made from scratch, starting with heavy cream and sugar, and whipping it into a thick, rich mixture. The strawberries, I marinated in brandy (peach, apricot or plum) mixed with honey and brown sugar, which kept in the refrigerator before slicing some of them up and incorporating them into the whipped cream. I would then scoop the whipped cream unto the slice of cake, garnishing it with whole strawberries. I used other fruits as well (cherries, blueberries, raspberries), but the strawberries seemed to make the most impact with customers.

Marinating the berries was not only to impart flavor to them; it would also make them stand out from the cream. The different brandies imparted an undertone to the strawberries' flavor, and made this dessert a popular favorite. Mimi was a huge fan of it, and always took some home for his family whenever he came to visit, telling me, "They send me out here to get this back to them."

I had also started up an escort service, the legit kind, with male and female escorts. One thing about Los Angeles was that there were plenty of beautiful bodies and faces to select from. Mindful of the pending charges in Florida, I found the perfect manager to keep all the libidos and drama in check. Mary Jo, or simply Jo as we called her, was a stocky no-nonsense lesbo who didn't tolerate shit from anyone. I knew the trade and its pitfalls, and I didn't mind the boys and girls hustling as long as they were discreet about it. If they were too wide open, I'd put them in contact with a madam to go into business with, as I had no intention of adding pandering charges to my other woes.

Mary Jo made certain the business was a straightforward escort service, and only that. I had used some of the money from the mad money account and my regular savings for the escort service start-up, which was a subsidiary of PKM Ltd. The business took off immediately, making money like you wouldn't believe. Soon we were able to pick and choose among the escort applicants, looking for minds as well as beautiful faces and bodies.

I even had a bunch of staff members aside from Jo who was vice-president of operations. There was Harvey, an accountant acting as our chief financial officer keeping the books straight, and an office manager, Louise (one of Jo's friends), to do the bookings.

My assistant's name was Ken, a light skinned black with fine features and startling bottle-green eyes, who had wavy brown hair with reddish tints. You would think he would be any woman's wet dream, but Ken would jump over a hundred women for a man; he was just geared that way. He was in demand as an escort and a model with photographers for magazines, for both women and gays, even where the women knew he didn't swing their way. He was beautiful to look at, yet also had a fine intelligence; Jo and I thought he was totally going to waste as an escort and model.

I was grooming him to be the personnel director and corporate manager to fill in for me, as it seemed likely that I would end up doing some time for the charges in Florida. The hotel itself had backed off when sources informed them of Chef Stevens' gambling addiction, and that they hadn't been his first victim, just his latest.

However, the state attorney still wanted to pursue the matter, stating that the fact that the invoices and paperwork had my signature couldn't be gotten around, and insistent that I serve some time. Therefore, we were in the process of negotiating a deal. One thing about Florida is that they have no problem sending an innocent person to prison; all they are concerned with is their conviction rates.

Ken's nickname among us was Ken-Toy. I couldn't recall how that came about, whether we gave it to him or he came with it, but it suited him well. There was nothing sexual between us; as I said, I had other plans for him.

I hadn't seen Mimi in months, as both of us had been busy, when I got the call from one of her brothers - Devlin. "Poison, Mimi asked me to call," he informed me, "he's had an accident and he's at the hospital."

Startled, I asked, "What kind of accident? Car wreck? I always told him he drove too fast. He's a good driver, but he can't account for the other idiots on the road. How bad is it?"

"Not a car accident. He was parasailing and the harness gave way. He had a nasty fall with multiple fractures. He is still in the intensive care unit at Memorial and he was asking for you."

"Is he going to be okay?"

"The doctors think so, but it was touch-and-go for a minute."

"When did this happen?"

"A couple of days ago."

"And you're just telling me now?"

"Mimi was unconscious, and we were more concerned as to whether he would survive at all. Daddy said to hold off on contacting you as there was no need to worry you, and that there would be plenty of time for that. Either way, however, when Mimi woke up today you were the first person he asked for."

"I'll catch the first flight out. Just have someone at the airport to pick me up."

'No need, Daddy sent the Learjet. It should be touching down in about an hour out there. Be at the airport ready to go."

"Then I better get packing. I'll see you when I get there."

"Yeah, the family really appreciates your coming."

"There's nothing to appreciate, Mimi is my friend, and he'd do the same for me, "saying goodbyes we hung up.

I called Ken Toy. "Ken, I'm going to need you to bring my car to Florida. I'll give you a plane ticket back. I don't know how long I'll have to stay, and I want to have it while I'm there."

"You're the boss," he replied, "It won't be a problem. Just leave it to me."

I packed as quickly as I could, keeping a carry bag with me and loading everything else I thought I might need into the car. I got two of the stacks of hundreds from the shoe box in the closet, one of which I stuck into my shoulder bag, while putting the other in my jacket pocket. I picked Ken up on the way to the airport, putting his bag into the back with mine.

My car was a sixty-three model Plymouth Sport Fury, with a 383 CI aluminum block engine, police interceptor model. It was an old California Highway Patrol supervisor's car - unmarked - that I was planning on restoring. Its body and engine were fine, but the interior needed to be done over, as well as a new paint job. I had gotten it a few weeks before, and it was my pride and joy. I don't know why I loved the car, perhaps because its looks were so deceiving; it didn't look like it could move fast as it did. Plus, it was compact, and a perfect fit for me. The trip to Florida would be a fine way of finding out if it had any problems.

I handed Ken the stack of hundreds from my jacket pocket, to which he replied, "This is way more than I need to get to Florida."

"Take your time. Get there in one piece, and I want to make sure you have enough to cover any emergency on the road," I replied, adding, "If you need more, I'll call Joe from Florida and tell her to wire it to you. Just call her if you need it."

"This should cover anything that could possibly come up."

"Let's hope nothing does." I gave him the map and address in Florida, as well as Mimi's home phone number.

At the airport, he got in the driver's seat as I got my carryall and shoulder bag out.

"Give me a call every day. If am not there, leave a message and I will get it, drive safe and don't rush, it will take you some time to get there. I don't need anything happening to you or my Baby," I said.

"Don't worry," he said with a smile, "I will take good care of her for you."

The jet was waiting for me, already refueled and cleared with the flight plan filed. Tom, the pilot who had taken us to the islands, was waiting, as well as Dave, who had come along as co-pilot for the flight time. I climbed aboard and settled in as the plane readied for takeoff.

The flight to Florida was uneventful, leaving me with plenty of time to worry about Mimi's condition. At the airport in Palm Beach, both of Mimi's brothers, Kevin and Devlin, were waiting for me with one of the ranch's station wagons.

"We appreciate your coming so quickly," Kevin said.

"Nothing to appreciate, Mimi's my friend. I appreciate you sending the jet to pick me up, as it saved me a lot of time. How's he doing?"

"Fine, he's alert and talking more now they've removed the breathing tube. They should upgrade his condition if nothing happens."

"How bad are his injuries?"

"Mostly broken bones. He'll be in casts for months and there will be rehab once he's released from the hospital. You can stay in one of the guest cottages at the ranch, and use one of the ranch's vehicles to get around, or one of us will take you where you need to go."

"Thanks, I have my car coming," I replied, "I expect I will be spending most of the next few days at the hospital."

"Whatever you need, let us know and it's yours," Devlin assured me.

We were silent the rest of the drive to the hospital. Kevin parked the car while Devlin and I went inside the hospital. "He's in a private room, so you can go straight in. I want to get something to eat from the vending machines. You want anything?" Devlin asked.

"Bring me a soda when you come."

"You got it. Mimi's in room 329. It's upstairs, and turn right when you get off the elevator."

Waiting for the elevator to take me to the third floor, I was dreading what I might find when I got there. I had imagined all kinds of scenarios on the flight from the West Coast: Mimi paralyzed or worse off, or his face messed up along with everything else.

Before entering the room, I took a couple of deep breaths. Going in, I saw Mimi lying there watching TV and drinking a glass of water through a straw. One of his arms and legs were in casts, the leg cast extending to his waist, with the leg and arm suspended from overhead.

"That contraption must be hell on your sex life," I said by way of greeting as I entered.

Water erupted from his nose and mouth as he began to laugh. "Ow, ow. It hurts when I laugh… You bitch."

"Didn't you know you were supposed to land with the thing, not fall out of it?"

"Don't make me laugh," Mimi said, while trying to suppress a laugh, "something was wrong with the buckle on the safety harness. It let go at the wrong moment."

"Obviously it wasn't the fall that hurt, it was the sudden stop at the end of when you hit the ground. Just call me when you want to see me. You don't have to fall out of the sky."

"Ow, you bitch, stop with the jokes please. It really does hurt when I laugh."

Other than the broken bones and a little swelling of the face, he seemed to be alright. But I would have hated to see him when he first got to the hospital.

"I'm glad you came," he said, "I didn't know if you would. You're so busy out there and with the matter in Tampa is still pending."

"Doesn't matter what's going on, I still would've come even if you hadn't asked me to. As soon as I got the news, I would have been on the first thing smoking in this direction."

"Come here -," he said, "- and let me get a good look at you. My God, what have you done with yourself? I almost didn't recognize you."

"A little of this and a little of that. Improving on perfection."

"Your face is so different, your nose is straight and your lips are fuller. You never did have a beard. But now your skin is smoother and softer. You've been at the hormones haven't you?"

"Guilty! As you know, California is the land of the lotus eaters, beautiful people and plastic surgeons who will correct the slightest imperfection."

My nose had had a slight lump which gave it a slight twist, from a broken nose which had never been set, courtesy of a foster parent flinging me down a flight of stairs when I was very young. The break had also affected my breathing on one side. The plastic surgeon had fixed all of it, made my lips fuller and added a few other touches here and there to make me more feminine looking, as did the full regime of hormones I was taking.

"And are those breasts real?"

"Yes, Mother Nature, not implants. You can credit them to the hormones."

California was not as homophobic as some places were, and my appearance had nothing to do with my ability to perform the job expected of me at the restaurants. Therefore, I could be myself and not worry about it. I had started on the hormones before coming to Tampa to be arrested. I liked the way they made me feel and look.

"You're beautiful, I'm so jealous."

"Eat your heart out. If you had come on out, you could have gotten it too."

"Yeah well, I won't be in this bed forever. You've just given me something to look forward to."

"I wouldn't be too certain of that, it's not painless you know."

"I can handle the pain. You've to tell me about the hormones and how they make you feel. I had started them a couple of times, but I keep forgetting to take them."

"Count on it girlfriend. I'm not going anywhere until you get better."

At that point, Devlin came in, carrying an armload of drinks and snacks from the vending machine.

"I thought you might want something to eat after you flight."

"Thanks," I said, reaching for one of the drinks and a candy bar.

"Me me… me too," said Mimi from the bed, causing all of us to laugh.

"I don't know if you should be eating this kind of food right now, maybe I should check with the nurse first," Devlin teased.

"The hospital food is killing me. I need food, real food."

Kevin came in, carrying another armload of snacks and drinks. "I see someone already beat me to it," he said, indicating the snacks and sodas on the bed table and dresser next to Mimi's bed.

"It won't go to waste. The munchkin in the bed will take it all or what's left over when we finish," Devlin said. They stayed a few minutes before getting up, with Kevin saying, "Visiting hours will be over soon, so we'll give you two a few minutes to talk among yourselves and wait for you downstairs."

After they left, Mimi and I talked for a while, and before I left, he asked, "How are you getting around?"

"Your brothers said I could use one of the ranch vehicles while I'm here. I also have my car coming from Cali, so I will have transportation."

"Another one of those junkyard rejects you normally drive?"

"Not quite," I said dryly.

"How is it getting here?"

"My assistant is driving it from Cali to here. I figured I would need it for a trip to Tampa to see Benny."

"Assistant? Coming up the world I see. Next time you come, bring some real food. I can't live off the vending machine and hospital food."

"The plot thickens. So that's why you wanted me here in Florida, to smuggle food in for you while in hospital," I joked.

"Of course, that's what friends are for."

"Yeah well, I'll see you tomorrow," I said, giving him a hug around the IV's and plumbing attached to him.

"Ciao," he said.

"Ciao back at you."

Devlin was waiting in the lobby for me. "Kevin went to get the car, he should be back in a minute."

"Any good butcher shops around? One who caters to restaurants and hotels?"

"Yeah, there's a wholesaler not far from here."

"You think we could stop by there on the way to the ranch?"

"Sure, but I don't know why, we have everything you need in the house. I'm sure the cook won't mind you getting the stuff you need from the kitchen."

"Your cook might be a little put out; they tend to be very territorial, and like to know exactly what and who is in their kitchen. Doing that would be like invading someone's personal space. Besides, I would like to have my own things so I can try out new recipes and things when I have a mind to, and I want to get a few special items."

At the wholesaler's, the butcher sold me a quarter side of beef, some scallops, lobster, crab, tuna, grouper and salmon. I had him run twenty pounds of top sirloin through the grinder for ground beef. "That's sure a waste of good steak, that's some prime beef," he said.

"I know, but this is for personal consumption," I replied, while requesting specific cuts on the side of beef he sold me. Then, I asked him about where I might find some of the other items I wanted. He said, "You got to be in the trade, those are specialty items. You're a chef right?"

"You got it on first try, although I'm still in the process of learning the trade."

"Doesn't sound like it to me. I'll have your meat and other things ready for you by the time you finish rounding up the rest. He continued, "Hey Arty, come show this... this guy, where to find the things she needs," being a little confused as to what to call me. My appearance, with the long hair, feminine features and shape had a tendency to befuddle people who met me for the first time; normally, they would mistake and take me for a woman.

Arty took me around the store with a cart, and we ended up with two carts, as I soon had more than I originally planned. However, it wouldn't go to waste. I even got a couple of coolers with ice for the meat and seafood, as well as thermal boxes for prepared food to keep it warm in transit, plugging in to the car lighter.

When I got back around to the butcher who had my order ready, he told me, "I got a side of aged beef back in the cooler. You want some of that?"

"Yes please, and thank you," I replied, pleased he had some; most of the time only really exclusive specialty shops carried it, and you usually had to buy a side of beef and age it yourself. The difference between fresh and aged beef is taste and tenderness when prepared properly - the former will burst with flavor and almost melt in your mouth. I left the butcher with a good tip for looking out for me.

Devlin and Kevin were at the check-out when Arty and I arrived with the two carts. "Glad we brought the station wagon," Kevin said. When it was totaled up, I was reaching into my shoulder bag for cash, when Devlin handed the cashier a credit card, saying, "We got this, it's at least we can do."

"But I have money," I protested.

"Don't worry; you can pay us back in food. From the way Mimi raves about your cooking, we figure it to be a good investment. We left the store with our load and stowed the bags and cooler in the back of the station wagon; I made note of the store address and location in case I needed to come back for something else.

At the ranch, they helped me unload the supplies from the station wagon to the guest house I usually stayed in when I visited, which had a state of the art kitchen with a walk-in freezer (cooler) and a double door reach in - all I needed.

"Just set it down anywhere in here. I will have to put it up. I like to know where everything is so I can put my hands on it in an instant," I told the two.

"Okay, come on up to the house later and see everyone. Mom and Dad want to make certain they see you while you're here this time. Mimi usually keeps you for himself when you're here; not that you've gotten down here much lately," Kevin said.

"Been busy with work, school and business really keeps me busy."

"Well come on up and see everyone when you finish here."

"Will do."

I sorted everything out and put it away, keeping out ten pounds of the steak burger. Taking a sheet pan and some waxed paper, I mixed some spices into the meat, and then made up eight ounce patties, sprinkling the first layer with some balsamic vinegar and separating the layers with the wax paper. When I finished, I set the patties into the reach-in cooler, lowering the temperature to the required value.

I then made up some bread dough, letting the yeast work the dough to rise before working the dough and sectioning it out- sprinkling it with flour, wrapping it in wax paper and setting it in the walk-in cooler; I had made enough dough to last a week. When I wanted to make some bread or rolls, I would pull out a section, and once it warmed the yeast would make it rise again. I could then form and bake it.

It was the easiest way of keeping fresh baked rolls and bread on hand because once it was baked it had to be eaten, because after a couple of hours it would no longer be fresh. You could extend its life by placing it in a bread box or cooler, but still the taste was different; I preferred fresh rolls. I whipped up some butter with seasonings and spices for cooking, as you want to work with fresh product as much as possible.

There's a world of difference between how the average person prepares food and how a chef does it. Most people don't realize how much of their food is prepackaged with preservatives and additives added as time saving devices. "From scratch" for the home owner cook means from a package or can; for a chef, it means exactly that with no shortcuts, which is why I went to wholesalers. Even then I would do extras like re-sifting bread and cake flour a couple of time before using it, to improve the taster and quality of the end product.

I sliced up some Pepper Jack cheese and grated some cheddar from the wheel I had gotten. Pinking out some goose-sized Idaho potatoes, I set them in the cooler after washing them along with the other vegetables I had purchased. Once I had prepared everything I would need for the following morning, I went up and joined the family for the evening meal, and conversation.

I was up early the following morning, showered, and put on a pot of coffee from fresh ground beans. I had pulled a section of dough from the cooler before taking my shower, to allow it to warm up for the yeast to begin its work. I scrambled some eggs and made toast for myself before setting to work.

Pulling five of the steak patties from the cooler, I cracked a few eggs and separated the yolk from the albumin; the yolks, I placed in a bowl with a lid and set it in the cooler. Taking a clove of garlic, I put it in the press and squeezed the juice into the egg white, along with some white pepper with a dash of cooking sherry, whipping it together then mixing it into the patties and reforming them.

I had preheated the range and oven, and from the bread dough, I made up some overlarge rolls and set them to bake. While they were baking, I took some of the butter mix I had prepared the day before and put it in a couple of skillets with a little balsamic vinegar. When the butter frothed, I put sliced mushrooms and chives in one, and green peppers, onions and scallions in another; sautéing them until tender. Once completed, I set them in a bowl to the side.

Using the same skillets, I cooked the patties, turning the heat down for a longer cooking time. Turning to the potatoes I had selected, I peeled them, and then sliced them into french fry strips. I had some extra virgin olive oil heated on the range, and used it to make several batches of french fries.

When everything was done, I put the burgers on the fresh baked slice buns, topping two with Pepper Jack cheese, two with cheddar and one with both, before spooning the still hot mushroom chives, green pepper, onions and scallions over them. Closing the bun, I wrapped them in wax paper with markings to indicate which was which. Then, I set them in the thermal box I had picked up the previous day, to keep them warm. The fries were set to drain onto paper towels before putting them into a container with a lid, which went into the box with the burgers.

Separately, I sliced some tomatoes, jalapeno peppers (freshly pickled), pickles(sweet and dill) and onions into separate containers and put them on ice in one of the coolers I had gotten the day before, along with some store-bought ketchup and mustard, as I hadn't yet had the time or inclination to make my own. I was about through cleaning up and putting everything away, when Devlin and Kevin showed up to drive me to the hospital.

First off, Devlin said, "Something sure smells good in here."

"I got you one made up," I told him, "You can eat it either on the way, or at the hospital with Mimi."

"I guess I'll wait then."

At the hospital, I walked the thermal box to Mimi's room while Devlin and Kevin carried the rest. Mimi was up watching the television news when we walked in the front of the bed, which was inclined so he could see through the contraption which kept his leg in a cast suspended.

"Room service," I said as we came into the room.

"I hope you brought me something to eat, I'm starved," he replied, delighted at the sight of what we were carrying.

"Your wish is my command, madam. Now, what kind of burger do you want? Jalapeño jack, cheddar or a combo of both?"

"A jalapeno jack and a cheddar," he replied as Kevin left to get some drinks from downstairs, while Devlin and I put the bed table in place over Mimi's bed. Putting the burgers he'd requested, fries and garnishes on plates before him with the condiments, I said, "Dig in before they get cold."

"These are huge, I don't know if I can handle two," Mimi said, before munching into one.

"How you tell which is which?" Devlin asked.

"They're marked 'JJ' for jalapeno jack, 'CC' for cedar... and 'JJ/CC' is the combo," I replied to Devlin, who was looking in the thermal box. Then, Kevin walked in with juices and sodas.

Mimi had two burgers while everyone else got one. I made up plates for each, then we dug in - Mimi had a head start on the rest of us. I opted for coffee while the others got soda or juice. I had used sea salt on the fries.

"Now I see why Mimi raves about your cooking," Kevin said.

"Yeah," Devlin agreed, "I didn't know a burger could taste like this."

Mimi had his mouth too full to say anything.

"That's because it's from a different cut of meat. Most ground beef is just scraps and end with some extenders added. These however, are nothing but pure beef."

"I'm not talking about the meat. It's not just the meat, it's how it's prepared and tastes," Kevin said, "people should pay top dollar for something like this."

"They do," I replied.

Mimi could only finish one burger, "I'm going to save the other for later, "he said, "with some of those fries."

"They won't taste the same cold."

"It'll taste a whole lot better than what the hospital plans on serving me."

We visited for a while, then left. Before leaving, I told Mimi, "I'll be back this evening with another meal for you."

That evening, it was salmon fillets and scallops on rolls with lettuce, tomatoes and onions, with fresh tartar sauce and a side of wild rice with egg yolks, green peppers, tomatoes, onions, leeks and chives stir fried. The tartar sauce had fresh horse radish grated in to give it a little bite.

By then, Mimi's condition had upgraded to satisfactory, although he still had one IV for pain medication.

The fourth evening, Mr. Cleary called me up to the house, saying, "You got a call from your assistant, Ken."

"I'll take it; he's driving my car from Cali. I hope nothing has happened."

Nothing had happened except that Ken was in Florida, nearby and wanting directions to the ranch. I directed him, and he showed up shortly thereafter. I was preparing Mimi's evening meal, shrimp fried rice with scallops and tomatoes, to be finished with apple turnovers and chocolate-blueberry tarts.

"You must have flown up here. How many tickets did you pick up?" I joked.

"None, I mostly drove straight through, only stopped for gas, taking a leak, or to eat or sleep when I got too tired to drive."

"I told you to take your time. How did my baby hold up?"

"Like a champ, you have to watch your foot with her because she likes to go. If you don't watch yourself you will be twenty miles over the speed limit before you know it. Once I blew the Carbon out of the cylinders, she ran like a charm. It's really a sweet car."

"You up for a trip to the hospital?" I asked, "I'm about to take Mimi his evening meal. You'll give him someone new to talk to." Kevin and Devlin had returned to their homes once the crisis had passed, though I still saw them at the hospital during visitation hours, as the family took turns going to see Mimi. So someone was always there, and was why I took along enough food.

"Sure, why not?" he answered, and noticing the food, said, "Sheesh, you got enough food here to feed a small army. Mimi must be as big as a house."

"Not yet, have you had anything to eat? If not, either fix yourself a plate or wait and eat with us at the hospital. I am going to take some of these pastries up to the house, and then I'll be on my way."

"I guess I'll wait then," he said, grabbing one of the turnovers from the pile, "except I have to have one of those now. The smell is driving me mad."

On the way out the door with the pastries, I spotted the young tabby cat who had started hanging around the house looking for handouts; I thought she was one of the many barn cats the place had. But she had taken a shine to me, or at least the food I provided her with.

Speaking to Ken, who was eating the turnover, I said, "and would you feed the cat, there's some salmon leftovers in the reach-in cooler, give her some of that and some cream."

"Gotcha covered Boss," he said, then, "I didn't know that you like cats?"

"I didn't either. This one however, seems to like the handouts." Saying 'shoo' to the cat rubbing itself on my leg, I told it, "He's going to feed you, I'll be right back."

Mrs. C told me to leave the pastries with the cook; they would eat some later. Their cook and I got along well; she was a mainstream-fair to middling cook who hadn't had the training or experience I had been exposed to, and who realized this and appreciated the pointers I would give her to improve her style, while also improving mine by experimenting and trying out different things. As a chef, you never stop learning or evolving your style and talent.

Returning to the guest house, I found that Ken had unloaded the car, bringing the belongings to the house; we loaded up the car with the food and pastries for the trip back to the hospital. Meanwhile, the cat was too busy eating to notice me.

"You want me to drive?" Ken asked.

"Nah, you have done enough for a while, I'll drive." It was a change from the ranch vehicle I had been driving.

At the hospital, I gave Ken the thermal boxes and cooler which kept the pastries, which were on platter with covers, telling him, "You carry those to Mimi's room. Its room 328; you go right when you come off the elevator on third floor."

"You are going with me aren't you?"

"Yes, but I may have to stop and talk to the nurses. If one of them calls me, you keep going and I'll meet you up there. Mimi will be the fat one on the bed, by the window."

However, I didn't get stopped by the nurses as I expected. By this time, they knew I was Mimi's friend who brought him goodies. They usually waved and said hello, but were too busy to chat, which was just well.

The door to Mimi's room was open and Mimi was sitting with the bed elevated, watching television. Seeing only me, as Ken was behind me and blocked from his view, he said, "Hi girl! You brought anything sweet?" then spotting Ken who had moved out from behind me, to find a place to set the boxes down, "Who is that?"

"Yes, I have apple turnovers and chocolate blueberry tarts," I replied, just as Ken said, "There's no fat guy in here. There's only one bed."

"You told him am fat? You better be glad I can't get out of this bed," Mimi said.

Laughing, I said, "It was just a joke. Anyway you're not fat, just plump," which was a lie as he was rail thin, having lost fifteen pounds because of the accident, with great big eyes in a waif face.

"Blueberry or apple?" I asked Mimi, moving aside so Ken could put the boxes down. Mimi hadn't taken his eyes off Ken since spotting him, and after a noticeable pause, he said, "huh… what?"

Then Ken spoke up, "I'm Ken, I work for Poison in California. I brought his car up from Los Angeles for him."

"I told you my assistant was driving my car here," I added.

"Yes, but you didn't tell me everything!" Mimi said.

I asked Ken, "You mind going from some juices from the vending machines down stairs? You want a soda Mimi?"

"No, juice will be fine."

"Be back in a jiffy," Ken said as he left. As soon as he was out the door and far from earshot, Mimi said, "He's gorgeous, where have you been keeping him?"

"He's part of the escort service. Lately we've been grooming him for better things."

"How come I've never seen him before?"

"For one, you haven't been out to Cali in months. Second, he worked at the escort service and you wouldn't have seen him except by accident, until lately that is. Like I said, we've been working with him, getting him some modeling assignments and working as my assistant."

"Is he legal?"

"Over the age of consent, if that's what you are asking."

"Is he taken?"

"Not that I'm aware of."

"Girl, what's wrong with you? Don't tell me he doesn't swing that way."

"Oh, he most definitely does. One of the problems we had with him at the escort service is with women wanting to jump his bones. And he wouldn't give them a sniff. Besides, I thought you didn't go black," I said, while handing him a blueberry tart.

"I said 'hadn't', I didn't say wouldn't."

"Don't let the pretty face fool you. He's very intelligent as well," I told him.

"Is that so?" taking a bite of the tart, "God they are so good. All the nurses are crazy for your cooking."

As I had suspected, Mimi was sharing the food with the nurses. "Which reminds me I will have to make Ken Toy a plate," I said, he's probably starved." Taking a paper plate, I placed a portion of the shrimp fried rice in its center, and the tomatoes and scallops around it. As Chef M, said, "It not only has to taste good, it must also look good."

I had made up little containers of hot sauce blend for it, to season more if they want to, if like me, they like it spicy. On another plate, I put dinner rolls, butter, and a couple of the turnovers and tarts. "Ken Toy?" Mimi asked.

"Yes, that is what we call him at the escort service."

"Indeed," Mimi replied.

As soon as I finished setting the plates, Ken came back, interrupting the conversation Mimi and I were having about him.

"Sorry I took so long. I had to get a nurse to show me where the vending machines are," he said, which meant that the nurse had detained him in a fruitless effort to work her wiles on him.

"No problem," I replied, "I made you up a plate as I know you're hungry."

"Yes... Starved."

"I'll take a plate too, if you don't mind," Mimi said, "just a little bit. I can't let the poor dear eat alone."

"I figured you'd like the orange juice rather that the other," Ken said to Mimi, handing him the juice bottle and a straw from the dresser by the bed. From the sappy look on both their faces, I knew where this was heading. I made a plate for Mimi, put his plate on the bed table, and made an excuse to leave, saying, "It appears I forgot napkins. I'll go get some from the hospital dining room," leaving the two alone in the room.

I was of two minds concerning what had developed between the two, as I wanted Ken to stand for me at the escort service while I did my time; something which might not come about if he took up with Mimi and got his heart broke, given Mimi's notorious track record with lovers. However, the casts Mimi had on put him at a disadvantage, and I thought a few weeks of lust might do him some good.

Although Ken was due to catch a flight back to Los Angeles within a couple of days (the day after or the next), I wouldn't take any bets on it happening, knowing Mimi as I did. And I would be there to pick up the pieces when she'd dump him, and get him back to Los Angeles in good time.

I made enough noise while coming back to alert them of my impending return. From the guilty looks on their faces, I knew something had happened while I was gone. My money was on Mimi getting what he wanted; poor Ken didn't know he was going to get steam rolled.

Some of the family showed up while we were eating, most of whom had already eaten, although Mimi's sister, with her husband and children, made inroads on the turnovers and tarts. The family soon left. Before we did, I cleaned up and put the thermal boxes on Mimi's dresser, plugging it in to keep the food warm, the platters of turnovers and tarts on the bed table now at Mimi's bed. I knew he would be sharing it with the nurses as soon as we left. I told him I will pick up the platters and boxes up the next day when I brought lunch.

As we prepared to leave, Mimi asked, "You are going to come to see me tomorrow aren't you Ken?"

I said, "Ken's got a flight to catch tomorrow, don't you Ken?" Mimi gave me a little 'move' face behind Ken, mouthing the words I'M-GOING-TO-KILL-YOU at me.

"I thought I'd stay over for a couple of days, rest up and catch the sights. I've never been to Florida before," Ken replied, as Mimi stuck his tongue out at me. "I'll come to see you tomorrow if you want Mimi."

"Oh please do. It's so dreary in here, being all by myself," Mimi replied, giving me a mean look that said I better not say a word. I knew Eros had set the hook and when to stand aside for lust or love, whatever was going on between them.

"Good, you can help me with Mimi's lunch tomorrow, and do let me know when you're ready and I will book your flight," I said, sticking my tongue out at Mimi behind Kens back.

"I will… I'm glad to have met you Mimi and I will be here tomorrow," Ken said. And every day thereafter, for as long as Mimi was in the hospital, it was Ken who took over, pushing Mimi's wheelchair from the nurse at the front door of the hospital when he was released a couple of weeks later, complete with smaller casts on his arm and leg.

I was busy out at the ranch, preparing the food for Mimi's welcoming party. Mimi would be staying at the ranch during his recovery. Ken never did catch that flight back to Los Angeles, having his things shipped to Florida, arranging it through Jo at the escort office. He had given me back what remained of the money I had given him from the trip to Florida. I had returned some of it to him, and he still got his check from the escort service as my assistant.

Nonetheless, I was still uncertain of how long the affair between the two of them would last. Therefore, before catching a flight to L.A. to tidy up my affairs there and returning to face the music in Tampa, I went to see Mrs. Cleary, telling her, "If something happens between them while am away, could you make a certain Ken has a ticket to catch a flight back to California?," trying to hand her the money to cover for the cost. She waved it away, "You don't need to give me that. Of course I will make sure he reaches home. Ken's a fine man and that scamp of mine better treat him right. But if you ask me, I don't think Ken will be going anywhere."

I had three weeks in California to settle up my affairs, before having to be in court in Tampa for a change of plea to one count of grand larceny; the state would dismiss all the other eight counts. The maximum time I could receive in any event was five years. The State had offered three years in and two years on paper (probation); I wasn't dumb enough to fall for that one, as I would end up doing the whole five years if I violated the probation; miffed, the State would ask the court for the full pound of flesh, of five years. Meanwhile, Benny was hoping to convince the judge that a two to three year sentence would be more appropriate.

I hated to plead out to something I hadn't done. But as Benny told me during the conservation in Tampa before I left for California to wind up my affairs there, "Two to five is better than forty-five. If they stack the sentences, they have you dead bang with your signatures on the invoices. Chef Stevens is not going to take the stand to incriminate himself in order to clear you. His past history is hearsay, and wouldn't be admissible in court at trial, therefore any jury would bring back a guilty verdict based on the evidence. There's a chance I could get the convictions overturned on appeal. But that would be three to five years down the line, if it could even be done. Then, we would still have to go through the process all over again. This way you're in and done with it, and you can get on with your life."

"The State knows I'm not guilty, yet they are still pushing it. Why?" I had asked.

"Because it's not about truth or justice, the law is a political animal. It's about looking good for the voting public. Sure you might be innocent..."

"But I am!"

"Sure, I know that, you know that, and very likely Bernie (The State Attorney) knows that. But, look at it from his point of view. The evidence which would be admissible in court clearly implicates you as being the guilty party. He wouldn't be doing his job in the eyes of voters if he lets you off scot free with just a slap on the wrist. Had he done so, you can be certain those facts would be gotten before the voters come election time. You happen to be a pawn in a much bigger game. Besides, in the backwoods redneck perspective of justice, Florida has a saying that 'while they may not always be right, they are never wrong.' Even if you are innocent of this, you are guilty of something you never got caught for. So, in their minds, it all evens out. Your lifestyle also doesn't endear you to them either; they still have the hard shell southern Baptist mentality. To them, you are just a faggot trying to look like a woman. That in itself offends those Christian sensibilities and morality. You can talk equal rights all you want but it's not going to change what they believe inside. If you had been indicted and with a court appointed public defender, you would have been extremely lucky to have gotten off with a fifteen to twenty year sentence. So take the deal and count your blessings."

"Oh I know, but does it mean I have to like it?" I had questioned him.

"Yeah, well there it is. You have your whole life in front of you. You have a fine career and a business started. Take the time in prison to further and broaden your education so the time won't be a waste. And when you get out, you will never have to look back."

In California, I gave notice on the lease of the apartment, placing the items I couldn't part with in long time storage, while giving the rest away. At the escort service, I had an attorney draw up partnership papers, giving Mary Jo minority ownership in the escort service.

Jo protested, "You don't need to go that far. You pay me well enough as it is."

"You are going to be the acting CEO and running the company while am gone. It's only fair you receive adequate compensation. This way, non-one can question your authority or the manner in which you conduct the company affairs, except me. And I think you are entitled to a minority ownership of the business; you're going to be running for the next couple of years or so."

Jo went ahead and signed the documents, giving her part ownership of the escort service. We also discussed how our business operations were doing, and what the business's future plans for expansion were, telling Jo, "Look around for a limo service in need of a partner. It wouldn't do for us to buy one outright. A partnership where they handle cars, personnel and business, while we provide finance and clientele." We already had deals with a couple of limo services, as escorts and limos went together. A new partnership with a limo service would permit us to arrange packaged deals.

I added, "Oh and you will have to find another vice president for operations to take over for you, and a personnel director, as I believe Ken will not be coming back to us any time soon, if ever."

"Your friend Mimi better not break that boy's heart or she will hear about it from me. What do you want to do about Ken?"

"Keep him on the payroll as my assistant; I can have him run some errands for me in Florida. Do you have any contacts with modeling agencies in Florida who might throw him some work?"

"Yes! Matter of fact, I do. And they would love to use him," she said, and continued, "I'll move Lou up to vice president of operations and get Ronnie in as office manager to do the bookings."

"Whatever you think is best, you'll be running the show out here for at least a couple of years."

I pulled two of the remaining stacks of hundreds from my bag. "Put this in the petty cash. I will let you know if and when I need you to send it to me or elsewhere." I had never gotten around to spending much of it, as I considered it as being the getaway money. I made a good salary with Chef M. - way more than for my needs anyway. Between my salary and the escort service, the money had been piling up in my savings account.

Jo replied, "You don't need to put that into petty cash, we make enough money from the escort service that I can wire almost any amount to anywhere you might need it. I would take it from the corporate account. Your salary goes into your personal account at the bank."

We talked some more, then I left for the restaurant on Sunset Boulevard. Chef M. had been understanding about the time I had spent in Florida while Mimi was in hospital. I had been working hard since coming back. There wasn't much I could do about the bread and the pastries, but each day I would make a different batch of cakes, which I would wrap, label and deep freeze. There would be enough to last the restaurant for a few months after I was gone, if they didn't get freezer burn.

Chef M. said, "We're going to miss you around here. Your job will always be open. So hurry back to us as soon as you can. I'm going to lose business while you are gone as the customers really love your breads and desserts. We will have to muddle along as best as we can. Keep at your studies so you don't get stale. You need to keep the edge you have now. We are throwing you a farewell party at the restaurant at Hollywood Boulevard. Just act surprised when you show up."

"How many will be there?"

"All the workers from the restaurant, and some from your escort services, why?"

"I want you to invite one more guest. He's staying over at the Hyatt. He's the father of my friend in Florida, and he's giving me a lift on his plane on his way back to Florida. I want him and the rest of you to try out some of the new cake recipes I came up with while I was in Florida."

I had called Mimi the night before, to tell him, I would be coming back, and to have someone to pick me up at the airport. He had informed me that Mr. Cleary was in town, and instructed me to catch a ride with him. I gave Chef M. the number of the penthouse suite at The Hyatt, to invite Mr. C to the party.

The gathering at the restaurant the following evening was bittersweet, as only a few people there knew I would be going to prison and not to a fancy culinary arts school. So I had to acknowledge the congratulations on me being accepted there, an ironic twist if there ever was one. Everyone raved about the new line of desserts and pastries I introduced. There were three cakes: a Devil's Food cake with chocolate toffee and caramel, an Angel Food cake with chocolate truffle, and a Strawberry Crème. Then there were tarts and popovers: orange delight, strawberries, banana, blueberry and raspberry chocolate crèmes. The trick with them was to mold the chocolate into the shell before pouring in the fruit and crème fillings of the tarts, so that every bite would produce a medley of flavors.

I saw Mr. Cleary speaking with Chef M. during the affair. It was a sad leave for me to take. This had become my family and home, with only others being Mimi and his family. I had left the streets and prison behind, or so I had thought. I didn't really want to go back to prison, afraid of what I might have to do there.

I could survive, as the street was still in me. However, the difference was mainly in the quality and the character of people I would be dealing with. It's hard to describe to anyone who has never been to prison; it was all the foibles and imperfections of humanity compressed into a small area, and magnified under the glass of both prisoners and staff.

During the flight back to Florida, Mr. C said, "Chef M. is quite taken with you as his protégé. He says you are starting to become known as an up and coming chef in the culinary arts field. He said if you had a mind to, you could give any chef in the field a run for their money in a few more years. He also said there were many top chefs who breathed a sigh of relief when you decided to specialize in desserts, pastries and breads, and it was a shame you went that route."

"I went with my heart. While I love everything about culinary arts, the desserts, pastries and breads are what speak to me. I would rather follow my heart doing something I truly love and enjoy. As then, it's not work at all but joy."

"I understand that, totally. What business arrangements have you made for your accounts on the islands?"

"Keep reinvesting it. All I've touched is the mad money account for starting up the escort service. But that money has been replaced. I paid for Benny's services out of my regular savings."

"What I mean is there are some really good financial management firms who could handle all your affairs while you are away, leaving you free to pursue your studies. It would be difficult for you to conduct your business affairs from prison as you won't have the access or communications you need to handle business matters. Plus, I would like for you to invest the money in real estate I have in California, since it appears that is where you'll be living. It's an investment which will take a couple of years to come to fruition, but will prove quite a windfall for you about the time you get released from prison. I would just use the accounts as collateral for a loan with the banks, you wouldn't have to put up any actual money."

"Sure, just let me know when and where you need it," I said, knowing I could trust him, which was a measure of how much I had grown since meeting Mimi.

At the ranch, I headed for the guest house, with Ken and Mimi following. I was greeted by the barn cat, who twirled and wrapped herself around my legs. "What's the matter, they ain't been feeding you?" I crooned while petting her.

"Ken feeds her every day. I think she missed you. What do you call her anyway?" Mimi asked.

"Call her? I don't call her anything," I said, nonplussed. It seemed strange to give animal a name.

"You have to give her a name."

"For what?"

"Cause that way, she will know it and come when you call."

"She comes when she's hungry. I don't have to call her for that." I had never had a pet of any sort growing up, so I didn't know the first thing about having one, nor did it seem to be an appropriate time or place to start, considering where I was headed in the next week or so; although I had always loved animals, which is why I had considered becoming a veterinarian.

Mimi insisted, "You have to give her a proper name."

"Alright her name is…is… Doris."

"Doris? Where did you come up with that?" Mimi asked.

"I don't know, it just popped up from the Wizard of Oz."

"That's Dorothy, not Doris… but Doris it is."

The cat followed me into the house where I said, "Everything should be frozen," and addressing the cat, "I don't know if I have anything for you."

"Sure you do, Ken and I shopped for you yesterday, as we knew most likely you'd be here today."

"I dread seeing what you put in the pantry."

"Oh hush, we just got you the basic stuff. I know you would want to get your own stuff, Ms. Picky. There's some canned tuna and some milk in the cooler that you can feed Doris with."

While the cat ate, the three of us chatted, as I checked out the kind of supplies I had on hand and what I might need to get.

"Don't even think about it," Mimi said.

"Think about what?"

"Think about cooping yourself up in here with your witch's brews for next week. That is so not going to happen. You are going to have some fun before you go back into that hell hole."

"But there's things I want to check out -," I protested.

Mimi interrupted me, saying, "And they will keep… you can work on them when we get home from the day's activities. But you are not going to hide away in here. There's a whole world of things to do out there. You've done nothing but study and work, work, work these past couple of years."

"We had some good times..."

"Only when I dragged you out by your ear. There's no telling how long you'll be gone for this time, so loosen up and live a little. It won't kill you to spend the next week enjoying yourself."

For the next week, each day we did something different, sailing one day, seeing the sights the other, and when Ken and I got sick of horse riding, Tom flew us up to Orlando in the Beechcraft, where we spent the day at Disney world (with Ken pushing Mimi in the wheel chair when he got tired of using the canes, as the casts had kept getting smaller).

It was at Disney World that I realized I had also been living near the Disneyland in LA - a matter of few miles; yet in the two years I had been out there, I hadn't even given a thought to go there; ditto for Busch Gardens in Tampa in the year I spent there.

Doris would follow me everywhere around the ranch, and be waiting for me whenever I got back from the day's activities. She would lie where she could watch me working in the kitchen, and only made a demand when she wanted out, standing by the door and meowing, doing the same when she wanted back in. I kept telling her I wasn't her personal doorman, to which she paid not the slightest attention; whenever I would sit to watch television or read, she'd crawl onto my lap and lay there purring, sleeping on my bed at night. I was going to miss her too.

Thoughts of absconding did cross my mind, but were quickly dismissed as impractical, as so much had changed in my life. Now, I had friends and people who cared for and about me, whose trust I wouldn't want to betray. If I left, it would mean I leave them as well; it wasn't worth losing everything I now cherished.

At the change of plea and sentence hearing, the judge listened to the state attorney who argued for the maximum sentence of five years. When it was our turn, Chef Paul came as a character witness while Chef M. had sent the judge a letter describing the work I was doing out there, and how much I had progressed and accomplished in such a short time. Mimi and Ken sat in the courtroom to provide moral support.

Benny asked the court to place me on probation outright, a split sentence of a year in prison and a year on paper, or a sentence of no more than three years.

Then it was the judge's turn. "I have given a great deal of consideration to this matter. While the young-ahem - man seems to have turned his life around, there still remains the offense he is pleading to. It's a very serious offense, and nor is it his first. The state is asking for five, Mr. Lazzra says no more than three. I will split the difference and impose a four year sentence. However, with the stipulation that should the defendant continue to do well, I will entertain the motion for a reduction of sentence on a future date." He continued, "The defendant is remanded to the custody of the bailiff," rapping his gavel to indicate he was finished.

Well, I didn't get the whole enchilada, but got a big chunk of it (four out of five). While others might give credence to the mitigation aspect of possible reduction at a later date, I though it to be so much hot air.

I would be storing the car at the Cleary ranch, along with the other items I had accumulated while there. Ken would care for the car and my culinary arts and cooking books. The bailiff got me and escorted me to the holding cell behind the courtroom to await transportation to the county jail. I spoke with the Clearys, Mimi, and Ken while I was in the holding cell waiting to be transported to the jail.

Ten days later, I was on the transport bus from Hillsborough county jail as part of the shipment of newly sentenced prisoners being sent to the north Florida, in Union county, twenty miles from The East Unit and Rock.

END OF PART I

554
3THE DEVIL'S COURTYARD

Part II

Boss Willie

I was seated at the far end of the front row of hard wooden benches facing the reception officer's desk, with a five foot gap between me and the next prisoner seated on the otherwise crowded benches, other prisoners having to stand along the back wall as there was no room for them to be seated on the benches.

I was wearing only a pair of men's boxer shorts, and the two t-shirts that one of the intake sergeants had insisted I put on to cover my breasts; whether from outrage or arousal, I couldn't tell. The rest of the convicts being processed in with me wore boxer shorts with their chests bare. Like me, they had their personal clothing and belongings they had brought with them from the county jail in brown paper bags between their feet.

I had gotten my share of curious and ogling looks on the transport bus bringing us from Hillsborough County Jail to the Lake Butler Reception and Medical Centre, especially since I was the only one in the cage separated from the rest of the prisoners while at the county jail (because of my feminine features and shape).

It was only when I got off the bus with them in the unloading bay at the reception center that the debate as to whether or not I was a woman ended. The strip search in the long west corridor leading to the reception area from the loading/unloading bay resolved any lingering doubts. I looked like a woman, with breasts and feminine features and my long hair done up in a pony tail, but I was obviously male.

After the strip search, we were given a pair of men's boxer underwear to put on, and then escorted to the receiving area. I was instructed to take a seat at the far end of the first row of benches where I could be observed through the windows of the intake officers station; I don't know what they thought might happen.

The officers made certain I was one of the first in line for the barber chair; my long tresses were soon a thing of the past, lying on the floor by the barber's chair, only leaving a quarter inch of stubble covering my head.

I was then directed to the shower to bathe. There was already a large group of prisoners taking a shower, but the officer told them to clear one of the shower heads so that I could shower alone. Before my shower ended, I noticed more than one erection among those in the shower with me. I looked like a woman from behind and the waist up; it was nice to know I was appreciated.

I took the erections as a compliment, making me feel better about my nearly bald head. I had known they would cut my hair at Lake Butler, but it felt like I was missing something nonetheless. Some of the erections in the shower probably belonged to guys who thought of themselves as strictly heterosexual. But where I came from, I knew a hard dick had no conscience and any port in the storm would serve if push came to shove.

After the hot shower, I returned to my seat on the bench. The cool air in the receiving area made the nipples on my breasts stand out; that's when The Sergeant told one of the orderlies to get me a T-shirt to put on. Then a second one, when my nipples continued to poke through the material of the first.

I was called first for everything in the intake processing routine: finger printing, medical, photo. When they called my name to come to the property officer's counter, I carried my bag of belongings to the desk where I was told to dump it out, and the Property Room officer sorted through it all.

The only things I was permitted to keep were photos, legal papers, a bible, watch, personal letters, and a medallion and chain; everything else, I would either have to mail home within thirty days, or dispose right then in the donation box behind me. Since I hadn't brought anything else I really needed to keep, I chucked what I couldn't take into the bin.

The property officer gave me a receipt for the twelve hundred dollars which had been in my account at the county jail, which they had forwarded to me in the form of a check, and a property receipt for the few items I had been permitted to keep. I was also given a bedroll and a brown grocery sack with a roll of toilet paper, toothbrush, toothpaste, a bar of state soap and a razor.

The property officer then directed one of the convict orderlies to get my clothing sizes and bring me a prison uniform. I had to guess my sizes at five-foot-six and one-twenty-five pounds. Prison sizes aren't street sizes - just as men's and women's clothing differs. The orderly brought me a set which was a little baggy, but it fit alright with the pants legs rolled up and the web belt clinched tight; I wasn't on the runway for no fashion show.

It was a given fact that a lot of minor indignities and humiliations they put you through in prison were forgotten after release, although others are burnt deep within your psyche. I could understand the psychological imperatives of stripping you of your individuality and symbols of your former freedom, and the need to attempt to separate the wolves from among the flock of sheep (those new prisoners most likely to cause problems to and for the officers and other prisoners).

It was a weeding out process, which was only effective with the wolves who hadn't learned to keep the sheep façade in place during their stay inside. Any prisoner who objected to the many indignities and humiliations they were subjected to during the intake process would immediately be classified as a potential trouble maker, and would be an object lesson for other prisoners, given their first lesson in the proper decorum for a prisoner in prison from the fists and kicks of the intake officers; a lesson which would be repeated and reinforced within the cell-block's confinement cells by shifts of officers in the days and weeks ahead.

However, I could never understand why some of the officers thrived and took great pleasure in subjecting a prisoner to such abuse. I guessed it had something to do with breaking their spirits or will to resist, to render the individual into a servile automaton or a corpse.

These officers would pounce on the slightest excuse to administer beatings, often deliberately provoking some young brash prisoner, new to the system, to make some wrong comment or objection just so they could have an opportunity to beat them down. The rest of us, who would see and hear it taking place, would have to stand helplessly, unable or unwilling to interfere in the defense of the convict being beaten. It was a sense of shameful helplessness, and guilt as you were glad it wasn't happening to you, leaving a bitter taste.

The prison population had expanded greatly since my release. It appeared the state was sweeping the streets and mental hospitals and filling the prisons and jail cells up faster than they could be built. It had become an assembly line process, with periodic breakdowns as prisons closed their doors to the countries, unable to accommodate more prisoners due to the lack of space to process all the bodies through.

They completed the intake process with me in what must have been a record time (usually a day long affair). I was lined up with a small group of prisoners who had come from other prisons for medical treatment or were just transferring through to another prison; all they required was a dormitory and bunk assignment.

My departure from the reception area was a relief to some and a disappointment to others. Frankly, for me it was a relief, with all the curious stares as if I were an alien who just landed on Earth, or sideshow freak at a carnival; it had given me an uncomfortable feeling which made me want to tell them, "I'm a chick with a dick, get over it!"

I had expected to be locked up in the cell-block and segregated from other prisoners as done in the county jail. However, to my surprise, when the officers dropped me off, the Housing Sergeant over the cell-block said to me, "Put your property up, and make your bed, then catch the yard." I was only to be housed on the cell-block to sleep and otherwise I would be on the open compound with the rest of the prisoners; my, how things had changed since I had been gone.

The only reason I was being housed on the cell-block was that the staff felt my presence in one of the open bay dormitories would be too disruptive. I was assigned to cell one, on G-wing, just off to the right of the counter where the cell-block officers did their paperwork; all they had to do was glance towards the G-wing to see the front of my cell. I didn't have a cell partner, and as I was to learn later, they would only house me with another Queen.

On the walk over to the cell block from the reception area, under the escort of two officers, there had been wolf whistles and ribald comments made to and about me. Word of my presence in the compound had preceded me; not me personally, but as a chick with a dick, one who "looked like and acted as a woman, even having tits".

As I headed down the stairwell after stowing my property and making up the bed in the cell, I marveled at how much the system had changed in such a short period of time. My last time through Lake Butler, I had spent my entire time there locked down on the cell block until I transferred to The Rock, and I didn't have breasts or other hormonal and cosmetic changes back then.

Now, for the most part, I was free to mingle with the other convicts on the recreation field. I fended off some blatant crude passes and offers of delights behind the bleachers or in the bathrooms, along with offers by others to get something from the canteen for me.

I heard my name called by a few prisoners, and soon found out there were a lot of them there with whom I had served time with at The Rock or East Unit. Prison was like a revolving door which never stopped turning; I met up with some of them on the Recreation Field.

I had brought some cash, reefer and hormone pills in with me, the money secreted among the photos, personal letters, legal papers and bible (things I knew they would let me keep). The reefer and hormones, I had brought in my ladies' carryall. I had known it would be a few days before I could access the money in my account at the prison and five weeks before I could get a visit (for that period of time, you are quarantined from the outside world until the intake processing is completed and you are classified and awaiting transfer to your assigned prison). This isolated you from the outside world while reinforcing your status as a prisoner solely at the mercy of the state.

Anticipating the isolation period, I had brought with me the things I required or those I could trade for what I needed. I knew refer was better than money in the prison system, and could get you items that even real currency wouldn't. I had found some prisoners I knew and could do business with on the recreation field, and before I left there that afternoon, I had broken a fifty dollar bill into tens, fives, ones and coupons, and bought two nice pieces (knives) for a dime bag of smoke. I also obtained two large canteen bags of soap, deodorant, shampoo, lotion, some perfume, and things someone like me would need. In addition to food items and sweets to snack on, I had made arrangements to sell a couple of fifty pieces of smoke for canteen items on the evening yard after the dinner meal.

I had figured that if I was going to be here, at least I would live as comfortably as possible. To paraphrase a famous actor, "A girl's got to do what a girl's got to do" to get by. The smoke I had brought with me was the California Red Bud, almost purple with dark resin. And a couple of tokes would get you high, so it sold like hot cakes. If I were so inclined however, I would conserve it until I could arrange to get more.

On the cell block that evening, the officers had me shower first and alone on my floor. When I was finished and had returned to my cell, he released the rest of the tier for their showers; sixteen cells with two people each, to share three shower heads in the shower in a hectic process of taking turns getting wet, soaping up and rinsing off, in the time span allotted to shower within. Once the officer shut the showers off, you were done; the showers weren't coming back on. If you still had soap on you or hadn't gotten to take a shower, it was "oh well, too bad". You would have to rinse the soap off or bathe in the cell's sink.

After breakfast and the morning count, it was mandatory for all prisoners on the cell-block (who weren't in confinement status or call-outs to Medical or intake processing) to go to the Rec field until the yard was called in for afternoon count and lunch. Coming out of the dining hall after lunch, you went straight to the Rec field, where you stayed until dinner, when the yard was called off for the change-of-shift count at four in the evening.

During the summer month of daylight savings time, you were to go from the dining hall to the Rec field after you finished the evening meal. They would close the yard around eight, just before sunset, with everyone returning to their respective housing, whether dormitory or cell-block. For the first two weeks, during the days, I was kept shuttling from one call-out to the next. At the physical, I had the doctor prescribe some allergy medicine for me, which I promptly dumped out and replaced with my hormone pills; any officer doing a search of my belongings would check the label to be certain it had my name and prison number on it. They wouldn't know they weren't allergy pills.

I wasn't able to get to the Rec field much during those first two weeks, maybe an hour or so during the day and for the evening yard. I could always make the canteen even with long lines of prisoners waiting a turn; certain convicts would have influence with officers to get you to the front of the line, usually for a price, but I often got to the front with a smile or thank you.

If I had wanted to turn tricks, I could have made a fortune. As it was, a lot of the convicts would give me items from the canteen just for some conversation, or to have a connection with me, as I was the closest thing to a woman they had. You really don't know how vital interactions with the opposite sex are to your psyche and mental/emotional health until you are deprived of it, for both heterosexual males as well as those of other persuasions like me.

You still feel a lack of being with those of similar minds and emotions, woman to woman so to speak; for the heterosexual male, it is far worse.

Some in the outside world would call the guys silly for giving in to the pretense that I was a woman, no matter how feminine I looked, acted or felt. Yet it would be best called a pragmatic, situational adjustment. They didn't want sex; just a connection or simply a conversation; people do what they have to in order to protect their mental and emotional well-being, no matter the circumstances.

By the second week, I got 'Peaches' as a cell partner. Peaches was from Fort Lauderdale, in on a shoplifting beef. He had been part of a boosting team, going around the malls and stores and walking out with shopping carts loaded with high end products; a trade a lot street queens seem to gravitate to; that, and credit card fraud.

There was good money in boosting, especially if you stole for orders, already having customers for the items you stole. Otherwise you would have to double your hustle, first stealing the item, then finding a buyer for it.

Peaches certainly knew how to work the men on the yard, as our cell soon looked like a canteen warehouse. Peaches wasn't transsexual like me, just a queen doing what he liked. Through him, I met Frankie out on the yard, though he wasn't a queen, but more of a bisexual hustler on the make, doing whatever it took to get by.

Frankie was 5'9", with sandy brown hair and blue eyes, and a gymnast's slender physique, a nice package with his looks. He was also street, and had the manipulative blarney, while always looking for an opportunity to get over on someone; totally manipulative, scheming and conniving. Once you understood that about him and let him know up front that you weren't lame to his game, he settled down and became alright.

We'd never be close friends, as I would never trust him to any extent, but we were on friendly terms. As I watched him hustle Peaches, I gave him a few dollars when he tried to hustle me, while telling him, "Baby, I know exactly where you are coming from. Been there, done that... and seen the elephant. Don't mistake kindness for weakness. I don't mind giving you a stake to hustle with, but I am not going to be hustled. I've been where you are." After that he kept his distance from me. We could talk as he ran with some of the people I knew on the yard, and because Peaches were infatuated with him for some reason.

The fourth week I was at Lake Butler, Frankie and Mac, whom I barely knew, stabbed a third guy in front of the gym. I saw it go down; Mac was stabbing while Frankie held the guy to keep him from running. I wouldn't know the significance of what I saw that day until much, much later; and I never did learn what the stabbing was about. The two of them were locked upon the cell-block for the stabbing, and then transferred somewhere the following day.

The Reception and Medical Center was also the place where I first met Koju and Frank T, both of whom were there from the East Unit for medical treatment.

Koju was very dark skinned, tall, slender, and black haired, with a wide mouth and white teeth; the type of person you would say was so ugly they were actually cute. He had an engaging grin and charming personality; he chatted with me up on the yard one day, and afterwards we would talk from time to time. I learned that he was in for some robbery charges, and had a life sentence.

Frank T was brown skinned with pleasant features, and about 5'9" and 175 pounds. He had multiple ninety-nine year sentences over a group of tourist and drug related robberies, shootings and killings in the Miami-Dade area. His crime partner, Willie Reed, was also at the East Unit. I did recall hearing about those crimes in the newspaper and on television a couple of years back, as their arrests and trials had been major news stories.

Frank and I talked about books and literature; he was very well read and erudite, and we had some very enjoyable conversations. With Koju, I knew he liked what he saw and would take advantage of it should the opportunity present itself (although Koju was a gambler and had little time for other things). Frank was more difficult to read. I ended up believing that he had no sexual interest in me; he liked my personality and intellect, and he was fascinated with the culinary arts field, constantly pestering me with questions after learning that I had a graduated from a culinary arts school and had worked as a chef.

When the five week quarantine was up, I started to get visits from Mimi, Ken and the Cleary clan, all of whom were on my visitation list. Mimi's father had somehow gotten permission for them to use the landing strip that ran behind the prison, and which could be seen from the Rec field. One of the institution's vehicles would meet the plane, and after ensuring it was secured properly so it couldn't be used in an escape attempt, would transport them to the front lobby to be processed in for visitation.

This was noticed by other convicts, who then made the assumption that I was either very rich or well-connected or both, which drew some unwelcome attention to me. Some prisoners were looking to scam me out of some money, or wanted me to finance some wild nefarious scheme of theirs, and would get mad when I couldn't go along with whatever they wanted. They wanted to believe that I was green, naïve and gullible, and it upset them when they found out it wasn't so.

At least they had sense enough not to push the issue, as by that time, word of how I had come to have the name 'Poison' had gotten around from some of those who knew me from the last ride at the prison rodeo. I did, however, make arrangements to be resupplied with hormones and reefer. This was simply a matter of coordinating with one of the convicts assigned to work on one of the outside crews, which went outside the fences to work.

I would have the package dropped off at a prearranged location to be picked up and brought in; it cost to have it done, most often with reefer as payment for bringing it in. The reefer sold well on the compound, so I would end up making money covering my expenses, even turning a profit. Koju had been dealing for me while he had been there, then I used others, so I wouldn't have to handle anything. I would receive the hormones and smoke for personal use, with the money being sent to my prison account or to a post office box outside.

I had no need of money, but since I wanted to continue taking the hormones, I thought I might as well make it pay. And the reefer facilitated everything, so it went smoothly; as I said, drugs in prison can get you things that even money can't buy. There was the additional benefit of not having to buy reefer off the compound to smoke, as I had my own.

Mimi was out of the casts and walking on his own, with a cane for nominal support. He was still undergoing physical therapy, but was much improved. Ken-toy was still an item, and it looked as if they were going to be a couple, which they confirmed when Mimi told me during one of the first visits, "Ken has decided to attend college here in Florida and is enrolling in pre-med classes." I could detect Mimi's fine hand behind all that. In addition, Ken's family, including his mother, two younger brothers and two sisters, were moving to Florida to be close to him while he was in school. Their home was provided by guess whom? Mimi was not about to let this one get away.

While Ken was at the canteen bringing food and drinks for us, I told Mimi, "You got it bad, girlfriend..." "Yeah, he's a keeper, and I intend on keeping him. Laugh if you want to, but just wait until it happens to you."

They also brought me up to date on how Doris was doing, "she misses you and looks for you every day", and about my car, the 63 Plymouth Sport Fury, which Mimi had decided to take on as a project. She was having it repainted in black metal flake, and the interior done over in red leather. It had a red interior from the factory, well worn, and Mimi had decided to redo it in leather. I coordinated with Mimi as to where the next package should be dropped off for the outside worker to pick up. Mimi knew some people in Jacksonville, who he paid to make the deliveries for him.

Although I hadn't planned on returning to prison, as they say, "shit happens", and I might as well make the best of it. I had only tried hormones sporadically before my first trip to the Florida prisons, but I had done them continuously for the past twenty months or so. This caused breast development and other feminine features; I liked the way they made me look and feel, so I wasn't about to stop taking them, not willingly at least.

Peaches transferred to a prison down south, and I got a new cell partner, Cupcake, a stocky queen out of Orlando, twenty years old, who was fascinated with the way I looked. He had always wanted to do the hormones, but hadn't built up the nerve to actually take them.

I knew that there might be a few problems for him since he had a coarse beard, lots of body hair and an already receding hairline; the hormones would help some, but it still wouldn't look right. I had been blessed with almost no facial hair, fine hair on my arms and legs, and none on my torso. I was thinking the hormones kept it that way as well as providing a little extra padding on my hips and thighs, in addition to the breasts and softened skin.

I didn't try to discourage him, for who knew, maybe laser hair removal would work on him; and often, you must do whatever makes you feel comfortable with yourself. To others, I may have looked like a freak, but to me, it was all part of who I was inside, which had nothing to do with what gender I had been born as.

The officers still made me wear two T-shirts to conceal my breasts; providing me with a bra would be too much of an admission to my appearance and femininity. With the uniform shirt on top of it all, it was very uncomfortable in the heart of sun. Nor was I permitted to take the T-shirts off and go bare-chested on the recreation field, like other convicts were, in order to get some sun; not that I would want to, as that would be putting myself on display, and inviting problems I didn't need in my life. I could and did, however, take the uniform shirt off and tie up the shirts just under my breasts to get some sun on my torso and legs. Even then I would get a lot of attraction, with a number of prisoners making it a point to pass by wherever I was in order to get a look.

After the first couple of weeks, I rarely ate in the dining hall, preferring to eat out of the canteen; or buy it off the yard, as the kitchen was next to the Rec field and the kitchen workers always had food and sandwiches which they had made off with out of the kitchen. Plus, I had some deals worked out with them, so I never had to go to the dining hall if I wasn't inclined to. You had to wait in the long line outside, and then finally when you got inside and received your food tray, the officers would rush you to get started and finish meal soon, so that another batch can sit down and eat.

Outside the chow hall, officers would randomly search the prisoners coming out to keep them from bringing food outside. Those caught feeding the birds (who waited outside the mess hall during meals for such handouts) would be made to spend the remaining time the chow hall was open shooing them away. A never ending task, as the birds expected that food would be available, and weren't about to leave.

Animated scarecrow or not, when the chow hall did close, the officers would make those chasing birds go back inside to help clean up, which for some prisoners wasn't such a bad deal, since they got to eat what they wanted of the leftovers.

The officers would also use other little gimmicks to amuse themselves at prisoners' expense. Whenever the dormitories and cell block would release their prisoners for the mandatory yards, the officers would be waiting to select the prisoners at random for their particular work details. They always seemed to target the younger prisoners, or ones they had had problems with in the past, or those caught doing something they weren't supposed to.

Once selected, the officer might tell the prisoners to get a "Cadillac", which was an empty no. 10 can, and go pick up trash and butts off the compound. Another officer would tell his selected group to get "Porsches" (street brooms) and sweep the sun off the side walk. Another officer would have his group get "Rolls Royces" (wheelbarrows) to transport dirt from place to place around the compound. The rest of those selected would end up in the kitchen for the day, to help out, the last being a good deal, because while you had to work, there was plenty of opportunity to eat and steal food while doing it.

Prisoners, when handed lemons, will make lemonade; some prisoners would deliberately try to be selected, or volunteer to pick up trash and butts, as doing so also gave them freedom of movement in the compound, opening up opportunities for hustling and moving around contraband in the no. 10 can. The officers were aware of this, but would mostly ignore it on the part of some prisoners. I'm sure there was some form of quid-pro-quo going on there.

However, the intent of the officer in selecting prisoners for their squad was a minor form of sport for them, and also a harassment of the prisoners, to see if they could generate an objection or negative response from the selected.

On the cell block during the evenings, especially during counts, the officer would divest themselves of keys, shoes and anything capable of noise in order to creep around the wing floors trying to catch prisoners off their bunks or talking during the sacrosanct counts, which at times took hours. The officer would either make a note of the cell number, or release the offending prisoners from their cell to go to the quarterdeck, where attitude adjustment for the violating prisoners would take place inside the lieutenant's office (which occupied a small portion of quarterdeck). Some of the beatings the prisoners received were quite severe for some minor offenses.

But then, it wasn't about what the prisoners had done; it was about what the officers wanted to do. They always wanted to whoop some convict's ass for their own entertainment and pleasure, and it also worked as an object lesson to other prisoners. The beatings administered in the confinement cells late at night were deemed as being too removed from the sight and hearing of the open population prisoners to serve as object lessons.

Through the banks of windows which fronted the cell-block, I could see the officers as they beat prisoners in the lieutenant's office, near enough to hear every blow and cry as well as to watch the officers as they began their creepy crawls around the cell-block wings trolling for the victims.

I was spared such indignities, in part because I never provided them with any excuse to do so, yet I think my appearance also played a role. However, what they would do was, whenever there were officer trainees on the compound, the regular officers would call me over to where they were standing, then have the trainee conduct a pat-down search of my person. The baggy prison uniform which I was given to wear, and the uniform shirt over the two t-shirts, disguised my form. The pat-down never went past the chest - when the trainee felt my breasts.

Some would take their hands away as if burned, to the great amusement of the officers. Or the trainee, uncertain as to what they had encountered, would grope my breasts while trying to figure it out, or would ask me outright, "What's this?" Either way, the regular officers would get hysterical with laughter at the trainee's moves, telling the trainee, "We told you to pat him down, not to feel him up."

The officers would then quip to the trainee, "What's the matter, you've never felt tits before?" Usually the trainees reply would be, "Yes, but not on a man." I would go along with it good-naturedly, not that there was much of a choice ever involved, yet it made me fell dirtied and ashamed, as if I had been somehow violated.

I was with my third cell partner 'Peggy', and on my twelfth week at the reception center, when on a Friday morning, I was told to pack up; I was being transferred. I had learned the prison's transfer schedule by that time, and knew that the prison buses went south on Mondays and Wednesdays, north on Tuesdays and Thursdays, and that Friday was the local run. Thus, I knew I was headed somewhere within the "Devil's Triangle", as the collection of prisons in the surrounding counties in and around Lake Butler (including the Rock and the East Unit) were called by the prisoners.

I left a lot of the items I had accumulated with Peggy, yet was left with quite a load which would be going with me. The reefer and hormones went into the ladies carry-all, while the money and coupons were scattered throughout my paperwork. The Rock and East Unit were the only two prisons to issue canteen coupons to prisoners, with Lake Butler accepting them at their canteens. I had kept some coupons as I thought there was a possibility of my going to the Rock, but I never expected to be sent to the East Unit. However, at the receiving area, one of the convict orderlies told me I was Unit bound.

It was the result of typical bureaucratic knee-jerk reaction; because of my appearance, the classification and administration couldn't figure out what prison to classify me to. Figuring my presence would be disruptive while posing problems for prison administration wherever I was sent, they had classified me to the last prison I had been in prior to my release.

I kept two of the culinary arts magazines I had subscribed to, but left the rest, as I was aware that I would be expected and required to tote my own property, and didn't want to be burdened like a pack mule; I could easily replace whatever I left behind when I got to where I was going.

The perfume, I mixed with my lotions. I was also taking a few pairs of panties, and had a pair or under the boxer shorts, on which I had sewed up the fly - otherwise it made me feel too exposed. I couldn't see how men could stand to wear them like that.

It was a short bus ride to the Unit, but the long Bluebird bus I was on made several stops at prisons within the Devil's Triangle, picking up some more prisoners while dropping others off. The bus stopped at the Rock before heading for the East Unit. I had grabbed a window seat towards the front of the bus, where the officers transporting us had told me to sit so that he could look through the wire mesh screen separating the driver's section from passenger section of the bus, and also keep an eye upon me; although it wasn't me he needed to watch.

As we entered the river sally port gate, where all deliveries including those of prisoners passed through before entering the compound, I noted that the Unit had been given a makeover of a new paint scheme. Gone was the former pinkish beige, replaced with a light-green color. However, the aura of the place was still as malignant, maybe even more so now; a new coat of print didn't change that.

Also, the dogs were gone from between the fences, replaced with a row of razor wire at the top and bottom of the fence-line of the inside perimeter fence. I had heard that they had taken the dogs away after a prisoner had escaped by cutting through the fences, taking the dog with him; neither the dog nor the convict had been seen since. I had also heard his name, Billy.

I recalled Billy as being young and lanky, as country and backwoods as they get. Yet, he had been a very nice person. I hadn't thought he deserved the time he gotten for killing his step father, who had been beating his mother; I guess he hadn't thought so either. I wished them luck where ever they were, although I didn't think the dog would still be with him. It was a story I wished I could learn; I was willing to bet it would prove interesting.

The bus pulled up to the ramp and unloaded eighteen prisoners who would be remaining there, me included. It appeared that nothing had changed inside the west corridor leading to Times Square, other than an addition of a walk-through metal detector at the entrance. However, there had been some changes, as I soon learned.

We sat on the bench in front of what was now called the colonel's office; the department having added a couple more layers of bureaucracy and officer grade. Captain Combs, as the convict grapevine had it, was now the assistant warden at Cross City, one of the prisons within the Devil's Triangle over towards the west coast of Florida. He had been replaced by Colonel Hicks, who I remembered as being a Sergeant when I had been released.

As he checked us off the clipboard, Colonel Hicks said to us, "Welcome to the East Unit boys," and to me, "I see you made it back to us, Poison. Couldn't stay away?"

"Would if I could," I replied.

"Take care of yourself in the trenches."

"Yes sir, I will," I replied.

This time around, an officer escorted us down the main corridor from Times Square to the laundry, where we were given our clothing issue, bed roll and bag of toiletry issue. I had expected to go back to K-wing, before hearing that they had stopped segregating the gal/boys from the rest of the prisoners. Now it was pot luck; you went to the wing they assigned you to.

I had been assigned to the south side of W-wing; first floor, cell six. It was the first wing on the left, close to the canteen and directly across from J-wing. W-wing was one of the three wings at the prison with solid floors, the other two being R-wing (which housed death row prisoners) and Q-wing (for those considered troublemakers, as well as those awaiting execution).

Among the prisoners, death by electrocution was called "riding the thunderbolt in Old Sparky". Those prisoners would be housed on Q-wing's first floor, which only had six cells, three to a side (the two upper floors had six cells to a side). The first floor was also called the Dungeon, and the Death Chamber was just beyond the end door on the first floor, next to the last cells.

The two wings beyond gate thirteen, R and Q, also differed from W-wing, as the cells on the two confinement wings backed on each other with a pipe chase in between them. The barred cell-fronts faced a bank of windows across an expanse of floor, making an attempted escape less likely, whereas on W-wing, the cell fronts faced each other across the floor.

The officers at the prison didn't like working W-wing, as the prisoners housed on the first and third floors would remove all the hallway lights and cover their cell windows, so that any officer working the wing the wing would require a flashlight day or night to make his round on those floors. Even with a flashlight, there still remained pools of shadows all around, and any officer known to be an asshole would have glass jars, bars of soap and D-cell batteries flung at him out of the darkness; more than one officer was run off the wing in such a fashion.

So the officers stayed off those two floors as much as possible, and only officers known to get along well with the prisoners would be assigned W-wing as their post, which is exactly how the convicts wanted it. They thought W-wing was a sweet spot to be housed, as they were allowed to do almost anything they wanted to among themselves. There was no need of guard, since it was just that type of wing.

Many people there already knew me from my last trip through the Rock and Unit. Therefore, I knew that shouldn't have much of a problem, if any. And if there was a problem, I had brought a little friend with me that I had had a convict in the welding shop make for me while I was at Lake Butler; it was kept concealed among my legal paperwork.

If I had been a queen or young man new to the system, W-wing would be the last place in the world I would wanted to be housed on; at least until I got settled in and known, as W-wing was a death-trap and killing ground for the unwary as was proven time and time again. Under other circumstances, I probably would have been raped, and had a train run on me within the first thirty minutes after I hit the wing.

Guys kept dropping by the cell to check on me, and to check whether it was really me; scoping out the changes in my appearance since I was last there. They had already heard about it, and of course about the breasts, all of which they wanted to check by themselves. At the first opportunity I had, I rid myself of the second t-shirt, cutting it out to make a halter top out of it and covering it with the other t-shirt. The uniform t-shirt, I left off, as it was hot in the cell and wing.

My breasts weren't as large as a 32b, as they had been described, but they were still breasts. They also came by to let me know that the wing was alright, and that I wouldn't need a knife because no one wanted me leaving the wing. However, there's no accounting for a fool.

I got the cell cleaned and straightened out, smoking a joint with an older queen named Katz, who had dropped by the cell. We had been together on K-wing the last time I had been at the unit, and we had been on friendly terms then; she was a hustler also, albeit a little long in tooth now. She filled me in on all the gossip about the wing: who was alright, and whom should I avoid or look out for, as well as the whereabouts of the other girls on the wing with us. Duchess and Cherry were living on M-wing, Freyda had gotten a paroled and Grubworm had gone home, while others had been transferred.

When I went to take a shower, I took the knife with me just in case, as a girl couldn't be too careful in a place like this. As the convicts said, "it's better to have it and not need it than to need it and not have it", the others saying being, "it's better to pick twelve, then to be carried by six" (twelve being the number of jurors on a capital murder charge versus the number of pall bearers needed to carry a casket.) As it was, I got a lot of drive-byes going past the shower on one pretext or another.

The mentality of some prisoners was that since I was a transsexual, ergo a homosexual, any man with a penis would do, and that I should leap at any opportunity to engage in sexual activity, since I was a gay or wanted to be a woman. In their minds, I should be whore as well, giving sex to whoever showed up at my doorway with a hard penis.

My lifestyle was by my choice, because of what I felt myself to be inside, and not because of sex; I enjoyed sex, but only with people I chose to have it with. Even when tricking and selling sex, I would pass on some who just did nothing for me, and I didn't consider tricking as sex per se in any event; that had been about survival and getting by. I certainly wouldn't have sex with anyone and everyone who wanted it.

However, that being said, I could still be raped. They would pay for it dearly in blood, but it could happen; some people never stop for red lights or warning signs. I wasn't looking for a man, sex or relationship at that moment. Now that I didn't have to turn tricks to get by or survive, my goal was to complete my sentence as quickly as possible and get out to continue with my life.

Over the next few days, I adjusted to the routines while learning more about what had transpired at the unit while I was gone. Whitehead was dead, killed by 'Creeper' at gym, allegedly about a boy and disrespect. That was the cover story, as his death had actually been a contract hit. Creeper had taken the contract from Stonewall to finish Whitehead, and in the process of doing so, it had almost cost him his own life.

Creeper had stabbed Whitehead as he was lying on the weight bench in the gym, doing bench presses with heavy weights on the ends of the weight bar. After stabbing Whitehead for a few times, Creeper had left the knife embedded in Whitehead's chest, with the weight bar also on his chest, and walked away, thinking the job was done.

But not quite; as Creeper was walking away, Whitehead, who had been feigning death, had pushed the weights off his chest and set the bar on the rack quietly before pulling the knife out and catching up with Creeper.

Whitehead had also made the same mistake as Creeper, thinking him dead and leaving the knife on him. As he started to run to seek medical attention for his wounds, Creeper woke up, took the knife and finished Whitehead off; and this time he cut the throat to ensure it. Creeper fell out on the way to the clinic and died three times on the operation table.

After returning from the hospital some weeks later, Creeper was still in confinement pending charges, there being some confusion about who stabbed whom first; he would probably end up with a few years for the killing. I got the story from Creeper first hand when I was in confinement later on.

Whitehead's death had been a result of Captain Combs going to Cross City as assistant warden about the time of Mimi's release. Colonel Hicks had replaced Combs, and I came to know that Stonewall and Hicks had served in the same company, and had seen at combat together while they were in military.

With Combs gone and Hicks in the top spot, it had become open season for bringing Whitehead down, with Stonewall taking full advantage of the opportunity presented by sending Creeper to make the hit. Stone was now top in the spot, replacing Whitehead among the blacks, and he would also work as the food service director's clerk in the kitchen.

Among the whites, Mike, who held the top spot, had gotten a release from the prison shortly after I did; he had spent time in Lake City before going back to California. Skeet had taken over his spot, while also replacing Mike as the maintenance supervisor's clerk.

I got along with Skeet. He was an orphan like me, and had grown up in the same school of hard knocks, having also been to Vietnam while serving in the Marine Corps. He had lost his leg in a shootout with police and state troopers at a truck stop just outside of Starke, Florida.

The hustling was same, and as always, the tension in the hallways and cell-blocks was one you could taste and cut with a knife, the miasma of anger, rage, fear, despair and malignancy pervading the unit stronger than ever. Every time you heard the cell-block's outer steel door slam shut and the keys turn to lock it, you would know blood was being shed and perhaps a life was about to be taken at one of the wings.

The officers slammed and locked the wings doors whenever an incident took place, to isolate and confine the case in one wing. They had learned this the hard way, when a fight once spread to all the wings on the west side, crossed over, and was joined by the wings on the east side, with several officer injured in the melee; it had taken the State Troopers and National Guardsmen, in conjunction with officers from several surrounding prisons, to quell the disturbance and restore order. Ever since then, the doors connecting the cell-block wings and the day-rooms were kept locked.

The main reason for slamming and locking the doors was to wait for enough officers to arrive to handle the situation inside, but convicts died, whose lives might be saved otherwise; if the prisoner was being assaulted, and didn't make it off the wing before the wings doors were locked, they were left to their fates.

It was my third day back at the unit; I was browsing the books on the library shelves, looking for something to read, when I rushed to Stonewall, who was doing some legal research.

"How's everything going, Poison?" he asked.

"It's going, that's all I can say," I replied.

"I had heard you had changed some, but I see the descriptions didn't do you justice," he observed.

"Yeah, I've also hard some things about you since I got back," I replied.

"All good, I hope."

"All depends on how you look at it, and who is looking."

"How do you see it?"

"It is what it is," I replied, shrugging my shoulders, "It's the way of the world. The strong move up and the weak go over. What else is there to say?"

"True, true enough."

Stonewall continued, "Say, since you were so good at what you were doing in the restaurants on the street, may be you could come in and give our bakers a few pointers to improve the quality of stuff they make."

"I wouldn't mind doing that. I've missed it a lot, and it's something I love doing," I said.

"I didn't know you were interested in cooking when you were in last time," he said.

"It was something I had always wanted to try, and it turns out I am rather good at it. I would never have gotten the chance to do that if not for Mimi and her family," I replied.

"Ah yes, the other half of the Bobbsey twins, how's she doing anyway?" he asked.

"Would you believe that she has taken a lover?" I said.

"One of her usual flings?"

"No, I think this one's going to be around for a while. She's even moved his family to Florida from California so that they could be near each other."

"Sounds serious alright, well good for her. I'll talk to Mr. Curtis, and see if we can manage a time for you to come in and instruct the bakers," he said, turning to leave.

"Do that and take care of yourself. I guess I'll be seeing you around, it's been nice talking with you. "I went back to my book search and he to his research.

Later in the evening, I was returning from the canteen window with some items when I had a chance encounter with Frankie, who was coming out of the kitchen after duty. His appearance was a total shock to me and I didn't know quite what to make of it, as Frankie was dressed like a queen: arched eyebrows, makeup, lip gloss and tight pants. Frankly, he looked garish and not feminine at all, at least not in my eyes.

He looked more like a parody of a queen than the real thing. Nor, in spite of all the accoutrements, did Frankie try to act like a lady; whoever was responsible for him playing this tune had sure hit some wrong notes, because Frankie was at best a bi-sexual or a boy; he wasn't made out to be a queen. We spoke for a minute as we walked down the corridor, not getting into details, and parted at the W-wing doorway.

One of the guys on the wing who had seen us talking told me, "Frankie is Stonewall's bitch," which explained a lot; if you can't have a queen, you make a queen. I knew the feminine look hadn't been Frankie's idea, and that he wouldn't have made up like that unless he had been given no choice in the matter.

This was typical of some of the men in the prison, who wanted those whom they were fucking to act and look like women as much as possible, so no one could mistake who was doing what to whom. It was also a part of the macho male chauvinists image they projected, with antiquated concepts about a woman's proper place being a part of the package.

I also saw Frank T and Sugar Bear out at the recreation field the following day, working out with the weights, it being their day off from work. Both of them worked in the kitchen, Frank T in the bakery, and Bear in the butcher shop. Frank T's fall partner Willie, whom I hadn't met yet, worked thirteen spots, mopping and sweeping the main corridor running in front of the wings.

We spoke for a few minutes in between their sets with the weights, Frank informing me, "Koju is in confinement, but should be out by few weeks. He is working as a confinement orderly now, and should be released soon by the classification committee."

"I've got a couple of subscriptions to the culinary arts and cuisine magazines coming. When I finish with them, I'll make a point of getting them to you," I said to Frank.

"Great, they don't have much of a selection in the library, apart from the Betty Crocker kind of stuff," he replied.

"I know... It's a shame too, but that will change because I'll be ordering a lot of good books. You know what they say, 'those who can do it, do it, and those who can't read about it.'"

"Let me know when you get them, I'd like to check some of them out," he said.

"You got it. Just be certain I get them back."

"No problem, there's not that many people interested in that type of stuff anyways."

"Well, there's you and me," I replied.

"True," he said, "let me get back to working out, I'll catch up with you later."

We said our goodbyes, and I went walking around the fence perimeters, never alone for long as the other prisoners would stop me to talk, or catch up with me as I walked around. Most just wanted conversation, or to be seen talking with me, while a few expressed interest in taking a test drive of the goodies.

I was still in the process of feeling out the place, and didn't want to make any commitments, thinking that I would have plenty of time to do whatever I had a mind to do. I wanted to be more focused on learning as much as I could while I was in prison, which would advance my career when I got released.

I did have a few discussions with some of the major players about bringing in some packages of smokes and hormones. It wouldn't be a problem, just the time it would take getting it all set up. I had enough of the hormone pills to last me a couple of months, and reefer I could get off the compound. The quality wouldn't be as good as I was used to, but it got would get the job done. I also had some of the California Red Bud, so there was really no rush.

And just when you think everything is working out fine and going smoothly, someone will throw sand in the works and screw it up. First off, I found out through the classification runner that I was scheduled to be assigned at the garment factory. Me? A seamstress? Fat chance of that happening; it was another one of the typical bureaucratic fumbles, sticking the square peg in the round-hole.

The fact that I was a certified chief and baker had held no weight when it came to assigning me a job in the prison. Therefore, I did what any normal person of my means would do. Taking some money and reefer, I paid the chief convict clerk in the library to have me assigned as general library clerk.

The chief clerk went to the platform, raised so the librarian could see the entire library at a glance, not that it stopped any of the clandestine activity going on in the library. After looking around, I saw the clerk pass Mr. Lewis (the librarian) something, which I took to be some of the money I had given him.

Lewis then called me to his office, took my name and prison identification number, and told me, "You'll be on tonight's job change sheet." Having taken care of that little matter, I thought I was set. Then, they moved "Shorty" on W-wing.

Shorty had just got out of disciplinary confinement for fighting. He was shorter than me, but was stocky and muscular, about 160 lbs, brown skinned, and was as ignorant as the day is long. He got one look at me, and that's all she wrote; I was going to be his, end of the story. He ignored the brush-offs of being pointedly ignored, to being told point blank that I wasn't interested and to go away.

I wanted nothing to do with him, but to Shorty, all "no" meant was that he hadn't tried hard enough, or aggressive enough, and that eventually he would wear me down or force himself upon me. He started telling everyone on the wing that I was his bitch and to stay away from me; the obnoxious little creep was beginning to wear on my nerves.

As the days passed, he got even more aggressive and threatening towards me. I asked him politely to leave me alone, which he took to mean that I was playing hard to get. I asked people to talk to this fool, but he still wouldn't take heed, when they warned him that he was playing with fire, and would get burnt. His reply had been grabbing his crotch and saying, "She's poison, and I got the antidote right here."

I didn't want to get involved with a killing if I could avoid it, which meant I let this shit go on longer than I normally would have, which Shorty took as a sign of weakness. Finally, knowing how all this would end up if I didn't get away from him, I went up to Times Square and talked with Lieutenant Gaskins about getting a wing change to avoid problems.

"You brought the shit on yourself by looking and acting the way you do," he said, continuing, "I'm not moving you, go back down there and either find a husband or get a knife to take care of your business. But never come back here, because I don't want to hear it again. You do whatever you have to do to resolve the problem."

"Could you place me in the confinement, as I'm trying to avoid problems?" I asked.

"No, I am not doing that either. You get yourself a man, or get a knife. You're going back to the wing, because I'm not moving you," he replied.

"Well, I tried..," I thought, as I returned to the wing and got my little dagger friend out of its hidden spot, as there wasn't much sense in waiting to do what needed to be done. When Shorty came back on the wing and down the stairs, I met him by the front of showers. He thought that I was coming to talk or go upstairs, and stopped.

All I said was, "Since we can't get along, we'll just have to get it on," bringing the knife out and lunging at him. A little patch of water on the floor from shower spray caused me slip, saving his life and saving me from a possible life sentence.

I had meant to stab him in the junction between his ear and jaw, which contained a nerve plexus as well as major arteries. With a little twist and pull, the knife would have cut his throat vertically to the collarbone, with the next stop being the graveyard. However with the slip, the knife went into the trapezoid muscle to one side of his neck, close to his back.

When Shorty felt the knife bite into him, he spun and ran back up the stairs, with the blade slicing a path down the back of his shoulder and arm to his elbow, as it was tempered and razor sharp. He squealed and bled like a stuck pig as he went out the wing door, causing the officer to slam and lock the door behind him.

I picked up the knife and put it away, while other convicts came by my cell saying things like "you only did what you had to do", "I expected it to happen long before this," and "he got what he was looking for." I didn't know how badly Shorty was injured, but it looked serious from the blood trail he had left behind on the stairs and floor.

I was locked up under investigation later that evening, and placed on the first floor of Q-wing by the confinement sergeant, when he saw who I was; it was unusual, as the cells down there were for prisoners on death watch. My property was stored in the property room for the time being.

I was placed in the cell next to the execution chamber itself. The three cells on either side (east and west) were twice the size of the other cells at the unit. Some would consider that a luxury for a condemned prisoner; nonetheless, there was a pragmatic reason for its size, as it provided more room for officers to overcome any resistance or objections on the part of the prisoner about to be executed.

I liked the amount of space within the cell, yet never felt comfortable or at ease, feeling like there was a presence there, giving me chills and goose bumps; it was as though someone watching me through the six-inch port window set into the door leading to the execution chamber.

Later that same night I had a visitor in the cell; it was the confinement sergeant, who had let himself into the cell with his keys to have sex with me, which explained why I had been housed there. I had no choice in the matter, as it was either give it up, or he'd take it. I opted for the lesser of the two evils and went with the flow, having learned from past experiences with staff members in the boys' schools and reformatories.

He visited me for sex every night he worked, and I felt violated each time. He expected that I would comply with what he wanted of me, and there wasn't any option but to go along, and make the best of it. And it wasn't as if I was a virgin and naïve: I knew the score; I had no win. Even if I had said something, who would they believe, me or him? I already knew the ending to that story, it was better to just to go along and keep my mouth shut.

I was on Q-wing for eight days before finally getting my property and being moved to a regular confinement wing: P-wing, third floor, north side. I was still under investigation, but the confinement sergeant told me that the investigation would be ending in a few days, with Shorty's assailant listed as unknown.

No one had put me on the spot by saying I was the one who stabbed him, as all the convicts felt he had got what he asked for. The prison administration didn't want to open a can of worms with regard to Lieutenant Gaskins' statements to me just prior to the incident. The lieutenant had recounted exactly what he told me to the prisoner inspector investigating the stabbing, which is how I had become a suspect, as the incident occurred so close after that conversation. Shorty had said that he didn't know who stabbed him, either being stand up or not wanting to admit a transsexual sissy had stabbed him and made him run for his life.

My nightly visitor on Q-wing while I was housed there had given me a fat bundle of loose canteen coupons and coupon books, which the officers had confiscated from other convicts as contraband (loose coupons and books not being issued to the bearer). He had also fed me food that he had brought in to work from home. Sure, I had derived some benefits from having sex with him, yet I felt no less violated for it.

I was glad to be leaving Q-wing, not only so the nightly visits would be stop, but also because the cell really creeped me out. It had a haunted presence, and whatever it was, I was glad to be getting away from it.

Koju was the "run-around" (prisoner floor orderly) on the third floor of P-wing, scheduled to be released back to open population within few days. So I took the advantage, and used him to help rid myself of the soiled feeling I had inside from the sexual activity with the Q-wing sergeant. We had sex between the bars, and on the narrow bunk inside the cell whenever he could get the wing officer to roll the door open for him.

For both of us, it was just about sex; we were friends, and it was something we both wanted with no strings attached. Koju was already involved with a boy named Ricky; I didn't want any relationships, nor was I about to play second string to Ricky, so I would take what I could, and enjoy it while it lasted.

I did give Koju some of the loose coupons to gamble with some of the other prisoners in the cell; and a bunch when he was packing his property to return to open population, so that he could send me a care package from there once he was out. I knew he gambled and hustled for what money he had of his own.

In between sex, his gambling on the wings, and the work his job as run-around required, he would sit in front of my cell, and we should smoke reefer and talk. It was during one of our conversations that he let me know he was a part of Willie and Frank T's clique, who were vying with Stonewall for control of the Black prison rackets.

He also told me that he had served in the Marine Corps, and that they had a detainer on him for being AWOL, and for a robbery of a paymaster on the military base at Cherry Point, North Carolina. The military would come get him should he ever be released by the state; not likely, as Koju was serving multiple life sentences. He kept me laughing with some of his stories, telling me about going through basic training at Parris Island in South Carolina.

One of their drill instructors had told him and the rest of the recruits that "sir" was a military acronym which stood for "service inspired respect". The recruits had spent the rest of the day coming up with colorful descriptions of "sir", including "sibling incest result" and "southern inbred redneck". There were others far worse than these two that had me rolling with laughter.

Koju and I talked a lot, and I knew I could trust him; call it woman's intuition or what you will. Nonetheless, if Koju was your friend, he would do whatever he could do for you, being loyal to a fault; right or wrong, he would always be there, whatever came about. This is exactly how he proved himself to be in the ensuring years.

After he was released into population, I received the care package (of canteen goodies and smoke) that he sent. I sent him some more of the loose coupons for another, but a week after he had gone, I was told to pack up my property to return to population, assigned to be housed on U-wing; second floor, north side, cell eight.

U-wing was used as the kitchen overflow wing, to house the kitchen workers when V- wing was full. The rest of the wing was used for prisoners with other work assignments (I was still assigned as a library worker).

Mimi came up to see me that weekend and gave me a lecture.

"Girl what in the world were you thinking? You could have gotten some serious time if you had killed him."

"I intended to, and would have if not for the water on the floor," I replied.

"See, that's what I mean. You could have paid someone else to handle the problem for you."

"That would have created more problems for me in the long run. I went out of my own way to avoid it, but there was no choice. When I went up to see Lieutenant Gaskins that day, I pretty much knew what he was going to tell me before I even went up there. This is prison baby; no one's going to wet-nurse you. If you have a problem here, you deal it with head-on, or you lie down and let them roll over you," I explained.

"Yes, but still it was a quite a risk you took. Suppose you had killed him," Mimi said.

"I intended on doing just that. All of life is a risk if you don't stand up for yourself, and no one else is going to stand for you either. I resolved it so that I wouldn't have any further problems of that sort, so that I can do my time and get out of here," I said.

"Well, I'm going to see if Daddy can do something to help out."

"Just do what you think best, but I believe it's over, and I am done with it," I said.

We then discussed where, and to whom, the packages should be dropped off to; Jo was sending me California sinsemilla. Mimi said that Doris was still pining for me, and informed me that Ken was doing really well with his pre-med classes. Apparently he was considering specializing in gynecology or obstetrics, which made me choke on the coffee I was drinking. I looked over at Mimi, who shrugged her shoulders helplessly; she didn't know what to make of it either.

The rest of the convicts knew that I had done what I had to do, and most of them were saying I did the right thing, with comments like, "We tried to warn that fool, but he thought he knew better. They say experience is the best teacher." I wasn't so sure that would apply where Shorty was concerned; sure he had learned a lesson with me, but it didn't mean it would extend to others. As it was, Shorty was at Lake Butler, and would be there for some months getting physical therapy on the shoulder and arm.

Several people told me that I should have waited a couple more days, that Shorty's problem would have been taken care of for me, as nobody wanted to see me leaving the wing or going to confinement. I could think of several reasons for that other than my sexual orientation and appearance, none of them good. Still, if I had permitted it to be taken care of for me, someone else would have taken it as a sign of weakness.

In my situation as a transsexual queen with no cover (meaning I had no man), I had to earn my respect from the other convicts, not relying on someone else's reputation, or the respect others would show based upon some relationship.

A few days after my release from confinement, I was delivering some copies of food service documents to the kitchen from the library, having run the copies on the library's copy machine. As I was passing through the south dining hall, I saw a crowd of kitchen workers crowded around the mop room on the south side of chow-hall. They were laughing and joking among themselves.

I was curious as to what might be going on over in the mop room, but not enough to want to go over and investigate; it wasn't any of my business, therefore I should ignore it. Sugar Bear, who had let me into the dining hall and was the lookout for those around and in the mop room, noted me looking over there and said, "They're running a train on Stonewall's bitch Frankie."

"Why?" I asked.

"Stone caught him trying to pass a kite (note) to another nigga, and this is to teach him a lesson. If he wants to be a whore, Stone figures he can help the bitch. The bitch has to have sex with anyone who shows up and wants some, and the fellas are having themselves a god ole time. That punk won't be able to sit down or swallow for a week after this," he said.

There was nothing for me to say about this. I had been given a glimpse of a side of Stonewall I hadn't been certain was there. From the past experiences I had seen with other queens and their lovers, the man you met during the courtship phase wasn't always the same one you ended up with when it developed into a relationship.

By the time you found out the true nature of the person, you were either trapped within the relationship, or trapped by your own emotional involvement. Extricating yourself from the mess you had gotten yourself into always proved to be a tricky proposition, with the only exit door sometimes being the graveyard.

Sugar Bear was shorter and smaller than me. Nonetheless, he was just one of the fellas who amused and entertained others with his antics. Bear had narcolepsy, and had been known to fall asleep standing up with a broom or mop in his hand, or while eating. He could usually be found sleeping under one of the food serving lines or in a store-room. So it surprised me that the others had him acting as a lookout for them.

But then, they probably weren't expecting to be interrupted as this was of Stonewall's doing; officers and convicts who didn't want to participate, or knew what was going on, would stay away. If the officers "didn't see it", it didn't happen, nor would they try to put a stop to it. It was another one of the realities of prison life, or as Orwell put it in the novel "Animal Farm", "all pigs are created equal but some are more equal than others", which was true for Stonewall in this instance.

I continued on into the kitchen to finish delivering of the copies, and never made mention of what I had seen to anyone else; neither Frankie nor Stone was aware that I knew about it. What I didn't know at that time was that there was a fiercely intensifying struggle brewing between Willie's clique and the Pensacola group for the top spot occupied by Stonewall. The two other crews were making inroads on Stone's grip on the reins of power.

While I had been in confinement, there had been a hit on one of Stone's lieutenants; three convicts had stabbed Sturgis in his cell on W-wing. However, the official version given out was that the stabbing had happened because Sturgis was an informant for the prison administration, and like Whitehead, had done some of their dirty work for them.

There likely was a smattering of truth to the last part, as Sturgis hadn't been killed outright. He had been alive and talking when he got to the clinic and was loaded on the ambulance to be taken to the outside hospital, but when the ambulance arrived after two hours of aimless driving, it had been too late to save him.

Prison rumor also supported that Sturgis held a lot of dirt on the current prison administration, and that they took the opportunity to ensure his silence - "Dead men tell no tales, nor testify". The three convicts accused of his death were in confinement awaiting charges for the murder.

The two factions were nibbling at Stone's power base and support as well, by robbing the gambling games and drug dealers operating under his aegis. But for the moment, Stonewall still held the reins of power.

Stonewall had arranged with Mr. Curtis for me to come in and provide the bakers with some tips on how to improve the quality of breads, rolls and desserts they prepared. So, a few days later, I found myself in the kitchen bakery showing them how to prepare large batches of bread dough for that day, and next two days' meals.

The kitchen had two industrial-sized mixers and a smaller one. I put the quantity of flour, salt-water and yeast the recipe called for, to feed 1200 plus convicts, into the two large mixers, adding extras to cover a couple of hundred more (the middle of serving a meal is not the time to run out of food). I had put the yeast in warm water to activate it.

When the dough was mixed to the right consistency, we broke it up into separate lager dough bins on wheels, and set it over by the ovens where it was warm for the yeast to make the dough rise. While waiting on that, I made the cookie batter for that day's evening meal, substituting peanut butter for some of the shortening, and some brown sugar in place of the regular sugar.

I had one of the bakers run some No. 10 cans of shelled-peanuts and almond-slivers through the smaller mixer to chop them up and mix them together. Once the nuts were mixed, I took half of them and set them to the side in an insert. The rest went into the cookie dough, before setting one of the bakers to portioning it out on greased sheet pans for baking.

I then prepared the peach-cobbler for the following day's evening meal. Once I had prepared the dough and rolled it out, placing it in the pans, I poured in the mixture of the peaches, sugar, brown sugar, honey, cinnamon and corn starch on the top, before placing strips of dough crisscrossing the tops. By the time those were completed, and in the coolers, the bread dough had risen.

I showed them how to work the dough and form the breads, and set them aside to rise again before baking. The only difference from what I did in the restaurants was the quantity of product I was making up and the quality of the ingredients.

We pulled the second batch of bread dough from one of the bins, worked it down, and then replaced it in the bin. We sprinkled some flour on top before covering with wax paper and the lid, rolling it into the cooler for tomorrow; the cold would keep the yeast inactive until then.

It really wasn't taking me much time to do these things, as I had plenty of eager hands to work once they knew what I needed, or had been shown.

Of course, the bakers wanted me to show them how to make some special stuff, for themselves and to sell to the other convicts.

Stonewall had gotten Mr. Curtis's "okay" for me to make up some cinnamon rolls, turnovers and Danish for the kitchen workers. I also made some strudel, which is like Danish, mixing up a sweet dough for the Danish and cinnamon rolls, and adding yeast to the cinnamon roll mix. The turnovers were just sweet dough, and while waiting for the cinnamon dough to rise, I rolled out sections of the flat turnover dough.

I had the bakers open two No.10 cans each of sliced apples, peaches and cherries. Draining the heavy syrup from each into separate pots, I added honey, brown sugar and cinnamon to the syrup, along with a couple of cups of water, and set it to simmer and thicken on the range.

I mixed half a can of cherries into a can of peaches and one of apples, adding it and other ingredients into a pot, and once it came to a boil, set it on ice before mixing the syrup with the rest of the fruit.

Taking sections of sweets dough (rolled and folded several times to make it flakier when baked), I rolled it out to make long pockets, which I filled with layers of fruit, alternating and mixing between the different types. Cutting strips of dough, I laced them across the top. Brushing butter across the top, I set them to bake after mixing up several sheet pans of them.

I rolled out some more dough and cut out triangles from it, spooning some of the fruit mixture into the centres of the triangle before folding it over, and using a fork to seal the edges. Once I had shown them what to do, the bakers would finish up and let me go on to the next project while they watched.

By this time, the cinnamon rolled dough had risen, and was ready to be worked (I poked it to make certain it was of the right consistency for working). I had one of the bakers mix some cinnamon, sugar and honey into some melted butter, and another mix a couple of large boxes of raisins into half of the remaining peanuts and almond slivers.

After rolling out the dough, I separated it off and trimmed the edges, brushing the top with the butter-mixture before sprinkling the almond, peanut and raisin mix across the entire section. After sprinkling cinnamon and brown sugar on top, the dough was rolled up into a cylinder and sectioned off into individual rolls, which were set on greased-sheet pans and set by the oven for the yeast to work again before baking. Again, we brushed the tops with butter mixture.

By then almost the entire kitchen, drawn by the enticing smells coming from the bakery, had made it a point to stroll by and see what was up. Even Mr. Curtis stepped out of his office upstairs to watch for a few minutes. While we were waiting for everything to bake or get set up, Stone came from the office upstairs, telling me, "Mr. Curtis wants you to put aside a batch of everything you're making for him."

"Sure, there is no problem. I made plenty." I replied.

When the strudel, Danish and turnovers were done and set out to cool, I took the pots of syrup mix I had had simmering all this time, which had reduced to a thick mixture, and dribbled it across the tops of the turnovers and Danish. Once the syrup mix cooled, it would be a thick layer of sweet glaze with the taste of fruit that had been in it.

When the cinnamon rolls were done, I used the rest of the glaze mixture over the tops of them, then helped with the cookies and bread we had baked for that day's meal. As the cookies were cooling, I had the bakers sprinkle the rest of the raisin, almond, and peanuts across the tops of the cookies, to set as they cooled. I set aside two sheets pans each of the Strudels, Danishes, turnovers and cinnamon rolls and cookies for Mr. Curtis, which we set on racks inside a hot box, which was secured with a padlock to ensure what was inside didn't disappear.

As it was, the bakery was mobbed by the kitchen workers and staff as the bakers handed out the pastries to them (except for the cookies, which were for the prison's evening meal). I ate a couple of cinnamon rolls with a mug of real perked coffee that an officer had brought me from upstairs.

I was cleaning up and getting ready to leave when Stone came and said, "Mr. Curtis would like to speak to you for a couple of minutes, before you leave." I followed him upstairs to the office, where the director had a plate with variety of pastries in front of him, and was eating a piece of peach strudel. He said, "Come in, and have a seat Poison. I must say I'm quite impressed with both the quantity and quality of your product. You've had some good teachers, because you've prepared two days worth of food in just a few hours. Not to mention the side work," indicating the pastries, "with little or no wastage at that."

I was beginning to think he was about to offer me a job, the prospect of which had me in two minds; I loved to bake and cook, but didn't like to have someone dictating how it should be done; institutional cooking inside a prison was sheer drudgery for a chef.

Mr. Curtis continued, "Don't worry, I'm not about to shanghai you to work in the kitchen or bakery, and frankly speaking, I couldn't afford you. We operate on a budget here, and if you worked in the kitchen, there would be more food down on the wings than would be served in the chow halls. I'm already getting calls from officers on the population wings about some of these pastries and cookies having found their way down there, and some officers wanting some for themselves. I probably couldn't afford to have you working in one of my restaurants outside either, as I'd have to raise my prices." Mr. Curtis had several family-type restaurants in the area.

"That being said, what I'd like to ask you to do is to come in a couple of days a week, and prepare the breakfast and lunch meals for the staff," raising his head before I could interrupt, "Hear me out. I'd give you the menu, you prepare it as you want, just let me know what you'll need. I separated the budget for staff meals. I would also like for you to come and help in the holidays for preparing the holiday meal for the prison population."

He further added, "I can arrange with Mr. Lewis for you to get time off when you will need it. You would still work for him, but you would come in to work the staff kitchen. I have a staff meeting up front, I have to go. So think about it, and let me know."

"I don't have to think about it. If I can prepare the food the way I know how, I would love to do it. It would provide me with the chance to keep so that I don't get rusty, while helping to perfect my craft at the same time," I replied.

"I thought you might. Well, I have to go to my meeting with the warden. I will call you in a day or so, and we can work out the details. I'm sure you'll want some items we currently don't have on hand in the stock room," he said.

"Yes, and thank you," I replied as we both got up to leave. Going down the stairs, I saw that Stonewall had placed some of the pastries reserved for Mr. Curtis onto platters, and into a serving cart. Mr. Curtis and Stone went out the west corridor doorway with the cart of pastries, while I exited the kitchen through the north dining hall with a bag of pastries and cookies (taken with permission), going to the library and sharing with the library workers and Mr. Lewis, while reserving some for myself to snack on later.

Needless to say, my activities in the food service bakery were the talk of the prison. Those who hadn't had a chance to taste any of it were told to be sure to go to chow that evening, for the cookies and bread. Those who already had a taste gave me compliments. I had just enjoyed the experience of being able to do something like that for the first time in months, making me realize how much I missed it. Now, I would have the chance to do some more in staff.

The following day, people who had never spoken to me before were saying "hi" and greeting me. The dining halls did landmark business when they served the peach cobbler for the evening meal.

At the library that morning Mr. Lewis received a phone call then called me to his office, where he told me, "Mr. Curtis wants to see you right away. I hope you aren't about to leave us to go to the kitchen."

"Oh no, I like working in the library. The kitchen would have me washing dishes or in the pot room."

"That's good to hear, as I'd hate to lose a good worker," he said.

I didn't mention anything about working in the staff kitchen on my days off, thinking that it didn't count. I left the library and went to the kitchen through the north dining hall; seeing me approach, the officer on duty told me, "Go right on up, he's expecting you." Upstairs in the office, Mr. Curtis said, "Grab a cup of coffee, and have a seat. I have something to discuss with you."

When I had gotten the coffee and a seat across from Mr. Curtis, he said, "At the staff meeting yesterday, everybody there couldn't get enough of your pastries. The warden even took some home with him for his wife and daughter. He called me up this morning, and that's the reason we are having this talk. His daughter Rachel's tenth birthday is coming up this weekend, and they're having a birthday party for her at the warden's house. He wanted me to ask you if you could make the birthday cake for it. I'll get you whatever you need to make it with, if you'll do it," he said.

"Sure, I'll do it. How many are going to be at the party?" I asked.

"You know, I forgot to ask, hold on a second," he said, picking up the phone and calling the warden's office. "Hello Mr. Strickland, this is Mr. Curtis in food service. Yes, he's here with me now. He wants to know how many will be attending at the party. What's that, forty children and about ten adults? Yes, I'll get whatever he needs, and I am certain he will do a bang-up job for you. Yes, thank you sir, I'll get back in touch with you." He hung up the phone.

While he had been talking, I had drawn up a list for everything I would need for that many people, which I handed over to him when he got off the phone. Reading the list, he said, "Hmm, yes, yes, pectin preserves, strawberries, chocolate, Skittles, M&Ms.... ", then looking up at me, "some of this stuff I'll get at the restaurant supply wholesalers. The only thing on the list I am curious about are the Skittles and M&Ms, six one pound bags of each?"

"You did say she was going to be ten, right?" I asked.

"Yes," he replied.

"You ever known a kid who didn't like candy? I plan on using them for the decoration on top. Two cakes for the kids and one for the adults. I'll have to use larger pans and make them sheet cakes. Easier that way, as I will have to watch them closely, with your large ovens," I said.

"What kind of cake you are planning on?" he asked.

"Chocolate Velvet, a Strawberry Delight and a Double Dutch Vanilla, all layered cakes," I replied.

"Those would be interesting. I'll have to check them out," he said gladly.

"I'll make smaller versions for in-house," I said.

"Yes, do that. I'd like to see what they taste like."

Mr. Curtis brought in all the things I would need the following day and kept everything in his office, except the strawberries, which were kept in lock box in the cooler.

I spent most of Friday in the kitchen making up the cakes, and the miniature versions which would be the size of a regular cake. I first re-sifted the cake-flour Mr. Curtis had gotten a couple of times until I was satisfied. I roped Frank T as my helper and assistant with Mr. Curtis's approval, and Frank jumped at the chance to help me.

For the layers in the chocolate velvet, I used a large pot, combining cocoa butter, cocoa, butter, honey, molasses, cream, chocolate and sugar to heat on the stove, stirring frequently. I was making a type of chocolate candy that would be softer than a Hershey bar, soft enough for the cutting knife to glide through, yet firm enough in consistency to where you wouldn't get the full chocolate taste until you started chewing.

It was just a matter of getting the proportions right. I would dip a little out from time to time, let it cool, and then check its consistency before making adjustments to the mixture until I was satisfied.

It was chocolate velvet cake, so the chocolate between the layers and used as frosting wouldn't be noticed until eaten. I thinned the chocolate out for the frosting, so it would resemble normal frosting.

For the strawberry delight, between the layers, I used strawberry preserves and fresh pureed strawberries simmered with some brown sugar, honey, pectin and rhubarb lathered thickly. I used the rest on the top of the cake, which I then covered with conventional strawberry (pink) frosting, with strawberry halves around the outer edges as a garnish.

I used the M&Ms on the Chocolate Velvet to spell out "Happy Birthday Rachel" as the chocolate frosting was setting, and used the Skittles on the Strawberry Delight.

On the Double Dutch Vanilla, I had used fresh vanilla beans, pure vanilla extract, marshmallows, heavy cream and sugar to make a thick crème for spreading between cake layers. Dividing the cake into horizontal strips, I used the chocolate I had made as a mortar between the strips as I reassembled it, before laying the thick crème between the layers. I used rest of the thick crème as frosting to disguise my handiwork. No matter how the cake was sliced, you would end up with a bit of it all; chocolate and marshmallow crème.

I made four of the miniature versions of each, about half the size of the ones I had made for the birthday party (which were kitchen sheet-pan size, three and a half feet by two feet). There were six large cakes altogether, two of each, which went into a lock box and were placed in the cooler and locked away, to keep them from disappearing before they could reach warden's house.

I carried six miniature versions (two of each) up to Mr. Curtis in his office after they had cooled and set. When he had tasted a bit of each, his remark to me was, "My God, whatever in the world are you doing in prison? Talent like this is just going to waste. I'm going to carry one each of these up to the warden for him to see, and I'm certain that he'll be pleased with the result."

I ended up with one cake of each. I don't know what the warden did with the three that Mr. Curtis took up to his office. Mr. Curtis took most of his home with him, after sharing some with the kitchen staff. Frank T got the fourth batch, which he really didn't want to accept at first, until I told him he could make at least fifty dollars off each cake. I took a thin slice of each for myself, reserving some for Mr. Lewis and library workers, while making certain Stone got a large piece of each.

The cakes were really rich and moist, almost melting in your mouth. The strawberry delight was tart and sweet, which was the taste I had wanted to complement the Skittles I had used, the rhubarb adding tartness to the strawberries. I also ended up with several bars of chocolate fudge from the rest of the chocolate mixture I had made, along with the remaining Skittles and M&Ms, which I took back to the wing with me after stopping by the library to drop off the cakes for Mr. Lewis and the library workers.

At my request, Mr. Curtis assigned Frank T to assist me in the staff kitchen, and work in the staff dining hall. After I had prepared several breakfasts and lunches for the officers and staff in the staff kitchen, as well as a holiday meal for the prison population, anyone wanting to do me any harm or give me a problem would have had a very bad day.

The officers, staff and prisoners alike appreciated my culinary skills on the days I worked in the staff kitchen, preparing the meals that all the officers, medical and administrative staff ate. Prisoners down on the wings would have standing orders with prisoners on kitchen duty for any of the leftovers. I got to prepare and eat what I wanted, plus I had become well known among the officers and prisoners for my cooking ability.

I started correspondence courses with a college on the outside, in Business Administration and Restaurant and Hotel Management. Mr. Curtis also kept me busy making birthday cakes for staff families, and I believe he was making money from it as a sideline, as he never commented on the fact that I would sometimes come in and show the bakers how to make things like peanut brittle and granola bars to sell to the other prisoners.

Being so busy, I hadn't paid much attention to all that was going on inside the prison among the prisoners, especially between Stone and the two factions attempting to usurp him from his position. Creeper was still in confinement, Sturgis was dead, and then Michael Pane, who was out of Pensacola, took out Stonewall's enforcer "Mongoose Shorty" down on M-wing (allegedly over a sissy name, "Luscious") early one morning.

Frankie had gone to confinement shortly after the mop room incident in the dining hall. You might as well as say that he checked in to get away from Stonewall for a time. His being in confinement like that wouldn't last more than a few weeks, as there was no such thing as protective custody at the East Unit at that time. If you kept getting disciplinaries while in confinement in order to stay, the prison administration would figure it out in short order, and send you back to open population. As one senior official put it, they "weren't going to hide in the back (confinement) to avoid dealing with their problems in open population. This prison is not a day care center."

In any event, being in confinement would grow old pretty quickly; its concrete and steel would wear you down, and the isolation and loneliness would get next to you until you had to get away from it. It would build to the point where it made the problems confronting you in open population seem insignificant, no matter what you might have to do to resolve it. In Frankie's case, it was returning to open population and Stonewall, as his bitch. Frankie's only other option was to kill Stonewall, and didn't have it in him to do that.

Frankie moved unto U-wing (third floor, south side) when he was released from confinement. Willie and members of his faction were already living on U-wing, including "California", Sugar Bear, "Gangster" and a hanger-on named Tick. Tick was the guy Stone had caught Frankie sending a kite to. The following day, Stone was moved from V-wing to U-wing, third floor, to the last cell on the south side, thus setting the stage for the final acts to come.

I never learned whether Stonewall's move onto U-wing was following Frankie or to set up a confrontation with Willie, as Stone had members of his faction living on the wing as well. Whichever it was, it was a mistake which cost him his life.

I was friendly with Willie by this time, having been introduced to him by Frank and Koju. The fact that I was alright with members of his crew, and that I had heart to stand on my own within the prison, scored points with him. Willie was very street savvy with leadership charisma, charming and cold-blooded. We got along, as we had both grown up out in the streets, and survived. He respected that about me, even more so because I was a queen, knowing what I had to have gone through to survive as I was.

There was nothing sexual between us, as he wasn't into white flesh, no matter how tempting the manner it was packaged; nor would I have been foolish enough to involve myself with him. The only member of his crew I didn't like was Tick, whom I thought to be a cowardly blowhard and parasite. Whoever had given him the nickname had had great insight into his character.

I was quite aware, in a distant sort of way, of all the violence taking place in the prison. The slamming of the wings steel doors and rattle and clank of the keys turning in the locks kept me informed that the prison beast was still getting its share of blood offerings and sacrifices from among the prisoners. Kenny Ford had killed a sissy named Space Monkey on J-wing, Joe and Gator had killed J.B. on K-wing, Trip and Jake had killed Ninety-Nine on L-wing, Michael had killed Mongoose Shorty on M-wing, Coney had taken out Nasty T on M-wing, Cue had killed Dirty on T-wing and Bam had killed Donnie on U-wing. Seven killings in five months, and that was open population wings. A couple of other killings had taken place in the gym and on the recreation field, not to mention all the stabbings which hadn't resulted death.

All of this really had nothing to do with me. It was one of those things where shit is taking place all around you while you're existing within an insulated bubble; aware and yet not aware, with nothing immediate to draw your attention to focus upon it all. Plus, I was busy with my studies and work.

Two things occurred which made me realize I might want to pay closer attention to what was going on around me; the first occurred as I was coming back to my cell from visiting one of the people I used to stash contraband for me within their cells, as I would keep very little in my cell (nothing I couldn't swallow, flash or toss out the window, should officers suddenly appear on the wing). I wasn't worried about my knife, as it was well concealed, and had gotten by other searches.

But no matter how much pull or connections you might have within the prison, there is always a measure of uncertainty and inconvenience. I probably wouldn't go to confinement, and the disciplinary report either wouldn't be written or wouldn't be processed. Still, why go through all that when I didn't need to?

I found older convicts who had been down for a while and had no money coming in, had no real hustle about them and never got into trouble or went to confinement. They would hold my contraband for payment on a weekly basis, in canteen or smoke. They were more than glad to do it, as it gave them something for themselves while making them feel as if they were now part of something bigger, with no real risk on their part.

They also knew that if they got caught with any of the contraband they were holding for me, I would send care packages for them the whole time they spent in confinement, and take care of them with canteen and smoke when they returned to population.

"Nubby", the stash person I had visited that particular day, wasn't in that category. True, he held stuff down, but he also sold smoke for me. Although he was short and only had one arm (having lost the other up to two inches below the elbow in some childhood accident), he had a good heart, and earned his respect among the other convicts. And though he had one arm, he still could use a knife.

I had suspected I wasn't the only one he held contraband for. However, that was his business and none of mine. As long as what he was holding for me was there when I wanted it, his business was his own. The only thing I required of those who held my contraband is that they don't tamper with any of it. If they needed something, they could ask for it from me. If they did tamper with anything, I wouldn't use them to stash things for me anymore, as I couldn't trust them not to get slick. As the saying goes, "I'd rather be swallowed by a whale than be nibbled by a crab."

I was coming down the catwalk going back to my cell after visiting Nubby, and as I passed Willie (who was standing at the railing with some of his crew), I touched his back as a way of greeting. This caused him to jump with shock, which hadn't happened in the past when I had done it. His startled response let me know he was keyed about something going on the wing; I knew it had to be big, because Willie wasn't usually on edge like that.

One other incident took place on the wing, which raised my awareness of the dynamics and tension between those living on the wing with me - a fight with lengths of steel pipe between Stonewall and Tick under the quarterdeck on the first floor one evening, with Stonewall and Willie's crew standing by to ensure it was a fair match.

Allegedly the fight was over who Frankie would be with, Stone or Tick. I figured Frankie had to be pretty desperate to escape Stonewall if he was using someone like Tick as his knight in tarnished armor, for Tick was a slimy self-serving coward. In the one conversation I had with Tick up to that time (which was one too many), Tick had bragged about tossing some woman's baby down an incinerator chute in an apartment building in New York.

Just based upon the vibes I got from him and my feelings as to the nature of his character, such an act would be right down his alley. However, I couldn't fathom why in the world he would tell anyone about doing it; I could only think he was trying to impress me as to how cold blooded he was. But killing someone's helpless child would and could never impress me at all. I could only believe Frankie was using Tick as a pawn, hoping Stone would kill Tick and end up in confinement, with a murder charge or under investigation for it.

Willie was also using Tick as his pawn to force Stone into a confrontation, and directly challenge his authority and power; Frankie was just the excuse to see who would reign as top dog within the prison. I was certain Tick would have gladly slunk away from the pending confrontation.

However, Tick was caught between a rock and hard place, and his Hobson's choice was to face Stonewall with the pipe or Willie with the knife. I imagine Tick believed his chances of survival were greater with Stonewall, as he was on the first floor with his pipe attempting to make it look like it had all been his idea, running off at the mouth with bluster, and boasting as a cover for his fear.

I could see clearly under the quarterdeck (where the fight would take place) from the railing in front of my cell. The grandstands were fine with me; it wouldn't be a good idea for me to be downstairs with a ringside seat, for the tension between the two factions was almost palpable. It wouldn't take much of a spark to set off a general melee, which certainly wouldn't be the place for Ms. Poison.

The fight took place during the evening meal, when the wing officer was out in the corridor monitoring prisoners off the cell-block wings going to and returning from the chow halls and the canteen. I had just returned to my cell and wing from the canteen when I spotted the two groups gathered around Stonewall and Tick. Both had pipes about twenty inches long wrapped in black electrical tape, and were eyeing each other inside a circle someone had drawn.

The two squared off and went at it for a good little while, the muted "thunks" of the pipes coming together the only noise being made. Tick, however, grew desperate to end it, knowing he was outclassed by Stone in the fight. He took a wild swing which Stonewall easily avoided, and while Tick was still off balance, Stone stepped forward and clobbered him on the jaw with his pipe. The blow broke Tick's jaw and laid him out cold, and the fight was over that quick, with Stone as the clear winner.

Even from where I stood on the railing, I could see the tension in Willie, as if he didn't want to accept Stone's victory. It appeared as if he would set it off, seeking to wrest control from Stonewall by direct means; Stone was alert for such a possibility and stood ready with the pipe.

Finally, after what seemed a long time, but really only seconds, I saw the tension go out of Willie. Thinking this wasn't the time or place for it, he gestured in disgust to some of his crew to pick up the unconscious Tick and carry him to his cell.

Later in the evening, Tick went to Medical with the now grossly swollen jaw, reporting that he had fallen in the shower. He was transported to the Rock hospital, then to Lake Butler, to repair the damage.

Stone had to know the fight with Tick would not be the end of the bigger conflict, yet he might have retained control except for his involvement with Frankie; he couldn't think straight, or past his image. It was one of those macho Stone Age carryovers: Frankie was his bitch, and his bitch alone, and no one was going to come between them.

Frankie's feelings or what he wanted wasn't even up for consideration; he would do what he was told and stay in a bitch's place. It was this blindness about it, and his jealousy, which brought about his death a couple of weeks later. I remember pondering, "men and their egos, which blind them to so much when it comes to dealing with emotions and feelings that conflict with the macho image they project."

Mimi was visiting on a regular basis, usually with Ken in tow, sometimes with one of her sisters or mother. About once a month, the whole clan would show up. Mr. C had talked to someone within the department to provide me with an umbrella of protection, of the sort Mimi had had when he was in prison. However, in my case, it had become almost a moot point, what with everyone's affection for my culinary skills, and the warden and others making use of them. But still, in all, the gesture was appreciated.

I say almost moot, for there is no accounting for fools or madmen; "Crawdad" had killed "Rooster" in the day-room of J-wing for changing the television channel when he had been watching the afternoon soap operas. The tension and pressure of the prison had prisoners would so tightly that there was no telling what minor little thing would light the fuse; you could become the unfortunate victim of being in the wrong place at the wrong time. It was something you always had to bear in mind at the prison, for there might be little or no warning signs that such an eruption was about to occur.

Mimi had sent me many photos of the family, Doris and the car. He would tell me about Doris (who still looked for me) and the latest additions and modifications to my car. He had now replaced the 383 CI engine with a

427 CI and 425 HP motor, while making over the suspension and rear-end and adding traction bars. He had also installed a Hurst Competition Plus shifter on a four speed transmission, modified the braking system and changed the tires.

Mimi had lost me at the part about the engine. He did tell me they had kept the original engine, which was being stored in the garage. It was getting so I wouldn't be able to recognize, much less drive my car when I got out, although it did look pretty in the pictures he sent, with its black metal flake paint job and real leather interior. As I told him, "you can't expect me to drive that on the road, it's a police magnet."

She replied, "Oh, you... No it's not. You can't tell what's under the hood by looking at it, fools a lot of people. I've had it out at the track and got some pretty decent times out of it. It does 160mph easy just the way it is now, yet it doesn't look anything of the sort.... And besides, it wouldn't even be noticed out in California with all the beauties I saw on the road out there. Your car would be one of the last the police would look at, because it looks restored. Nothing unusual about that at all."

The weekend of the battle of the pipes between Stonewall and Tick, I had told Mimi about it at visitation on Saturday, and he had said, "Girlfriend, you should stay out of it, you hear? Let those cavemen do their thing. None of it concerns you, and I want you out of the devil's courtyard as quickly as possible... I don't want to attend your funeral, or visit you here for next twenty years."

"The devil's courtyard? Are you getting religious on me, Mimi?" I had asked suspiciously.

"No... there is just something totally evil and malignant about this place... don't tell me you haven't felt it," he had replied.

"I have, I just thought it was me."

"It's not just you. This place gives me the creeps. Every time I think of doing something stupid, I think of this place and it changes my mind every time. I want you out of here the soonest."

"You and I both….."

"So, whatever they got going on in there, you stay out of it."

"I'll do my best."

"You'll do better than that. This is no place for you, you have too much going for yourself to wind up staying here. So please, for my sake, keep clear of it."

"Don't worry, I will."

"Promise?"

"Yeah, promise."

Mimi knew I didn't give my word lightly, and having it would ease her mind, knowing I wouldn't get involved unless I couldn't avoid it. Mimi had also started hormones, not really needing any cosmetic surgery as he looked feminine enough without any. But, like me, Mimi liked the way the hormones made her feel and look.

I never did learn how Willie or his crew communicated with Frankie, although I could think of a couple of ways they could have done so without letting Stone knowing about it (even with Stone keeping close tabs on Frankie at all times). Both of them went in to work in the kitchen on the early morning shift, which prepared the breakfast and lunch meals, and whenever Frankie was on the wing, he would constantly be under Stone's watchful eyes; when Stonewall couldn't watch him personally, he had others to do it for him.

However, Willie and his crew managed it, and it was done so smoothly that Stonewall never had inkling about the trap Willie was setting it up for him. Three weeks after the fight between Stone and Tick, everything was in place.

That morning, Stonewall and Frankie had gone into work in the kitchen at 3.00 am. The cell lights were turned on and the cell doors unlocked at

5.00 am for the convicts to rise and start getting ready for breakfast, if they were going. Frank T would make me a couple of egg omelets and send them with one of the kitchen staff, so I didn't have to immediately wake up when the cell lights came on.

Normally, any convict with sense will get up when the cell doors are unlocked; just as a simple act of prudence and safety, to be alert and ready for any danger that might come their way. It would be foolish to be caught unawares and sleeping under the covers should someone (or several someones) come rushing through the unlocked cell door with knives, intent on robbery, assault or murder; all of which was common practice at the prison.

I, however, had two other locks on my cell door, which would prevent it from opening because it was controlled by me only. The first was a piece of metal inserted into the runner at the top of the door, and it was jammed in to prevent the door from opening until removed. The other was two tightly rolled up magazines placed at the door's bottom, as a brace keeping the door closed.

Not that I had any worries or concerns about anyone coming into my cell uninvited. However, it was always better to be safe than sorry. One body isn't different from another under a blanket, and more than one prisoner had been assaulted or killed because the assailants got the wrong cell or cell number. As they said, an ounce of prevention is worth a pound of cure, as "oops I'm sorry" just doesn't cut it when you are dead.

I did get up about fifteen minutes after the doors were unlocked to wash up, make my bed and get dressed to breakfast. I puttered around in the cell, smoking a joint, before removing the inside locks on the door so I could go get some hot water from the water fountain to make a cup of coffee.

As I was returning to my cell with the hot water, the wing was called for the morning meal; this meant there would be peace and quiet on the wing until the prisoners who had gone to breakfast returned. I made my coffee and got a sweet roll out of my locker to snack on, and walked out of the cell, going out on the catwalk that fronted the cell to stand by the railing and enjoy the coffee and roll.

I was standing on the rail when I saw Frankie come through the wing doors and shoot upstairs to go to his cell. From my cell, I had clear views of all three floors, front and back. A couple of minutes later, I saw Willie come on the wing with his mop bucket to put it on the mop room before going upstairs. Since Willie had a couple of his crew living on the third floor above me, I thought he might be going to see Sugar Bear or "California". There was nothing strange to arouse my curiosity.

The wing officer was out in the main corridor monitoring prisoners going to and returning from chow. I, however, was curious as to what Frankie was doing back on the wing that early, when he was supposed to be at work, but dismissed it as being none of my business.

I hadn't spoken with Frankie any extent in a few weeks, not waiting to get caught up in any of the dramas swirling around him during that time. We would exchange greetings when we ran into each other on the wing, but that was as far as it had gone since Stonewall and he had moved into the wing.

I had finished the sweet roll and was savoring the coffee, when I saw Stone come unto the wing and head upstairs. It occurred to me he might be coming to check on what Frankie was doing back on the wing; I was to learn later that one of Stonewall's crew had told him that Frankie had left the kitchen through the dining hall doors when breakfast was called for the open population prisoners. Stonewall had immediately left work to return to the wing, probably with the intent of catching Frankie cheating.

Stonewall was armed with a knife tucked into the waistline of his pants under his shirt, whether from habit or to use on Frankie or whomever he was with, I couldn't really say; nor would Stone, for he would be dead within a few minutes, and would carry that information to the grave with him.

Stone reached the third floor landing and started towards the south side of the tier to go down to Frankie's cell. He was between cell two and three and still on the landing when Willie and Gangster stepped from the shower, where they had been concealed, with knifes drawn, looking all business.

The third floor differed from the other two floors, for on the south side of the third floor, the cells started at the top of the stairs (so that first four cells would be on the landing), whereas on the north side of the third floor and the other two floors, the cells didn't start until the landing ended and the catwalk began (the wing being an open square, three floors of cells facing each other across open space, with only a catwalk and railing for movement to and from the cells).

Each cell had a large window in the back wall for looking out over the area between the wings. The first four cells on south side of the third floor looked out over the rooftop of the day-room and main corridor, the shower area being on the north side of the landing just before the catwalks began.

When Willie and Gangster came out of their hiding place within the shower with their knives out, Stonewall squared off, facing them with his back turned to the cells behind him. Stone had his knife on his hand, and distracted by Willie and Gangster, didn't notice the cell door behind him being eased silently open. California, wielding a small length of pipe, closely followed Sugar Bear, who had a blade, and crept from the cell behind Stone.

California hammered the crown of Stonewall's head with the pipe, using an overhand with his weight behind it. The blow caused Stonewall to drop to his knees, where California struck him on the head again. I could hear clearly the muted thunks of the blows hitting Stonewall from where I was standing, on the tier below and opposite to them. The second blow dropped Stone bonelessly to the ground.

Stone had been so focused on the two in front of him that he had never realized the danger behind him; it had been a skillful ambush. I suppose I could have given a shout of warning, but the thought never would have gotten past my lips. It happened so fast that there was little time for any warning to do him much good; it also had caught me by surprise. I hadn't expected to be a witness to murder taking place before my eyes, in any event.

It also wasn't any of my business, which is why I would have kept my mouth shut even if I had wanted to shout a warning out, as one of the strongest prohibitions of the convict code was to "Mind your own business and stay out of others'". If you were foolish enough to interfere or involve yourself, you had better be ready to carry it all the way to the graveyard, as their deaths or yours would be the outcome.

Willie and Bear caught up Stone by his arms, while Gangster got his feet to carry him down to his cell. They were followed by California, with the pipe still in hand (I don't know whether Stonewall was unconscious or dead at this point).

The group, with Stone's limp form, started down the south side catwalk and tier at a fast pace, before noticing me standing at the railing of the second floor. I had forgotten cup of coffee in my hand by now, and they paused momentarily with Stone's body, looking at each other as if uncertain as to what to do about it. When they looked back at me, I raised the cup of coffee as if in a toast before turning my back to them and returning my cell, thus telling them it was none of my concern and to carry on like I hadn't seen a thing.

Inside the cell, I got my blade out of the stash because I couldn't say with any certainty how it would all play out. I was a witness to their killing Stone, and I wanted to be ready for whatever might come my way because of it.

Willie and the others were operating within a time constraint, as they needed to be finished with what they were doing before the prisoners who lived on the wing returned from breakfast. From my cell, I could see them continuing down the tier upstairs, carrying Stone's body to his cell.

They put Stonewall in his bed, and I saw Willie going into Frankie's cell to bring him. I later learned that Willie had made Frankie cut Stonewall's throat as he was laid out on the bed, so that he would have a direct role in the actual killing. Once that was done, they had covered Stone completely with his blanket and closed the cell door behind them as they left.

Frankie and Sugar Bear went back to the kitchen for work, while Willie and California put the weapons and bloody clothes in a mop bucket of bleach water in the second main-floor mop closet. After sticking a mop into the water on top of that, and pushing the bucket out into the main corridor to be disposed of elsewhere, Gangster returned to his cell on the wing.

None of them said a word to me at the time about what I had observed. I hadn't known what to expect, so I had been ready to sell my life dearly. Having killed one, they could have easily decided to eliminate the witness as well. "In for a penny, in for a pound", as they say, for the state can't execute you twice, nor can they execute you at all if they can't prove you did it.

Willie and Bear both told me later that they knew I wouldn't say anything, and that they had been more concerned about Frankie talking. However, there had to be a brief time when they must have considered it; they needn't have worried, as I would keep my mouth shut. Stone was dead, and whatever I could have said wouldn't have changed that.

Also, saying anything about what I had seen wouldn't serve my purpose. Stonewall had known what he was into and how it would end. As I had told him about Whitehead's death, "The strong move up, and the weak move over and make way". Nor was I a snitch of any sort.

Stonewall's body wasn't discovered until the morning count at shift change. His blood had soaked through the blanket and formed a pool on the floor of the cell, the blood being what caused the officer to notice something amiss. Otherwise, he might have passed by thinking Stonewall was asleep with his head covered with the blanket.

The clearing of count that day was delayed as first, as the prison investigator had to do this thing. Colonel Hicks also came on the wing to go see Stone's body in the cell, and the investigators had to finish taking pictures of it all before medical was able to remove the body. Only when Stonewall's cell door remained secured was the morning count closed for the wing, and we were released from our cells.

It wasn't until the evening of the following day that prison administrators rounded up all the usual suspects, locking them up in confinement under investigation. Those rounded up included all of Willie's and the Pensacola factions, as well as Frankie.

Over the next couple of weeks, some of those locked up were released from confinement as Sergeant Bell, the prison investigator, cleared them of any involvement in Stone's death. Frank T had been working on the line in the staff kitchen dining hall during the period when they believed Stonewall had been killed, with a number of officers he served breakfast to that morning verifying the fact.

Willie, Sugar Bear, Gangster and Frankie remained in confinement while California had been released with others, either because whoever was feeding details of the murder to the investigator hadn't known of his involvement, or it was a play by Sergeant Bell to create confusion among those involved in the killing, to cause them to think that one of them might be talking (California). The intent of such a ploy would be causing one of the others to break and tell what happened, fingering the others for the murder in exchange for a deal or immunity, which was a pretty common and obvious tactic police used.

Obvious or not, it didn't work in this case, at least not in the fashion it was intended to. Colonel Hicks did let it be known that none of those still in confinement would be getting out until someone came forward to take responsibility for the killing.

Shorty C and Tick returned to the unit about this time as well, Tick being placed back on W-wing while Shorty was housed on M-wing. I did have some concerns at first about Shorty C's presence in the unit, on the chance he might want to retaliate for my stabbing him, although other convicts told me I needn't worry about him. I wasn't raised in the streets to be a fool; no matter what anyone else had to say about the matter, I wasn't about to be foolish enough to turn my back on, or sleep, on him.

But I figured someone must have had a discussion with him concerning me, as he avoided even looking in my direction when we encountered one another by chance. I believe Shorty was glad, in a way, to be absolved of having to uphold his manly honor by seeking revenge for my stabbing him; it gave him an out. In any event, the issue resolved itself in short order, as he was in confinement within a few days of his return. I was given to understand he wouldn't be returning to open population any time soon.

I guess others were concerned with his presence at the unit as well, not so much for what they thought Shorty might do to me, but rather because they thought I might take the initiative and complete the job I had started on W-wing. I wasn't known for my restraint when it came to perceived threats to my person, nor was I a rattlesnake, in providing warnings as to my intentions; I would eliminate the threat without hesitation if I felt there was a need to.

Needless to say, I felt relief as well when Shorty went to confinement. Say what you will do about it, but with me it was all about survival; I did what I had to do to protect myself, and wasn't into gratuitous murder for pleasure or ego.

Now, Ticks return to the wing was a whole different story. The obnoxious creep didn't even realize how he had been used by the involved parties, and that and this was the only reason Willie had let him hang around. With Willie still in confinement, Tick strutted around the wing with his chest poked out like a pouter pigeon as if he was personally responsible for Stone's killing, and because of his association with Willie's faction. But he was too dim to realize that the others convicts were laughing at him and his presentations, and that they only tolerated him because of Willie; for now that is.

About a week after his return to the unit, Tick somehow learned that I had seen Stone's killing by Willie and the others, probably from the talk of other members of Willie's crew among themselves. He then took it upon himself to come to my cell to warn me to keep my mouth shut about what I had seen that morning, telling me that there would be repercussions should I speak out about it.

His entire presence and attitude irritated me. First off, I didn't know how he had gotten to know that I had witnessed the murder, as I had told no one of what I had seen. Thus, it had to have come from one of Willie's crew. Second, he had no business even speaking to me about it, for I was a convict, and wouldn't say anything regardless of the circumstances.

Now here this slime-ball was in my cell attempting to intimidate me with his blowhard bluster. I asked him, "Did Willie send you to see me?" I already knew the answer, but I just wanted to see if he would lie about it.

He hesitated for a second, as if considering telling me the lie. Then thought better of it, replying, "No, I'm just looking out for his interests."

"Willie certainly doesn't need your help with that," I said to him, before deciding that I had had enough, continuing, "What you do need to do, however, is get your slimy, stinking, psychopathic, parasitical self out of my cell before you find yourself joining Stonewall. When Willie has something to say me, he will say it... he doesn't need you to act as his spokesperson or go between."

Tick blustered a little, finally saying, "You shouldn't talk to me like that, and I'm just looking out for Willie."

"No... you're not. You are just trying to make yourself feel important... now get out of my cell," I replied firmly.

Tick slunk away from my cell, passing several of Willie's crew, who had heard the entire conversation in my cell, as all were trying to suppress laughter. Tick had reported to Willie that we had conversed, as he knew it would get back to Willie anyways, and was hoping to cause a conflict between Willie and myself.

Willie, however, had given Tick strict orders to stay away from me, and had Frank T apologize to me on his behalf. When Willie did get out of confinement, during one of our chess game he told me, "I never laughed so hard in my life until I heard what you had said to Tick in your cell that day. You called him to a T.... I was never even concerned about you saying anything, and that fool had no business even coming to you like that."

The investigation of Stone's death spanned several months, taking a strange turn when Frankie was transferred to the Rock. Rumor had it that he was going to turn state on rest of them, and I put some credence to the rumor, for at the sometime Frankie transferred, California was locked back up for Stone's killing. But whatever Frankie had thought to do didn't work out and he returned to confinement in the unit in short order, having changed his mind about being state witness against the others.

I believe Frankie thought he could get away from the whole mess he was in by turning state on others, for he had only exchanged masters from Stonewall to Willie. Frankie was now owned lock, stock, and barrel by Willie and his crew.

I learned from Koju that, when Frankie had got to the Rock and started to unpack his belongings in the cell he had been assigned to, several of Willie's friends and associates had stopped by to give him a message from Willie. They had said something along the lines of, "Boss Willie says to tell you hello, and that you had better stop with the foolishness and return to the unit."

It having been made perfectly clear to Frankie that he wouldn't be safe anywhere in the prison system and would never live long enough to get up on the witness stand to testify against the others, he backed out of his deal with the state and was returned to the unit.

Since Colonel Hicks was insistent about none of the group getting out of confinement until someone came forward to take responsibility of Stone's death, and Frankie had been willing to give the rest of them up, Willie thought it only fair for Frankie to confess and plead out to being the one responsible for Stonewall's murder; and that is what happened.

The prison investigator and the state attorney had to know Frankie was lying about being the only one involved with Stone's killing, yet it was the choice of getting one conviction or carrying all five to trial and seeing them all acquitted, as there was no evidence to link any of them to the murder.

From their point of view, one conviction was better than none; the state attorney's office at Bradford and Union counties were still smarting from losing a series of murder cases at trial one after another originating in the Rock and East Unit (although recently they had obtained a conviction for the Sturgis killing).

The Sturgis case had concluded with Kenny getting the death penalty while the other two received life sentences. This was Kenny's second trip to death row, having gotten the first one reduced to life a few years back. They might have beaten the charge but for the fact one of their alibi witnesses had changed his story at trial, spilling the beans about the alibis the convicts had manufactured for the express purpose of obtaining acquittals at trial.

Willie knew that the group could spend years within the confinement under investigation without ever being charged with anything. He also knew that the longer he spent in confinement, the weaker his hold on the reins of power he had acquired with Stone's death would grow; someone else could come forward and assume control of what was rightfully his.

Nor could he rely on the now defunct Alibi Inc. to ensure acquittal at trial in the event he was charged with Stonewall's death; there had already been one break in the ranks with Frankie's attempted betrayal. It was safer to resolve the whole thing by getting the bitch Frankie to cop to the killing and let the rest of them off. Why waste years in confinement or risk a possible death penalty when there was no need to?

With Frankie pleading to Stonewall's death and receiving a life sentence in exchange, Frankie would remain in lockup for a period of time. Willie and the others were released back to open population, and the welcome of a hometown hero from the other convicts, who were now referring to him as 'Boss Willie' in acknowledgment of his leadership role among them.

It was Koju who got Willie and me started on the chess games, telling Willie, "Poison's got a good chess game… you should play her one…" The one turned into several hundred over time, as I would never let him win unless there was no choice in the matter. This was very seldom; Willie could have been a good chess player, but he relied too much on his power pieces and not enough on game strategy. The only times he would win were when I was tired or too distracted to think.

Willie liked playing me because I would make him work hard for his wins, as he felt that a lot of the others he played let him win to curry favor, or because they were intimidated by him. There was always some of Willie's crew around while he played; they would be either in the cell watching us play or standing outside on the rail.

After Michael came into the picture, I watched as Boss turned from someone who held the reins of power benevolently and with a light touch, to an autocratic despot. The change was growing more and more evident with time.

With Boss's return to population, the prison returned to its normal routine of casual mayhem, with the Pensacola faction biding its time.

I was kept pretty busy with all my activities and studies, in the kitchen, library and around the prison. I was in no manner celibate; I was discreet, yet I got around. I kind of liked being a liberated woman, and never had any problem finding partners for sex.

Nonetheless, I wouldn't let anyone tangle me up in a relationship. I was having too much fun with my freedom. Not having to turn tricks for survival, I learned that there was much more to sex than I had thus far experienced, and that it could be very, very enjoyable. Plus, I liked the fact that I could pick and choose with whom to have sex with.

There were many among the prisoners who would have liked to have a long term commitment, but I stayed away from those types. This wasn't the time or place for Ms. Poison to put down roots, and without realizing it, I was emulating my sister Mimi's behavior while she had been in the unit (before Ken).

TWO YEARS LATER

So quickly had the time had passed, yet so much had happened, and now I was getting short again, my release date being less than six months away.

The mitigation of sentence for a reduction of time never worked out, because by the time enough of my prison stay had passed for it to be considered, the judge who had sentenced me had moved to another division in the courthouse. It was also an election year.

The judge who replaced him kept pointing out that the state had dropped eight other counts, and that it was my second conviction for larceny, and the state attorney opposed any reduction saying I had gotten off light with just the four years. They both completely ignored any of the positive aspects we tried to get them to look at.

Somehow, I had figured it would work out that way, and hadn't pinned any hopes on it. The system had schooled me to hope for the best, while expecting the worst. That way, no matter what the outcome is, you won't be disappointed. I considered it a mini- vacation from the unit.

The first year at the unit, I had prepared the Thanksgiving meals for the staff and prisoners. I pulled an all-nighter in the kitchen with roast turkey, giblet gravy, corn bread stuffing, cranberry sauce, peas, corn, and mashed potatoes. I had also made a fruit salad of sliced bananas, grapes, raisins and musk melon in mayonnaise (having dipped the bananas in lemon juice to keep them from turning brown before putting them in the salad), bread rolls and three types of dessert (pumpkin pie with a whipped cream topping, sweet potato pie with a butterscotch marshmallow topping, and mincemeat pie).

I had also prepared the warden's family dinner in addition to the other two, and instead of fruit salad, I had a tossed vegetable salad with French dressing and a sweet potato pie with peppermint marshmallow topping. For New Year's, it was candied yams and sliced ham with apple turnovers for dessert.

The prisoners liked the fact they were being served same meals that the officers and the warden and his family were eating, prepared by the same person (me). It provided them with a little taste of freedom with their meal. Vicariously to be sure, but to a man serving a life sentence and never expecting to see the outside world again, that little taste meant a hell of a lot; it was something that couldn't be wrapped and placed under a tree, nor taken from them.

Frank T was developing into a very fine chef. There were things he couldn't get from a book and which required the kind of hands-on training he couldn't get in prison, but he had the knack for cuisine (there are people who can't boil water without burning it).

I was learning to improvise and work around the limitations of institutional cooking and Frank T was teaching me how to properly prepare soul food, which we did for Martin Luther king Jr's birthday for the prison after getting permission from Mr. Curtis and the warden.

In February, I was given outside custody and classified to minimum custody, as the officers wanted me to do their cookouts at the officer training building out by the gun range. I couldn't go outside with close custody status, so the warden had the classification supervisor review my file. When it reveled I had no violent crimes and was serving a four year term for larceny, they dropped my custody from close to minimum. And presto I could now go to the gun range to do the cooking there, with an added benefit for the warden, as I could also go to his home to prepare meals for him and his family now.

I say I was learning to improvise, but I also cheated... by having Mr. Curtis bring me in items from the specialty stores, and by working out a deal with the inside grounds crew to grow herbs for me among the flowers in the prison's flower beds (I liked using fresh herbs or ones I had prepared myself as much as I could).

I could have been assigned to work in Classification or the administration building in front of the prison, but I liked the freedom of movement that the job in the library provided. I most likely could have moved about even without the library job, but this way it was official, if anything ever came up as to what I was doing in a particular area of the prison.

It was called CYA (cover your ass), and I would rather have permission to do it than to tell a lie or put an officer on the spot for allowing me to do something, or be somewhere the rules said I shouldn't (because then *their* CYA kicks in and I could find myself on the short end of a very shitty stick).

I had also developed a connection with Mr. Lewis, who was now bringing in some of my pills and smoke for me; we would smoke weed and have sex in one of the back rooms of the library. Plus, in the library, I had a coffee pot and coffee brought in from the outside, which I could make and drink all day.

One additional benefit of the library job was that it gave me access to all five confinement wings behind gate thirteen. Those confinement wings were set up differently than the cell-block wings of open population, whose cells faced each other across an open square (with each cell having a large window at the back of the cell). In the confinement wings, the cells backed on each other with a pipe chase running behind them. The entire cell front was bars, and the tiers faced outwards towards the outside wall and a bank of windows twenty-five feet away; a box within a box.

Only officers or the run-around prisoner wing orderlies had direct access to open the outer banks of windows, which is not to say that contraband didn't go from one confinement wing to the next or from an open population wing to one of the confinement wings.

The convicts inside the confinement cells had developed an art out of fishing from the cells, through the windows and across the intervening yard space between the wings, using the catwalk tier rails and those on the ranks of windows as the pole and reel. If the window was closed, it was often simpler to use a bar of soap on the line to break it than to attempt to get it opened, leading to some very cold winters.

The only wing which would require contraband to be brought in personally was Q-wing, because of its isolation. Extending out from the building's end, Q-wing faced east and west, whereas the rest of the wings faced north and south.

I could go into any of the confinement wings carrying legal work and books to prisoners in the cells, which is how I kept up with everyone. Some of the prisoners would also place me on call-out to use the writ-room with them to "help them prepare legal documents". Yeah right, more like a social hour arranging deals for smoke or other items, plus they wanted to smoke weed and talk with someone feminine.

Some just wanted to get out of the cell, and Sonny was all of the above. I had met Sonny when I had first returned to the unit, when he virtually ran me over. I had been coming from canteen when someone shot by me coming out of the barber shop, and headed up the hallway at a staggering run towards Times Square and the clinic. A couple of seconds later, a second person exited the barber shop and literally ran right to me. He steadied me with one hand, the other holding a knife, and said, "excuse me lil' momma," and took off chasing the first guy up the corridor.

The first one had been Jap, the barber, whom Sonny, the second one, had just stabbed about a gambling debt. When Sonny had stabbed Jap, his hand had slipped onto the blade, slicing the tendon of his ring and little finger. This had given Jap the time and opportunity to make a run for it, as Sonny had had to switch the knife from the cut hand to his good one before he could follow-up. When he had touched me, it had been with his cut had, leaving a bloody hand print on my shirt. I didn't know who he was at the time, only that he seemed twice as tall as I was.

I had had to go back to the wing to change shirts and put my canteen away, getting through the door just before it slammed and locked behind me. Because of the disturbance in the corridor, I had had to rinse out the shirt with Sonny's blood on it; that was our introduction.

I had seen Sonny around the prison, as it was hard to miss a lanky 6'9" brown-skinned black who was always talking trash and joking. Sonny was an unrepentant gambler who lived for the card games, and could be found anywhere there was a game going. Jap's stabbing had been about a gambling debt he had owed to Sonny, which he refused to pay thinking that Sonny wouldn't do anything about it because he had some size. Jap had found out to his dismay that that the blade didn't see size.

Sonny went to confinement under investigation for the stabbing, and soon after placed me on a call-out to use the writ-room with him. I admit to having some curiosity about someone who had the presence of mind in the midst of attempting to kill someone to not only recognize who he had bumped into, but also to be polite enough to apologize for it.

Sonny knew I kept weed, and had called me out to see if he could wrangle me out of some on credit. I didn't give him all he asked for the first time, as I didn't know if and when he could pay for it. This way, if it was a scam then I wouldn't be out much, and shame on me for being a fool, something which wouldn't happen twice as I would never do business with them again. They might believe they got over but really they set a price on what they were worth; cheaper in the long run, as they knew they could never come to me for anything else, and I was spared having further dealings with them. It was strictly about business and I didn't let personal feelings or ego get involved.

And as I said, I couldn't know when Sonny might pay for the weed he had gotten while being in confinement. He could still gamble there, but Sonny was a flush or bust gambler; flush with winnings one day, and busted broke the next, although he won more often than he lost because he knew a thousand or more ways to cheat, and wasn't above assisting lady luck when he felt she needed encouragement to see things his way at the table.

However, Sonny always paid me off as soon as he could, sometimes slowly or a bit at a time, as the siren call of the card table was too much for him to resist. This is how our friendship began; he would call me out to the writ-room to talk, smoke or buy weed, or to carry notes for others.

During the talks in the writ room, I learned that Sonny was from Pensacola, and that he was Michael Pane's fall partner. Michael (the one who killed Mongoose Shorty) was a friend of mine; well we had had sex, but we were keener on being just friends.

Michael was also a gambler and a hustler who used me as his bank and ATM. I would hold his money for him, to use as I wanted, and whenever he wanted some of it, it could be converted to smoke, coupons of cash, doing it as a favor for him as I liked him. But we had agreed it would best for us to be friends, as I wasn't housewife material and he wasn't into sharing.

Sonny always called me Lil' Mama ever since our first encounter in the hallway, and I called him "Sunny Boy". He had a droll sense of humor and had jungle fever bad; wouldn't even look at a black sissy, yet loved white boys. With Sonny it was all about the head; he wasn't into ass at all.

It was during this time that I was having my little fling with "Big West", another black out of Pensacola, very dark and ugly as sin, with a wide nose and mouth, but with a good heart underneath. He was only 5'10", but was big boned, weighing a good solid 270 pounds; his biceps was bigger than my thighs.

West had been in the Nation before having the fling with me, and there were those who felt I was responsible for his leaving. This wasn't true, as West had grown tired of all the strictures it placed upon him, such as not eating pork, for he loved everything about Willie including the squeal. I had just happened to come along when he had decided to part ways with the Nation for a time.

I came close to breaking my resolve about relationships with Big West; fortunately, he liked things the way they were, because even though he was out of the Nation for the time being, its calling was strong and there was no telling when he might return to its fold.

It was through West that I met many members of the Nation who were at the prison, who always treated me respect and recognized me as a person. I spent a lot of time with Musa, and their Imam, Mustafa, discussing religious philosophy, human psychology and business administration while playing chess. The Nation was strong on involvement in business to support them.

I found that I was attracted to men with strong personalities; no weaklings for me, liking my men to be men. I wanted to be the only bitch in the relationship, which is probably another reason Mimi and I had never indulged in sex; we both liked the same things and had the same tastes. It would have been like having sex with myself; neither of us would have been satisfied.

Sonny respected my pseudo-relationship with Big West, and never asked about the sex, although he let it be known that he wouldn't mind it at all if circumstances were different. The upshot with Sonny was that I provided him with smoke and carried his notes to and from whatever white boys he was chasing or having an affair with. I had no way of knowing how or when Frankie and Sonny met or got together, (most likely a writ-room call-out or while they were in confinement together), but they were hot and heavy with the notes for a long time.

The Pensacola faction, after Stone's killing and Boss assuming leadership and control of the prison rackets, seemingly accepted the way things were for the time being. They knew that trying to wrest control from Boss at the present moment would lead to a bloody free-for-all, with no one being able to predict which faction would end up on top. So they bided their time.

I was able to move freely among the various factions at the prison, both black and white, and was one of the few who could do so; I was liked for my personality and character, and none of them perceived me as being any threat to their interests. Plus, I had heart and earned my respect from them.

I was known as a "stand-up" convict, it being known among them that I had seen and knew the details of several killings that had taken place. Considering my sentence and charges, they knew that I could have easily traded the information to the prison investigators in exchange for a transfer to a road prison or work release center (to finish out my sentences in relative ease and comfort), but never did so.

Nor had the thought ever even crossed my mind; snitching wasn't a part of my character or makeup. It wasn't the manner I had been brought up in the streets, where the only thing you had was yourself and sense of personal integrity. No matter what the circumstances, I wouldn't trade either for a bit of comfort and ease.

For I had to live with myself, which I wouldn't be able to do by knowing I had betrayed those principles -trading them for nothing at all. Time was what you made of it, and I didn't need to steal pieces of another's life to be comfortable in mine.

My sexuality, feminine appearance, culinary ability, that I was rumored to have good sex game, the Clearys' pull in providing me with protective cover, my business sense and access to quantities of primo weed; choose among any of those and you would likely find the combination which permitted me to move freely among the prison factions. Since, I was also trusted, I would also act as an intermediary between the factions when they needed to work together or make trades or deals among themselves.

Frankie got out of confinement in the fall, and was reassigned to work in the kitchen. He was living on U-wing under Boss's protection and control, where Boss totally dominated him, not having forgotten his attempted treachery. Frankie was the crew's whore, and any of them wanting to have sex with him could do so, Frankie having no say in the matter. Boss wasn't into white flesh himself, so that Frankie didn't have to look the part any longer and could at least go back to looking like himself.

It was about this time that Michael Perry came into the picture and Boss's life, causing many changes in the way Boss dealt with everything. Michael had come from one of the gladiator schools for youth offenders, Sumter or ACI, having gotten into some kind of altercation there that had caused him to be sent to the unit. He was one of those who had the mistaken impression that having done something to another prison would provide him with some cachet with the convicts at the East Unit.

He was never more wrong. The other prisons were considered the minor leagues by those in the Unit, with the Rock and Unit as the major leagues. Whatever you had done prior to coming to the unit didn't count with them, and unless you were well known before you got there, you would have to show the stuff you were made of.

Michael's scrapes which brought him to the Unit counted for nothing. The real test would happen at the Unit itself, and was the only one which might count, because like the predators they were, the others could sense weakness if it was there at all.

An example of this was Mitchell White, who had killed Cody in the gym on movie night over twenty dollars. Mitch only had a few weeks to serve on his sentence when killing took place, and after spending time in Bradford County Jail on murder charges after his release from his sentence, returned to the unit with a life sentence, where the others turned him out on his first week back, having sensed weakness.

Michael had several things working against him at the Unit. He wasn't but eighteen years old, had creamy caramel colored skin, with good looks, pouty lips, big brown eyes with long lashes, curly black hair, and a shape and ass any woman would be proud to have. He was also not that big, being 5'8", and had a whole lot of feminine characteristics.

Michael was from Miami, and perhaps thought that his homeboys would help him out like in the gladiator school (which was probably why he hadn't been turned out before he got to the unit). He would get no such assistance at the unit, and he had hardly stepped onto the wing before the ass bandits were getting their blades out in order to be among the first to get some of that prime tail.

I happened to be on the wing the morning Michael arrived, and the commotion that his appearance on the wing caused drew my attention. From the movements of the other prisoners on the wing, I knew what was in store for him.

The bandits wasted no time, and within a half hour of his moving into the wing, rushed Michael's cell as he was putting his property away. Four bandits got in the cell with him with knives, and a line was forming outside the cell door of those awaiting their turn. The rapists had stripped the clothes from Michael's body and had him completely naked, and despite his struggles, had him bent over on the bed on his hands and knees with a knife at his throat.

They had greased his anus, and the train was about to pull into the station on him to break him in right when Boss strolled into the cell and told the would-be rapists to hold-up, and wait outside the cell; he wanted to talk to Michael. There was some minor grumbling about having their sport taken from them, but they left the cell to wait outside and see what would transpire within. The boy could still be theirs if he didn't get his mind right in a hurry.

Boss closed the cell door and put a curtain up in the door window, preventing anyone from seeing into the cell. I can't say exactly what Boss told Michael in the cell that day, but I had a pretty good idea. Boss had pretty much given Michael the option of becoming his boy, the alternative being Boss leaving and letting the others have him.

Take it or leave it were Michael's only options, confronted with the reality of his weakness while also knowing what would happen to him once Boss left the cell. Even if he attempted to fight the others, they would still overpower him and the rapes and train would happen to him, there being no doubts about that at all.

Michael had envisioned himself as being hardcore, but now being faced with reality, broke and told Boss he would be his boy. Boss then had sex with him to seal the deal, lest he gather courage once the immediate threat had passed, and try to renege on their deal.

You can't fault Michael for doing as he did, it being the lesser of the two evils confronting him. I've heard many claim that they would rather die than submit to being raped if faced with such a Hobson's choice. Those are fine words when you're not confronted with its reality, as they don't have to kill you to rape you, as I and many another can attest to; overpowered and unconscious, the outcome would be the same.

Rape, after all, isn't really about sex but power and control. Even if you killed some of those involved in the aftermath, you could never regain what was taken from you. I knew this to be true, having previously had to gather up the shreds of my dignity to find, like Humpty Dumpty after the fall, that it was never the same.

Michael did what he had to do - which is not to say he liked it, or didn't resent those who had put him in such a position and turned him out. After finishing, Boss came out and told those waiting by the cell that Michael was now his "nephew" and to leave him alone, "nephew" being the slang term in prison for someone's boy. The others smothered their disappointment at this turn of events although it had confirmed what they had believed about Michael, and left them alone in the cell.

I cannot say for certain that Boss put the others up to rushing on Michael that morning, but it is most likely what happened, as Boss's showing up at Michael's cell when he did was just a tad too convenient. Whatever it was, the outcome would have still been the same, Boss or not, as Michael was just too fine a morsel for the others to pass up.

It was after Boss got involved with Michael that I started to see changes in his attitude and behavior. He had always been a little autocratic, but now started to take it to the extreme, becoming more and more demanding and turning into a petty tyrant and despot, at least to those under him.

Boss, in order to give Michael the things he thought Michael wanted or needed, increased the house's take on the gambling games under his control, and raised what the other drug dealers and gamblers had to pay to operate with me. He was as cordial and friendly as ever, but they say, "power corrupts", and it corrupted Boss; Michael was just a catalyst. It made me think of the old movie called 'Little Cesar' with Edgar G. Robinson in it.

Under Boss's direction, the robberies, assaults and stabbings escalated, and the tension inside the prison grew as his rule mutated from benevolence to tyranny, this occurring within a environment already chaotic beyond imagining (with prisoners escaping, assaulting each other and murders). The beast continued to enjoy the rising number of blood sacrifices.

I wasn't alone in noting the changes in Boss after Michael's arrival, as I found out when I overheard Koju telling Frank T one day, "Boss's nose is wide open about that punk. That's not a good thing, as he believes Michael is a bitch and not a punk, and I'd trust Michael about as far as I could throw that dumpster out there."

As some of the more crass among the prisoners would put it, "there's Voodoo in the Doo-doo", meaning when you start having sex with a boy, your emotions become involved and cause you to change. Not always for me better, some losing perspective completely. In Boss's case, he became very possessive and jealous of Michael.

Michael contributed to a lot of this as well, because although he had been pressured into turning out, there was a lot of bitch in him. After a time, I could see that Michael was getting jealous of the relationship between Boss and me, although it only entailed smoking reefer, talking and playing chess.

Michael had the punk touché problem; he wanted to be a bitch, and had a whole lot of ho in him, yet resented the manner in which it had been brought out. Therefore, somewhere in Michael's heart there was a mix of both love and hatred for Boss.

Michael wanted to believe so badly that he wouldn't have become a boy if not for Boss, illogical as that seems given the fact that the train was fixing to enter the depot when Boss intervened. Nonetheless, Michael still wanted to believe himself to be hardcore - but then, we all live with some delusions about ourselves.

Boss's complete infatuation with him led Michael to indulge some whims and idiosyncrasies, including having sex with Frankie whenever Frankie was out of confinement. It appeared that Frankie was staying out of confinement more and for longer periods now that Michael was around to keep Boss distracted. I suspected some other ulterior motive as well at the time, but nothing clear came to mind.

Boss's indulgence of Michael's whims created dissent among the rank and file of Boss's faction, who felt that Boss was far too generous to Michael and needed to put him in his place as a whore, as it appeared they were doing all the work just so Boss could give it all to the punk.

I was busy with the holiday season from the end of October through the first of the year, with all the cookouts for the officers, preparing the warden's family meals, and making the holiday meals for the prison population.

The menu was the same as the previous years, except for the Christmas. I had gotten some of the other prisoners with money to chip in, and every prisoner left the chow hall Christmas morning with a brown lunch bag filled with fruit, an assortment of candy and candy bears, and a pack of bugler (roll your own tobacco). The confinement wings got a bag delivered to the cells.

There were a number of prisoners who didn't have money, never received any money from outside sources, and who didn't have much of a hustle game. The Christmas bag would give them a little treat, and give them something to hustle with, exchanging items in the bag for things they really wanted or needed.

I utilized some of the prisoners who had no means of income (aside from the holding contraband for me), and had too much pride to accept a hand-out, to clean my cell or wash some clothes. Both of which I didn't really need, as I had learned to be very orderly and neat as a chef, and I could get the laundry man to do all my personal clothes at the laundry.

However, getting them to do it was a contribution to the prison economy. There was always a high demand for the reefer I was having brought in, so I had to spread it out among the other dealers in order that there was variety. Yet, the quality was about the same among all of them.

I didn't want to corner any markets or cut into their profits either, as all I wanted was to have smoke available for my use and to barter with. Nevertheless, I always ended up with a profit, as the others couldn't get the same quality of smoke I was getting (most of what I got was home-grown sinsemilla bud coming out of California, with some pretty wild and exotic names, and very high in THC content, so it wouldn't take much to get you high and flying).

Jo was having the weed sent out of California, and the dealers in the prison were getting it from me, as they couldn't rely on the quality of the local grown weed. This was surprising given that there was a college right down the road in Gainesville; you would figure that if they could come up with Gatorade, they could also grow some decent pot. The weed coming into the state by boat or van was spotty, with periodic dry spells, so a steady source was nice to have around.

I also got a surprise for the holidays, when Mimi brought Doris up for a visit. Doris spent the holidays with the warden's family. Don't ask me how Mimi wrangled to get warden's approval, but as I was coming up the walk to the house after being dropped off by the prison van, Mimi released the cat from the carrying cage used to transport her. Doris spotted me in an instant and started racing towards me, leaping at me so I would have to catch her. Darcie, the warden's wife, remarked "Goodness gracious, I never seen a cat do that before."

Doris was purring and rubbing her face on mine as I held her, and wouldn't let me out of her sight during the time I spent at the warden's house. When I had to return to the prison, I would have to put her in her carrying cage to keep her from following the van back to the prison. To lessen her discomfort, I put a sweatshirt that I had been wearing inside the carrying cage.

I spent a lot of my free time at the warden's house playing with Doris or just holding and petting her; you never realize how much an integral part of your life an animal is until you are separated from them and they suffer as much as you do, if not more.

When it was time for Doris to return home with Mimi, I hated to see her go and I'm quite certain she hated to go as well. Mimi told me on the next visit that Doris yowled for most of the flight back, telling me, "You better get your ass home quickly, as that cat really misses you... She looks for you every day and sleeps on that sweatshirt of yours."

That Christmas is when Dave killed "Moon Dog" in the dining hall as Christmas dinner was being served. Moon dog was seated at the table eating when Dave came from the line of prisoners waiting to get a tray and be served their meal, ducking under the guard rail. Dave approached the unsuspecting moon dog from behind.

Pulling out his blade, Dave stabbed Moon Dog several times in the back and neck, holding the victim in his seat with one hand when he attempted to get up from his seat with the first sting of the blade. The tables in chow halls were steel four-seaters, the square table bolted to the floor and the seats welded to the table, making it easy hold someone down. The cross-bar holding the seat underneath the table kept you from being able to slide out, as your legs would be on either side of the bar, blocking you. Dave left Moon Dog face down in his mashed potatoes.

The killing had happened because Moon Dog had a little crew who were robbing other prisoners. They had robbed Dave twice already, thinking him soft, and an easy target. When they hadn't known was that Dave had three life sentences for murders outside and hadn't been in prison long. Dave had known that he wouldn't win trying to take on the whole crew, so he had bided his time until he caught Moon Dog without any of his crew around.

As it happened, the officers monitoring the dining rooms would run prisoners coming to chow to either the north or south hall, switching between the lines. That particular day, Moon Dog had been sent into the north dining hall while his crew was directed to the south. Dave, coming into the north chow hall's waiting line, had spotted Moon Dog without any of his crew around, seated with his back exposed. Figuring he would never get a better opportunity then this, Dave had done what he had to do.

I was out at the warden's house, where they were just sitting down to Christmas dinner, when he got the call concerning the dining hall murder. The officers had closed off the north dining hall and continued feeding prisoners in the south dining hall, with Moon Dog still seated with his face in the mashed potatoes.

The warden didn't get back until late. I had kept his dinner warm, and he drove me back to the prison himself after eating. I know he had a lot on his mind, and probably would have liked to talk about it or at least ask me some questions. However, we spent the drive in silence, for our respective roles placed a gulf between us that words alone could never bridge; I could not express them in terms he could comprehend, nor would I try, as we shared the same space but not the same world.

No matter what, I would still be a convict to him, what privileges he accorded me making no difference, as nothing could change that fact. And from my perspective, no matter how well I got along with him or respected him, he would always be guard; exchanging the uniform for a suit made no difference.

All of which placed us on either side of a chasm. Even if I could tell him, he wouldn't be able to understand or grasp the nature of my experience, as the minds and world of prisoners and prison was in too much contrast and opposition to the insular world of the prison official. It would be like a member of a cultured society trying to discern the rudiments of a primitive society, neither of us being able to comprehend or communicate with the other.

Tensions boiled over at the prison over the course of the next few months as Boss's despotic control grew ever more an oppressive burden upon the other prisoners. I believe it was when he had his crew begin robbing the white drug dealers and gambling games that he set in motion the events which would lead to his downfall.

The heads of the white factions, Skeet and others, sat down with the leaders of the black factions to discuss their common problem: the havoc Boss and his crew were causing among the rest of the prisoners, the whites being outraged at the violations of the long standing truce between black and white factions.

The whites wanted something done about Boss to rein him in and keep him on the blacks' side of the fence, figuring also that if Boss was out of the picture, the rest of his crew would fall in line, as they were followers and not leaders. They wanted the blacks to handle the problem of Boss initially, and if the blacks couldn't or wouldn't deal with it, then they would take over.

If the whites were to take care of Boss, it would raise the racial tensions at the prison, and escalate into a race-riot free-for-all. None of the factions wanted to see happen, as it was bad for business, while resulting in worse conditions and restricted movement within the prison. The black and white factions had reached these accords among themselves a few years ago, after the last riot along racial lines, so that everything could run smoothly.

Understandably, the whites believed it was the blacks' responsibility to handle the matter of Boss, but if it came down to it, they would take care of it by themselves and let the chips fall where they may. The leaders of the black factions assured Skeet and the other whites that they would take care of Boss, as they had something in the works already. They had been aware of the growing problem that Boss represented, knowing that eventually it would come to this, and had planned accordingly.

Boss wasn't aware of the sit down between the black and white leaders, and if any of his lieutenants or crew knew of it, they made no mention to him. The decisions within the ranks among Boss's crew were open to exploitation by the leaders of the Black factions, and you didn't require a weather vane to know the way the winds of power and change were blowing. Some of Boss's crew had already worked out deals for switching loyalties while others were in the process of doing so, based for the most part on Boss's putting Michael's welfare and well-being ahead of theirs.

Boss was so caught up in his own ego and infatuation with the punk, Michael, that he didn't even realize that the sands had shifted under him and that his time was running out. His hardcore cadre, consisting of Frank T, Koju, Sugar Bear, California and Gangster, were still for the most part steadfast in their loyalty to him. However, even they were uneasy, and didn't agree with a lot of what Boss was doing and having them do. Koju's dislike for Michael was intense, for he blamed Michael for the changes in Boss.

It wasn't until the following day when I learned of the meeting between the faction leaders, having spent the previous day out at the officer training building and on the finals of the college courses I was talking about, one for Business Administration and the other in Restaurant and Hotel Management. Next up on my agenda was to begin the study of Veterinary Science, thinking that if I was going to have Doris, I might as well bone up on her care; plus, it was something I had always had an interest in.

Once I did learn of the meeting which had taken place, I made no mention of it to Boss (even after I knew he had been the main topic under discussion), for it wasn't any of my concern. My friendship with him didn't extend to getting involved in the prison politics power struggles, and I assumed that Boss would hear about it from other source, and if not that he could handle it.

Nor could I talk to Boss about something like that, as his understanding would be zero and he would go off and create the very situation everyone else was trying to avoid. Also, foolishly, I somehow believed the blacks would merely get Boss and his crew locked up under an investigation of some sort, forgetting that within the prison, disposing of someone like Boss could only be done through violence. Violence had brought him to power, and only violence would remove him.

Jo and Mimi came up to see me that weekend, Jo having some business papers for me to sign. Over the past couple of years, the escort service had opened up branches in Fresno and San Francisco, and we had also obtained part ownership of a couple of limo services in the city. Now Jo wanted to open another escort and limo service branch in Jacksonville, Florida, and required my signatures.

Cities which host a lot of conventions and tourists are good places for an escort and limo service, and as a sideline, we had also gotten in with the modeling agencies, which would use our escorts. It was a very good business investment, although I told Jo to find someone to handle the day to day operations in Florida as I had no intention of staying after my release.

When I informed Mimi about the goings-on inside the prison, he reminded of my promise to him, saying, "You remember your promise not to get involved. You're short now and have too much to lose getting messed up with the internal power struggles of the prison. Doris and I want you out."

"Don't worry. I have no intentions of being involved in any of it," I assured them.

Nonetheless, now that I had been made aware of it, I would make it a point to keep a closer eye on things to protect my own interests, as those kinds of things have a way of getting out of control. I didn't want to end up as an unintended consequence of any of it by not paying attention.

Sonny had been released from confinement around the same time Frankie had been for Stonewall's killing, and could be found wherever there was a card game going on. I would see him in the library, gym or Rec field, and we'd talk for a few minutes.

I figured Sonny was caught up in his gambling passion and old routines. The affair between Sonny and Frankie had appeared to fizzle out once they both were in open population; I thought it was because Frankie belonged to Boss and his crew.

Boss would kill Frankie or have him killed rather than let him slip from his control. Part of it was ego, in keeping the treacherous bitch on a short leash, but also for another very good reason, that Frankie could incriminate him in Stonewall's murder. Thus Frankie could run to confinement all he liked, but he couldn't hide there forever, and when he did come back out, he was still owned body and soul by Boss.

I was in my cell eating a sandwich I had made for myself in the staff kitchen earlier that morning. The library was closed on Monday, so on those days I prepared the breakfast and lunch meals for the officers and staff. Breakfast was over with and lunch was prepared, and I had left Frank T to keep an eye on things there as I brought some sandwiches, pastries and perked coffee back to the wing to take a well-earned and needed smoke break, and to eat before returning to the staff kitchen.

I had finished smoking a couple of joints with "Nubby", and was munching on the sandwich when I heard raised voices in argument outside my cell, below me on the first floor of the wing. One of the voices was Sonny's distinctive tone, and the other Boss's. Curious as to what these two might be arguing about, I stepped to the railing lining the catwalk outside my cell to watch and listen to them argue from my vantage point.

At first I thought the argument was about money or gambling. Sonny was housed on M-wing, the last wing of the east side of the corridors just before gate thirteen, and he would violate the prohibition about being on a wing you weren't assigned to live on, in order to get into the heavy gambling action. This was probably the reason as to what Sonny was doing on U- wing.

However, Boss had been waiting for Sonny to show, and as I listened to them arguing, I learned that it was about some notes, as Boss was telling Sonny, "Don't be passing notes with my boy... Stop sending him notes..."

Sonny told Boss, "You can't tell me who to write. Tell your boy to stop writing me and I won't write back."

Boss would retaliate, "No you won't write him," so on and so forth. Back and forth the argument raged, their voices growing ever louder, Sonny telling Boss,

"You tell a bitch what to do, you don't tell a man. Tell your bitch to stop writing me."

I thought at first the argument was about Frankie, which didn't really make any sense because Boss didn't care who Frankie wrote or whom he did it with, as long as he toed the line and did what he was told. The thought never crossed my mind that they might be arguing about Michael.

Boss had told me one time, early in their relationship, that whenever they had sex, Michael had to make certain all the cracks, windows and door were covered, so no one could see into the cell and see what they were doing. I remembered Boss commenting, "Michael doesn't even want God to know he's fucking...," meaning that if no one saw it, then it didn't happen, at least in Michael's mind.

Plus, I knew Sonny wasn't into black boys at all. Nonetheless, Nubby, who had come out of the cell to join me at the rail said, "They're talking about Boss's boy Michael... Boss found a note Michael wrote to Sonny."

"Are you sure about that?" I asked, surprised by this.

"Positive, Boss has been steamed about it all morning. He's been waiting for Sonny to come on the wing in order to confront him about it."

Sonny was repeating the statements, "You tell a bitch what to do... You don't tell a man what to do. Tell that bitch of yours to stop writing me, talk to the bitch, don't talk to me," when Boss hauled off and slapped him across the face with his open hand, making a sound like the crack of a pistol shot. Rocking Sonny's head back, Boss told Sonny, "Pussy nigger, I told you to stop sending kites to my boy."

The whole wing had quietened at the sound of the slap, waiting to see what Sonny would do about it, as being bitch slapped in front of a wing full of convicts wasn't something you could just walk away from, not within this milieu. Yet it seemed like Sonny would do just that. After the slap, Sonny looked at Boss and said, "Okay, okay. There was no call for you to do that," before going to the cell where the card game was going on.

Sonny hadn't brought a weapon with him and Boss was armed with a blade. Sugar Bear, Gangster and California had gone to Boss after Sonny had gone into the cell to gamble, telling Boss, "You need to kill that nigger right here and right now. Don't let him leave the wing. We are telling you. You got to kill him. He will not let that pass."

To which Boss had replied, "Fuck that pussy nigger. He ain't going to do nothing."

"Boss, that's Sonny, you just can't slap him and let him walk away. If you don't want to do it then let us... but don't let him leave the wing alive," California had said, with Bear and Gangster nodding their agreement.

But Boss had remained defiant, saying, "You three stay out of it. It's none of your business. This is between me and that pussy nigger. The pussy nigger isn't going to do shit about it. I'm telling you three to stay out of it. This is between me and him..."

I didn't think letting Sonny leave the wing alive was such a good idea either, considering that Boss had the upper hand at the moment, having a blade while Sonny didn't. Not that I wanted to see Sonny killed, but there are certain things you just don't do to people in prison and let them walk away, unless you are willing to bet your life on there being no comeback later down the line.

Boss had gotten around so much by this point in time that he actually believed he could get away with doing anything he wanted, and that there would be no repercussions or consequences from the prisoners he did it to. This line of thinking made him think that Sonny was intimidated by his power and afraid to do anything about the slap. Sonny was still on the wing gambling and acting normal.

When I returned to the staff kitchen, the events on the wing troubled me, as something just didn't seem right about it. While I don't think Sonny expected to be slapped by Boss that morning, I smelled a dead rat somewhere because Sonny and Michael passing love notes to each other didn't jibe with the Sonny I knew. The whole matter of notes felt contrived.

I figured that someone had put Michael up to writing notes to Sonny, as a means to make Boss jealous and more amenable to give Michael what he wanted; a bitch's move to manipulate Boss with the power of sex and his emotions. It was likely that Frankie had been the one who had put Michael up to it, as part of some scheme of his, but that was just a suspicion on my part at that time, as being the only explanation to fit all the facts I had. I don't believe Michael was actively involved at this point in any of the scheme to do away with Boss; he was a bitch doing what a bitch does.

I don't know why Boss wasn't aware of Sonny's jungle fever fetish, but then I imagine you have to pay attention to that sort of thing to know about it. Sonny had never messed with black boys before, and it was unlikely he would start now. There was the outside possibility Sonny hadn't known anything about the notes until confronted by Boss about them, and then not liking to be told by Boss what he could and could not do.

When I returned from the staff kitchen later in the day, I found out that Sonny had made it off the wing alive and still in good health. However, Boss's slapping Sonny was the main topic of conversation among the prisoners, as news of the slap had been heard around the prison, with much speculation as to if or how Sonny would respond to the insult to his manhood.

For within the prison culture, to be bitch slapped like that was about worst insult you could give a convict. In fact, it would have been better if Boss had punched Sonny, knocking him down or out, as there was the possibility that he could salvage his pride and walk away. But not being slapped in front of an entire wing of prisoners; walking away from that would lead to other problems for Sonny later down the line.

Thus, everyone was waiting to see what Sonny's response would be, but as the days passed, it appeared Boss was correct in saying Sonny wouldn't do anything about it, at least to all outward appearances. Letting such an insult pass wasn't at all the Sunny I knew, but all Sonny seemed to be doing was bitching and complaining, going around to the various factions to talk about how wrong it was for Boss to slap him like that.

It looked as if talking about it would be all Sonny was going to do, unless you paid close attention and caught the nuances of what Sonny was really doing, making it clear to everyone that this was a personal matter between Boss and himself. Boss had even told his trusted lieutenants to stay out of it.

I had thought I knew what was going on, but there was a whole lot of by play behind the scenes that I never caught. In hindsight I should have caught it, but instead it caught me sleeping, my street senses having grown dull, as there had been a time I would have missed none of it.

Things were not as they appeared to be. First, Frankie checked into confinement, which everyone, including myself, took to be a part of his usual get away from it. Second, Frank T was placed in confinement with a disciplinary report for disrespect.

When I carried Frank T a care package of goodies and books in confinement, he told me that the officer had said something out of the way to him as he was serving, and that he had cursed the officer out. This had resulted in his being given a disciplinary report and placed in confinement.

Third, Koju and California got locked up under investigation for a couple of robberies Boss had them doing. There was nothing unusual in any of these upon which to hang suspicion, or to indicate in any way that it wasn't normal prison routine, and part of a plot to isolate and eliminate Boss.

I had decided to go to the gym that Saturday to watch some romantic comedy that I had planned on seeing, and to take care of some business. Gangster elected to say on the wing and not go to the movie while Sugar Bear went, as well as some of the kiss-ups (those always hanging around Boss, looking for handouts or making it seem like they were part of his crowd).

Frankie was normally the one who would carry Boss's knife to the gym on movie nights, but since Frankie was in confinement and thus unavailable, the job of sword bearer fell to Michael. Sugar Bear was armed as well. U-wing was the last wing in the rotation line that week to be released to go to the gym for the movie, which meant that all the choice seats (up along the top row, which put the wall at your back) would already be filled. I didn't mind, as I had planned on sitting out on the gym floor in the centre.

Boss and his little entourage took seats on the last section of the bleachers, nearest the bathroom, about three rows of seats up. It was standard procedure for whoever carried the knife to place it under the bleachers within the easy reach of Boss. Accordingly, since Michael was carrying the knife and seated next to Boss, he slid it under the bleachers between them.

I was seated thirty feet out on the gym floor with the centre section of bleacher seats behind me, and the stage and movie screen another thirty feet in front of me. Since we were the last wing to enter the gym, we had barely gotten settled in before the lights were dimmed, and the movie started.

I noted those who would be sitting around me before taking my seat, seeing Big West and a couple of others out of Pensacola. I knew that they would normally be seated up in the bleachers with the Pensacola faction, and even commented on it to Big West, "I see you're slumming with the best of us today."

"Change of pace…," he replied.

I was happy there would be people I knew near me, and thought nothing strange about Big West being seated so close by. I usually didn't attend movies but on the occasions I did, I liked to sit out on the gym floor, and a lot of people knew this about me.

The movie was running about fifteen minutes in when the commotion began in the section of bleachers over by the bathroom. I had completed my business, and was getting into the movie when the yelling began. You couldn't really tell what was being said with the movie soundtrack and the others talking, so it was mostly confused noise.

In response to the noise of a disturbance, the officers slipped out through the gym doors and locked them before turning up the lights inside the gym; they knew from past experiences that something was going down inside the gym.

Those of us seated out on the gym floor arose, and faced towards where the disturbance was coming from, just as Boss ran down the steps to the gym floor, scanning around looking for someone, with Sonny in close pursuit with his blade in hand.

Boss was searching for Michael, who had excused himself a few minutes before to go to the bathroom, taking Boss's knife with him and disappearing into the darkness. Sugar Bear was already in the bathroom smoking weed and talking with some others there when the attack started, so that Boss was left without a weapon to fight with or defend himself with when Sonny came from behind him in the darkness and began stabbing.

Giving up his search for Michael, Boss ran down the front of the bleaches on the gym floor headed for the folding chairs the officers would sit in during the movie, and had left behind. He reached the chairs just as Sonny caught up and stabbed him twice in the back, not giving Boss an opportunity to turn and try to wield the ungainly weapon.

Boss realized he couldn't get the chance with the chair, so he dropped it with a clatter and took off running towards the stage, where he knew another knife was hidden. Sonny was still following close upon him, still working with the knife, and after a few steps Boss knew he wouldn't reach the stage or the knife in time, so while running, he stripped off his shirt and turned, trying to use the shirt to trap the blade in its fold and strip it from Sonny's grasp.

But unfortunately for Boss, Sonny's height and long arms were just too much for that to work, as the blade kept penetrating Boss's attempt at defensive measures. Their movement across the gym floor had brought them less than ten feet in front of where I was standing facing the bleachers, when one of Sonny's blows with the knife struck Boss's temple, causing Boss to fall to the floor. Sonny never let him get up, stabbing and stabbing even as Boss tried to rise and fend him off at the same time.

I knew that Sonny would kill Boss if it didn't stop, and it was in my mind to go and to speak to Sonny, to try and get him to stop. I was friends of both, and felt he would listen to me, as he had done enough that he didn't need to kill Boss for payback. But as I was about to move forward, I was grabbed from behind in a bear hug by Big West, who locked my arms down by my sides so that I couldn't get to my knife.

He held me as if he was protecting me, while the others from the Pensacola crew closed around us to either side. Big West murmured in my ear, "Sonny said you had too much heart and you would try to stop him from killing Boss. He said this is the way it has to be. If you try to intervene, it would kick off a riot in here, which no one wants. This is strictly between Sonny and Boss. You've got to stay out of it and I was here to ensure you do, and don't get hurt."

I stood there wrapped in West's arms, totally helpless, and watched Sonny finish killing Boss. Boss was still trying to get up, as each blow from the knife plunged in to the hilt. I could see some yellow and gray matter protruding from the side of Boss's head around the temple area, where the knife had struck, and I shivered within West's grip; I know he felt it, as his arms tightened around me. I wanted nothing more than to turn around and bury my face in his chest so I wouldn't have to watch, at the same time needing to see it all.

I learned later that Bear had been in the bathroom, smoking reefer and talking, when one of the kiss-ups came running in and told him, "Sonny is out there stabbing Boss, aren't you going to help him?" Bear had responded, "Boss told me to stay out of it. It was none of my concern. This was between him and Sonny," and had remained inside the bathroom.

Boss finally grew too weak to continue attempting to rise, or fend off Sonny, and sank back to the gym floor. Sonny stood directly over him and plunged the blade into his chest, twisting it in a circular motion telling Boss, "See, pussy nigger, this is why you don't slap a man."

I saw the light of life leaving Boss's eyes then, and he died out there on the gym floor. Sonny pulled the blade free from Boss's chest and spit in his face before walking away, as the blood ran outward in rivulets on the gym floor.

Sonny kept the blade in hand going up the stairway to the gym doors, and pounded on them, looking through the window set in the door and telling lieutenant Gaskins, "Let me out. It's finished over here." He had kept the blade to prevent some of Boss's friends attacking him in retaliation, which they might have done if he had been unarmed.

Lieutenant Gaskins let Sonny out of the gym, unlocking the door for him while the crowd of convicts inside the gym remained quiet, still in shock and trying to absorb what they had just seen. Medical came into the gym with the stretcher and loaded Boss's limp from unto it, trying to force a sign of life out of him. I knew it would be wastage of effort, as I had seen Boss die out there on the gym floor.

All the Pensacola faction and their associates had come armed to the gym that night, and for good reason, as others had tried to come to Boss's aid when Sonny attacked him. Medical, still working over Boss, took the stretcher up the stairs and out of the gym, heading for the clinic, and Lieutenant Gaskins came inside telling the prisoners, "Shows over, line it up by the wings and head back to the house…. J-wing, let's go…."

Michael now came out from the crowd on the gym floor, close by me where he had concealed himself before the start of the attack, and went to the pool of Boss's blood which was glistening on the gym floor. He stooped down, putting his index finger into the blood, and then stuck the bloody finger into his mouth, licking off the blood and saying, "Mmm-sweet…"

In doing so, Michael signed his own death warrant, as many prisoners saw and heard him as he did it. His death was almost certain in any event for betraying Boss, in the matter of taking the knife and leaving him defenseless when Sonny struck; I couldn't say how they arranged for him to leave with the knife before the attack began, but I knew it had been done.

The entire episode in the gym had been a setup for the killing of Boss, and they had indeed gone lengths to ensuring everything went according to the plan. Most of Boss's lieutenants had been in confinement, or at least those who would have come to assist him in the gym. No matter what the odds would have stood against them, right or wrong, they would have stood with him, and there would have been a blood bath in the gym that night instead of just Boss's death.

Conversations of the prisoners filling out of the gym were subdued, but I heard parts of comments about how Boss went out like a true warrior fighting till the end; meaningless, trite words to me at the moment. I was still in shock and grief from watching one friend kill another.

Big West had continued to hold me even after it was all over to provide me with a measure of comfort, and released me only when he heard his wing called. Before leaving he asked me, "You alright? You'll be okay soon. You know it had to be this way since there was no other way…"

"I know…" I replied, though the knowledge provided little comfort right then. I kept away from Michael in the line as was going back to the wing, as the little gloating smile he had worn when tasting Boss's blood irked me, and I didn't want to see him at all just then.

M a cup of coffee, drinking the coffee and nibbling on a pastry as I listened to the prisoners on the wing talk to each other through the cell doors back windows. They were recounting to those across the open space on T-wing (who might have missed the action in the gym by not going to watch the movie that night) what had happened in the gym, while speculating as to whether Boss was dead or not. I knew he was dead, yet still, there remained a small hope that it might not be so.

All speculation ended about forty-five minutes later, when official word came down through the officer that Boss was dead. Word of his death spread like wildfire across the wings, and there arose a burst of cheers, applause and celebration from the prisoners in the cells at the news.

The sounds of celebration for Boss's death from the other prisoners, who had feared him when he was alive and who didn't have the heart to stand up against him or confront him while he was among them, broke something inside of me. I was reminded of something another prisoner had written one time, saying, "There are people, places and times in the prison, which exist outside and surpass human comprehension… Experiences which will tear holes in the fabrics of your soul…"

Now I understood what he meant, for up until that point I had felt part of the world inside the prison, its culture and people… And now all of a sudden, I was apart from it. I could no longer consider prison or prisoners as part of my world or being; this was their world, which I had no part of or claim to.

This being something which had been part and parcel of my life up to that moment, I began to consider what my life would have been if I hadn't met with Mimi. I would have never been given the opportunity to do the things I had with my life, and would have been through the revolving prison door many times until there was nothing left of my humanity that mankind would wish to put a claim to.

That night and the following day, the roundup of the usual suspects began. All of the Pensacola faction wound up in confinement under investigation. Michael, Gangster and Sugar bear also went into lock up until matters got sorted out.

I was still feeling the shock of watching Boss's death, and from revelations of the night before in my cell, so I couldn't really tell you how I got by the next few days. The other prisoners left me alone, knowing of the friendship

I shared with Boss. When any one tried to speak to me about the killing, I would just walk away from them as I didn't want to hear it.

To them, he had been a tyrant and oppressor; to me, he had been a friend, and I couldn't get out of my head the sounds of their celebration at the news of his death. Their attempts to talk to me about it seemed to be a form of gloating over it.

I had gone to confinement to see Koju and Frank T to carry them the news of Boss's death, although I knew word of it would have already reached them through the prison grapevine, which was faster than light. Still, I felt they would want to hear it from someone who was a friend, and I carried care packages to both of them among the books on the library cart. They looked downcast and saddened upon hearing the news from me. I passed notes between the two before leaving the wing.

Sonny was on Q-wing, second floor, west side. I left him some books, as there really wasn't much for us to say at this point in time. What was done was done, and nothing we could say now or later would alter that fact. Sonny was still a friend; I left him a little care package, and carried a note from him to Frankie, who was on N-wing.

I didn't even bother to try and find out where Michael and the others of Boss's crew were, as I didn't want to see Michael, knowing he had role in Boss's death. For a while I thought he had been manipulated and used, but I couldn't shake the feeling that he wouldn't have been a partner to it if it hadn't been in him all along.

Michael had never forgiven Boss for making him realize his true self, and hated himself because of it. Yet and still, there was a part of him which had never given up or surrendered the pretense and image of himself as hardcore and stand-up, giving him a wholly false sense of bravado, leading to such gestures such as tasting of Boss's blood in the gym. A childish gesture, yet in keeping with Michael's character, as was his betrayal to Boss.

Michael was due to finish up his sentence and be released a few days before me, but would never make it. Only a few days after Boss's death, Michael, Gangster, and Bear were released from confinement, Frankie being scheduled for transfer and remaining in confinement until it came through. The same offer had been given to Michael, who declined it. Why he did so will remain one of life's mysteries, as he took that answer to the grave with him.

It is entirely possible that those who had put him onto betraying Boss in stealing away with his knife had also assured him that no harm would come to him, that he would be free to do as he pleased for his remaining time in the prison. Michael's foolishness and callow youth would have made him believe those assurances.

There were other reasons were there as well, like Michael knowing that whatever prison he went to, it would be known that he had been Boss's bitch, and that the ass bandits wouldn't give him any slack. He also liked being in the centre of the drama which unfolded around him, and held the bulk of Boss's assets within the prison, which he could now use as he wanted, lording it over the other young blacks while using it as a means to manipulate them.

A transfer would have stripped him of most of those assets and whatever reflected glory there was in having been Boss's bitch at the time of his death; The role he had played in bringing it about would be unknown as well, leaving him with only the label of being a bitch in a man's world, his ego, the pretensions of being something he wasn't, and maybe a death wish for what he had become.

A few days after his release from confinement to open population, Michael had written a letter to his mother in Miami, telling her that there was good possibility he would be killed in the unit and never make it home. Whether it was a premonition, or some more of the exaggerating, posturing and false bravado he was prone to, it's hard to say. Michael's mother doted on her only child and would have made prison officials transfer or lock him up in confinement had she gotten the letter in time; as it was, Michael would already dead by the time the letter arrived.

Because Frank was in confinement, I was training another cook for staff and preparing some meals myself in addition to my work in the library. I was also sorting through the files and property I had accumulated since coming to the unit, deciding what to keep, what to give away and what to toss out in preparation for my upcoming release.

It was then that I remembered I had Frankie's files that he had asked me to hold a while back, of his personal and legal papers, which he added to periodically. But with him about to be transferred and my pending release, it was time to return the papers to him.

As I pulled the file from the cabinet, some of the papers slipped out and fell into the floor, and I recognized Sonny's handwriting as I was picking them up. It aroused my curiosity, and I shamelessly admit to have indulged my curiosity by reading it, then going on to read the entire file of correspondence between Frankie and Sonny, going back to when they both were in confinement and their affair was going hot and heavy.

Within the letters, Sonny promised Frankie he would take care of the problem of Boss for him, and later letters after Michael entered the picture discussed ways in which they might use the silly bitch. In one letter, Sonny described Michael as a "punk with pretensions", not having enough brains to fill a gnat's ass.

Reading the letters was like perusing an anatomy of the murder, as Boss's death had been years in the making. It also made me wonder as to Frankie's motive for keeping them all, and whether Sonny had a similar stash of notes from Frankie squirreled away somewhere; to what end and purpose I don't know; the notes read like a one way ticket to death row for both of them.

Putting the correspondence back into the files, I delivered them to Frankie without any comment, now knowing far more about him then I cared to know. Still, it was his file and his business.

Soon, Frank T, Koju, California and some of the Pensacola crew including Big West (to whom I had just delivered two care packages) were released from confinement. I was glad to see Frank T, as it would take some of the load off me in the staff kitchen. Frank was moved back into V-wing, and Koju into T-wing.

Michael had been on K-wing since being released from confinement, and when passing by, I could see him through the banks of windows on the corridor side of the K-wing day-room. He was usually playing cards and holding court with some of the other younger blacks at the card table, under the windows in the day-room which looked out onto the area between the wings. The blacks at the table with Michael were just playing along with him for what they could get from him (Michael was flush with Boss's money, smoke and things, using it freely and sharing with his new found friends).

Two days after Koju and Frank T's release from confinement, I had delivered some legal papers and books to the confinement wings and was returning to the library. On the way, while waiting at gate thirteen for the confinement hall sergeant to open the gate for me, I saw Koju leaving T-wing and heading down the corridor.

I had wanted to ask him something but didn't try to catch his attraction right then, thinking I would have enough time to catch up with him before he got to where he was going. He seemed intent on getting to wherever it was, as I had to hurry once the gate opened just to keep up.

As I was closing the gap, I saw Koju looking into K-wing's day-room through the windows facing the corridor, then taking a turn into the wing's open door. Suddenly having a sudden horrible suspicion as to what Koju might be up to, I sped up and entered the wing scant seconds behind him.

Officer King must have been making a round of the wing, as the quarterdeck was empty and the officer's station door closed with no one in it. I could hear the sounds of the cards slapping down on to the steel table bolted to the floor of the day-room, and the laughter and chatter of the card players there.

I stepped further onto the wing where I could see into the day-room, and saw that Koju was already approaching the card table at which Michael sat. He was facing the doorway with his back towards the outside windows that looked out over the area between K and L-wings, the other three players filling in the sides of the table's square.

I had hoped to catch Koju before he got to the day-room, in order to talk with him and see what he had on his mind, and perhaps divert his attention. I saw now that it was too late for any of that, for as Koju moved closer to the card table, he pulled out the butcher's knife that he had concealed in the waistband of his pants. Looking at Michael, who was still unaware of his presence, he said, "You killed my partner...."

At the sound of Koju's voice, Michael looked up saw him and the knife he held, and froze. The player to Michael's right also looked up and saw the knife Koju had; he got up suddenly, the folding chair clattering to the floor behind him, and held his hands toward Koju to show that he was unarmed and wanted no part of what was going to take place. As he scuttled sideways, away from Koju's approach, the other two players (who had their backs to Koju) turned, saw the knife and scurried away from the table, all three going past me in their hasty exit.

Michael was left alone at the table to face Koju. "I didn't kill Boss, Sonny did," he said, looking around and realizing everyone had deserted him. His only avenue of escape was past Koju and the knife, to get to the day-room door leading out of the wing. Koju replied, "You helped him, don't you deny it... I didn't come here to talk."

As Michael got up and tried to run, Koju moved forward quickly to block his escape, and stabbed him in the chest. I don't know whether it was fear or shock, but Michael didn't even put up much of a struggle for his life as Koju repeatedly plunged the blade into his upper torso. His lifeless form fell to the floor and it was over in seconds, the blood spilling from his wounds forming a small pool around his body.

Stooping down, Koju stuck his finger into the blood, sucking the blood off before remarking, "Too sweet... the punk always had too much sugar in his tank." He wiped his hand and the knife on Michael's clothing to remove the blood before sticking the knife back into his waistband, then turned and walked out of the day-room and off K-wing, returning to T-wing to dispose of the knife.

I had left scant seconds ahead of Koju, not wanting him to see me now. The killing had been done so quickly and smoothly that no one knew what had happened other than the other prisoners in the K-wing day-room at the time. Also I figured that someone must have told Koju about Michael's little gesture of sticking his finger into about Boss's blood that night in the gym, as well as the comment he had made. I passed through the gates, and was almost at the library door before I heard the slamming of doors and the sound of keys turning in the locks of the wing doors behind me.

Michael's body made the trip back to Miami, where his mother read his last letter to her to those attending the service. The letter was also published in the black newspaper there.

Koju was locked up under investigation for Michael's death later that day. Two days later, as Sonny was being escorted up the corridor going to the prison investigator's office concerning Boss's death, Frank T came off the wing and tried attacking Sonny with a knife. The attack failed, in part because Sonny, who was in handcuffs, spotted Frank T coming with the knife and took off running down the corridor, making good use of his long legs.

Frank T's pursuit of Sonny to catch and kill him was cut short by one of the Pensacola crew who had been out in the corridor mopping (but really in order to see Sonny as well as to keep an eye out for such an attempt made on his life). After Sonny passed him, the mopper from Pensacola spilled out the buckets of soap water across the corridor, causing Frank to slip and fall, and allowing Sonny to escape with only minor injuries.

By this time the prison administration had had enough. They locked up all of the Pensacola faction and most of Boss's remaining crew, and then started shipping them out to different prisons around the state to break up whatever was going on. They transferred Sonny to the flattop at the Rock, as he was to be charged with Boss's murder.

Gangster, Sugar Bear and California went to prisons down south, while Frankie went to Tomoka in Daytona Beach. The Pensacola crew were sent to prisons in north Florida. After the transfers, the prison quieted down somewhat, the leaders of the black factions deciding to share control of the prison's black market activities. It would remain to be seen how well that would work out.

Frank T was back in confinement for the assault on Sonny. My release date was approaching rapidly and I was busy training a new cook for staff kitchen, while also getting everything together for my release. I still made time to go see Frank T and Koju; I would carry them books and care packages of smoke and canteen, stocking them up on all of it as I wouldn't be around much longer. I gave Frank T a lot of my books on the culinary arts and magazines on fine cuisine.

Frank was on S-wing, third floor, south side, and Koju was on P-wing, third floor, north side. I would sit in front of Koju's cell and we would smoke weed and talk. He told me, "I saw you come on K-wing that morning... I thought you'd come to try and talk me out of it."

"The thought had crossed my mind. However, by the time I got there, it was too late... Nor do I believe I could have talked you out of killing him, for what he did to Boss," I replied. I didn't say anything about how pointless Michael's killing had been, or that he had been a victim of others' manipulation, as Koju's antipathy towards Michael wouldn't have permitted him to acknowledge it. Koju's loyalty to and friendship with Boss demanded that someone should pay for his death. However, I did ask,

"Why Michael and not Sonny?"

"If I had known Frank T was going to fuck it up and not kill Sonny, I would have done Sonny and Let Frank have Michael. Sonny's the one I really wanted, and the only reason I let Frank have him is because Boss was his fall partner. Now I wish I hadn't let it go like that. I should have done Sonny..."

I made no mention of Frankie's hoard of notes from Sonny, or their contents, as it would have served no purpose other than to let Koju know that he had been played, just like everyone else. Only three people knew parts of the whole story, and what the truth might be about what had taken place: Sonny, Frankie and I.

Of the first two, I didn't know who was playing and manipulating whom. Was Frankie playing and manipulating Sonny's emotions to get him to kill Boss for him, or was Sonny manipulating Frankie in order to get where he needed to be to take Boss out? Or did Sonny really care that deeply for Frankie? What I did know was that the two had worked together to bring it about.

Michael had been played by both, using his resentment against Boss, and his illusion of being something he was not, and never could be, to set Boss up and then betray him by leaving him defenseless on the night in the gym. They had also played Boss when they saw that his love for Michael was his weakness and vulnerability, exploiting it to isolate and take him down.

The entire prison had been played by the two of them; a move of expert misdirection. The prisoners all believed Sonny had killed Boss behind the slap, which, while true, wasn't even part of the whole story behind the killing. I doubt Koju would have believed me even if I had told him all I knew or suspected now about the entire matter, as he wouldn't credit sonny or Frankie with being that cunning or devious. It made me wonder whether we can ever truly know the people we think we know, or whether we are taken in by the façade they present to us, believing what we want to believe about them.

I told Koju and Frank T that I would keep in touch with them after my release. I don't know if Frank believed me, but he agreed to keep in touch, while Koju was a little more pessimistic saying, "Yeah, if I had a nickel for every time someone has told me that in here, I could buy me a helicopter to fly me out of here."

"You can believe it this time..."

"When I see it..." Neither of us wanted to make an issue of it with so little time remaining before my release, so we left it at that.

Mr. Curtis, the food service director, told me, "If you ever want to come live in Jacksonville, I'll provide the financial backing for you to open a fine dining establishment, for a partnership interest."

I thanked him for the thought and told him I would keep it in mind for the future, which was a lie, as I couldn't wait to get back to Los Angeles, smog and all.

Mimi had sent me a release package of clothing items, unisex, as the prison wouldn't let me leave dressed as a woman. Which was just as well, as it would be months before my hair would be long enough to be styled properly, and until then, I would have to remain with the boy look or wear wigs.

I gave away some of stashes I had scattered around, ensuring Koju's paramour Ms. Ricky would have enough to take care of both of them for a while. I also told those holding stashes for me to keep them, and just send Koju and frank T something. I knew that one or two, like Nubby, might actually do it, while the rest would forget about it the instant I left; I wasn't all that concerned about it.

The morning of my release, Jo brought two limos full of escorts, male and female, from the Jacksonville branch office, who accompanied Ken, Mimi and her to the prison to pick me up. On the way out of the prison the warden shook my hand and wished me luck, telling me that he appreciated the meals I had prepared for his staff and family, as well as the birthday for his daughter Rachel.

Outside in the parking lot, Mimi and Jo hugged me, Mimi saying, "You made it… I was so afraid you wouldn't ever come out of there." I looked for one other, but she was nowhere to be seen. I didn't feel my release was complete until I saw her.

"Where's Doris?" I asked.

"She's waiting for you at home. She's somewhat preoccupied right now, you'll see when you get there."

"Preoccupied with what?" I asked.

"Keep your blouse on, you'll see when you get there. This way I can be sure you won't jump on a plane for California right now," she replied.

"Oh, so you're holding her hostage to make me stay in Florida for a few days?"

"Just for a few days…. Now be a sweetheart and let's get the pictures you wanted, and get out of here."

Before we left, we took group pictures of the limos, escorts and me in the prison parking lot, with the unit wings looming in the background. I could hear the calls and whistles of the prisoners on the wings, who were looking out their windows at us out in the parking lot. As we were driving by P-wing, I had the drivers give a long blast of horns so Koju would know I was leaving.

We had a little celebration on the way to the airport, and when we arrived, Jo dismissed the limo drivers and escorts, passing out hundred dollar bills to them and promising there would be something extra in their pay checks the following week.

Mimi, Ken, Jo and I climbed abroad the Cessna, an eight passenger corporate model that Mimi had brought up. The pilot welcomed us aboard, and I looked at Mimi saying, "I thought you were going to be the pilot."

"Not today girlfriend… I flew us up here, Jerry can fly us back. We got some catching up and celebrating to do."

During the flight to Palm Beach County, we smoked some weed and drank a bit, but I didn't want to get too high as I felt this was going to be a long day. As the plane flew mover the Cleary ranch, I could see the big "Welcome Home" sign hung over the front of the house, and that the entire Cleary clan had shown up to welcome me home. We got into one of the golf carts when the plane landed, and Ken drove us to the main house, where I was greeted and given warm hugs by everyone.

The guest house where I usually stayed when at the Clearys' had been cleaned and readied for me; it had become my de facto residence, and they had kept it empty for me. I excused myself, got the few belongings which I had brought from prison to take at the guest house with me, as I wanted to clean up and have a bite to eat. Mrs. Cleary said, "Don't get too full. We're having a special dinner for you at the main house later…"

As Mimi, Ken, Jo and I neared the guesthouse, Doris came trotting up, meowing and rushing at my legs to brush against them. I stopped and picked her up, asking her, "Where have you been hiding?" She rubbed her face against mine before insisting on being let down; when I placed her back down, she trotted a few steps away and looked back at me, meowing. Mimi said, "It looks like she wants you to follow her."

Mimi had a secret smile on his face, so I knew there was something out there he wasn't telling me about Doris. So I bit, knowing it was the only way to find it whatever it was, saying, "Okay, just let me set my stuff down on the porch..."

"No, Ken and I will take it from here... You just follow Doris, I think she has something and wants you to see," Mimi said.

Curious now, I picked up the box I had set down, handed it to Ken, and followed Doris, who led me into one of the barns and to a spot behind some bales of hay. There, on the sweatshirt I had given Doris (when she visited me at the prison the year before) were three tiny kittens. Doris went to them and licked them before lying down so they could nurse. "Oh ho, I see you've been a busy girl, haven't you?"

I picked up the kittens one by one and looked at them as Doris watched. "They're beautiful... I imagine you expect me to support them, seeing that I don't see the father anywhere around," I joked, putting the last kitten down to where it could get nursed with the other two. The kittens' eyes weren't even open yet, so I knew from my studies they were only a few days old. I left Doris there with her kittens and returned to the guest house, where Mimi, Ken and Jo waited, Mimi with a grin for the secret of Doris's kittens, that she had kept from me.

We talked some more, then Mimi said, "We'll let you get settled in. The kitchen is stocked for you. We'll be up at the main house, when you finish here..."

"Yeah...," I agreed, "I want to make something to eat and wash the prison stink off me. I'll be up a little later..."

As they were leaving, Jo said, "Oh look", and I turned and saw Mimi open the door to let Doris in, holding a kitten in her mouth by the back of its neck. Doris didn't look left or right, taking the kitten straight into my bedroom (the door had been left open by me while putting my box of prison belongings there). When Doris put the kitten on the bed, Mimi laughed, saying, "Looks like she's moving the family in... she must know you're going to stay."

They and Doris left, the cat returning after a few minutes later with another kitten in her mouth, leaving it on the bed and going back for the third one. While she was gone, I checked the kitchen out and saw that it was well stocked - Mimi's brothers Kevin and Devlin must have remembered the butcher and specialty shops I had used when I had been here while Mimi was in hospital.

I began to prepare myself a snack, stopping to open the door for Doris when she returned with the last kitten and made one last trip, returning with the sweatshirt dragging alongside of her. She placed the sweatshirt into the closet then one by one brought the kittens there; she had taken over the closet as her nursery. I decided to take a shower before making the snack, and Doris stayed with her kittens in the closet as I showered.

Once finished, I dressed and went to the kitchen, where I prepared a light snack of buttered toast, peanut butter, sliced bananas and mayonnaise. As I was eating, Doris came in to investigate what I was doing, rubbing her face on my leg, so I got up and fed her some tuna with raw egg, and a bowl of cream.

Having finished my repast and followed by Doris, whose kittens were full and sound asleep, we went up to the main house to join everyone there. Mr. Cleary called me into the library, where we discussed what he had done with the monies I had invested with him. Doris climbed into my lap when I sat down, purring as I petted her.

Mr. C told me that the money had been invested for developing an apartment complex in the Los Angeles area, consisting of three hundred units. Then using the first development as collateral for financing, he had built a second apartment complex consisting of two hundred and seventy five units, leaving me with a minority interest in both, as well as in other properties he had bought for possible development in the future, or as investments.

The first apartment complex had been operating for over eighteen months, the second for over six months, the rentals being handled by a property management firm. Both complexes were at capacity, all units rented, and the return on investment was just starting to roll in. And I mean roll in, as these were high end units, gated, with security and all the amenities.

Mr. C explained to me, "We can both sell out now and get out with a decent profit, as we already have several officers on the table for the two complexes. Or we can wait a few years and sell out for four times as much, plus the properties would provide income the whole while. It's up to you, do we take the money and run, or do we wait? My advice is to wait… these are new units just coming onto line, and will be productive sources of income for many years to come."

As I nodded in agreement, he continued, "We have also bought an older apartment complex, which is centrally located in L.A. We're in the process of renovating them and converting them into condo units, which will take about a year to complete. Most of the units are already reserved with substantial down payments."

"Then I guess we wait," I agreed, before asking, "Where is all this money coming from, for all these projects? We certainly didn't put up that much?"

"Good… I was hoping you would ask about that… We're using other people's money other than our original investment, which we used to get the financial backing from the bank. Investment and financial groups, as well as the banks, loves a winner who is able to provide them with a good return on their money. You aren't hurting for money, as you haven't been spending any appreciable amounts in the past few years, and it has just been accumulating in your accounts. If I had known those escorts services, limos and modeling agencies were such cash cows, I would have started up a couple long ago."

"Let me know if you're still interested," I said, "as Jo wants to open branches in Tampa and down here in your neck of the woods. You can discuss details with her."

"I'll just do that," he replied.

It was time for dinner, and Mrs. C called us from the library to come eat. First, I had to take Doris across to the guest house so she could check up on her kitten, before coming back to the main house for the dinner and party which they had prepared to celebrate my release.

After the party at the main house, Mimi, Ken, Jo, myself and of course Doris retired to the guest house, where we smoked reefer, drank some Jack Daniel's Black Label, and talked. However, it wasn't long before I was feeling the effects and emotional toll of the long day, as my body remained adjusted to the rhythms of the prison. Therefore, we said our good nights with shared hugs, and I was left alone but for Doris and her kittens.

It was a while before I could drift off to sleep, thinking about everything which had transpired that day while reflecting on how lucky I had been and was. Doris would spend time with her kittens, and would curl up with me on the bed in between nursing duties.

Despite of going to bed late, my eyes automatically jolted open at 5.00 am, when the cell doors would normally be unlocked at the East Unit; mentally and physically, I was still on prison time. Knowing that I wouldn't be able to sleep, I got up and smoked a joint, played with Doris, put on a pot of coffee, and then jumped in the shower. Being able to take a shower whenever I wanted was a luxury I had missed while in prison; I made a mental note to take a bubble bath in the tub later when I got the chance.

I got dressed after my shower, feeling good to be able to wear a bra openly again, then going to the kitchen where I put food out for Doris, including some extra raw eggs since she was nursing the kitten. I also left the sliding glass door open so that she could come and go as she wanted.

I got a large cup of coffee, and then prepared my own breakfast. Dicing tomatoes, onions, green peppers, mushrooms and jalapeno peppers with minced garlic, I browned them in butter in the skillet. I left a few tablespoons of the mixture in the skillet before cracking some eggs into it so that more flavor would be incorporated into the albumin of the egg as it cooked. Then I made hash browns in another skillet and got some toast before sitting down to eat.

I had a lot of vegetable mixture left over, as well hash browns, for I wasn't used to cooking for one person. I left them on the stove to keep warm, thinking that Mimi or Jo might show up hungry. After washing the dishes I was at loose ends, so decided to make up some bread and cakes. Before long, I had everything ready, and was waiting for the bread dough to rise while the cakes were in the oven baking. The cakes were "Chocolate Banana Nut", one of my innovations.

Mimi arrived a couple of hours later, informing me that Ken was in class. He continued, "Sure can tell when you're home. Whatever it is smells delicious." I prepared her an omelet, toast and hash browns, then having to fix Jo some when she showed up, having just awakened a short time ago.

I mentioned to Jo what Mr. C had said about the escort service limos, and modeling agencies, and she jumped right on it. It looked as though we were about to open a couple of more branches in Florida and perhaps elsewhere. Jo would be leaving the next day, first to Jacksonville then back to L.A., to set everything in motion and take care of other matters, some for the company and some for me.

I stayed at the Cleary Ranch for almost two weeks, getting used to freedom, getting my bearings and also waiting for Doris's kittens to get big enough to be flown to California. I had already decided to keep one of the kittens while Mimi claimed the other two; I knew she would have to come to California to get them once they had been weaned.

I didn't want to drive my car out to California. After checking it out on the local roads, I decided that it could certainly move, and would fit well out in California, having all the bells and whistles. I just didn't want to drive all the way with Doris and kittens. Therefore, I had the car and the original engine shipped to L.A. on my first week out, arranged to be there when I arrived. I told Jo to put the original engine in storage.

Mr. C's corporate jet would be flying Doris, the kittens and me to L.A. In a way, I hated to leave the ranch and the Clearys, as this had become my home and family. Nonetheless, I didn't want to remain in Florida, despite of all the good which had come of it, because Florida was and always would be the stuff of nightmares for me. I would take Cali over Florida, mudslides, earthquakes, wildfire and all.

I paid a visit to Chef Paul in Tampa, just to pay my respects, where he roped me into giving an impromptu class to his students on desserts, pastries and breads. He was beaming when I left the school to return to the ranch.

On the flight back to California, the kittens were in a shallow basket on the sweatshirt with Doris in attendance. She split her time between them and my lap. Jo met me with my car at the airport, and I handed her the basket with the kittens and Doris while I carried the two bags of clothes and what not I had obtained in Florida since my release. I placed it in the car's backseat, telling Jo, "You drive," while taking Doris and the basket of kittens from her. I explained to her that, "Doris gets nervous if anyone else but me holds her babies."

"Sure, just don't sit on your photos," she said, indicating the large envelope on the front passenger's seat.

"Are those the one's we took at the prison?" I asked.

"Yep... with the enlargements you requested. I didn't realize how ugly that place was until I saw the photos," she replied.

"If you think the outside is ugly, try living inside there for a while," I replied.

"No thank you. It was bad enough visiting you there."

Jo moved the envelope so I could get into the car with the basket of kittens and Doris, then handed me the envelope before going around to the driver's seat. After getting in, Jo said, "This car is sweet. I wouldn't mind having one of these," and started it up.

"Well this is the AM version of it," I replied.

"AM? What's that?"

"After Mimi... Mimi had a lot of work done on the car. The engine you put in the storage is the original engine."

"I didn't put it in storage. The place I leased for you has a two-car bay, so I just had them put it in one of them. I'd still like to have one like this though. I like the power and the way it handles," she replied.

I made a mental note to start looking for another 63 Sport Fury model for Jo as I pulled the photos out of the envelope and glanced through them, before sliding them back into the envelopes. Jo had gotten 8" by 10" enlargements as I had requested.

"The condo I leased also has an option to buy. It has three bedrooms. I figured you would convert one of them into an office. It has the chef's kitchen you insisted on as well. I had my assistant arrange to have all your stuff in storage moved into the condo. It's all there waiting for you. It's also pet friendly, so there won't be any problems about the cats," Jo said.

"Thanks for handling all this for me," I replied.

"Por Nada, as they say out here. It doesn't even begin to cover what you've done for me," she said.

The condo was a corner ground floor unit. Jo parked the car and grabbed the luggage, telling me, "You have enough with the photos and the cats," opening the door and maneuvering past the stack of boxes scattered around inside. I took the basket of kittens into the large master bedroom and set it down, letting Doris out to start exploring her new home. As did I, spotting the large kitchen area with its centre stations, breakfast bars and the full accoutrements of range, stove and convection oven, as well as the large reach-in cooler, walk-in freezer and plenty of counter space for preparing food.

"You did say there was an option to buy?" I asked Jo.

"Yes, I figured once you saw its kitchen you would want to, so I had put it in the agreement," she replied.

"Then exercise the option. I won't be able to find a setup this good until I'm able to build my own."

"I was going to buy it for corporate purposes anyways, if you didn't want it," she replied.

Jo's assistant had stocked some food staples so I was able to put some food and milk out for Doris. I opened the closet in the master bedroom, Doris watching me as I slid the basket of kitten inside. The kittens' eyes were open now. They were still having a lot of problems with coordination, but Doris was an attentive mother, and they were getting pretty frisky.

Jo and I left the condo, and I drove Jo back to the escort service offices. Jo informed me on the way that, "Chef M. has been calling regularly. I told him you would be back today. There's a welcome home party for you scheduled for 8 p.m. at the Hollywood Restaurant. It appears your deserts have really been missed."

"You going to be there?" I asked.

"Are you kidding? Free gourmet food and lots of cute honeys, I don't get that every day," she replied.

"You want me to pick you up?"

"No, I'll drive my own jalopy... I'm hoping I won't be leaving there alone," she said.

I dropped Jo off at the escort services offices, which were only about a mile as the crow flies from the condo. I drove back to the condo to be greeted by Doris, who wanted to go outside. I brought her back inside when she finished her business, and made up a litter box for her as I did not want her going outside till she was familiar with the place.

At the welcome home party at Chef M's restaurant that evening, he asked me, "How soon do you think you can come and begin working?"

"It will take me a couple of days to unpack and get settled in. Why?" I asked.

"Because ever since you left for your unexpected vacation, I've got nothing but inquiries from the customers as to when I was going to get you back... And since word got out you'd be returning, I've gotten bunches of calls wanting to know when you will start work again."

"Don't you have a party and dessert chef?" I asked.

"Yes, but not like you. He never had your touch or feel for it," he replied.

"I might have lost my touch," I said.

"Oh bull, that's like Michelangelo forgetting how to paint. That kind of touch you never lose."

"Well, give me a couple of days and I'll give you a call and let you know when I'll start," I said.

I was actually eager to begin, as I had been missing work. However, I knew that if I didn't unpack first, get settled and stock my own kitchen, I might not get a chance to do later, since I had a tendency to get involved with work and lose track of things.

"Oh, and you will be in for a treat. I've developed a lot of new recipes in the time I've been gone," I told him.

"I can't wait to see what you've come up with, but be sure to include the Double Chocolate Devil's Food Cake with the strawberries and whipped cream. The customers have been hounding for that one, because no one can duplicate its taste," he said.

"I have others which will match that one," I replied.

"I bet you have. Now enjoy the party, we will discuss your salary when you return to work," he concluded.

I returned to work at Chef M's restaurant four days later. It would have been sooner, but the financial manager Mr. C. had placed me with prior to my going to prison insisted on giving me a full accounting of everything. I had done quite well over the past three years, since a lot was coming in and little was going out except investments, which were showing good returns. I also had to sign a lot of documents. There are a lot of responsibilities which go with having money.

I mailed copies of the 8" by 10" photos of me and the escorts to Koju, Frank T and Mr. Lewis, to let them know I hadn't forgotten about them and for Mr. Lewis to post them in the library for the other prisoners to see.

The day before my scheduled official return to work at Chef M's restaurants, I spent the entire day and night there, first prepping everything and setting up the production line to turn out product: the dough and batter for bread, pastries and cakes.

Chef M had posted signs at the restaurants saying "Chef P is back", which resulting in the restaurant being booked solid for the next month. He couldn't keep enough on hand of the Double Chocolate Devil's Food, Chocolate Banana Nut, Chocolate Velvet Layer with Caramel, Fudge Caramel, Double Dutch and the variety of chocolate fruit tarts, even though I was working most days. The tricks I had learned in prison stood me well now. I was back to do what I loved, and loved doing it.

The Devil's
Courtyard

Part III

Epilogue

The years have flown by, and it's so hard to believe four years have passed since I was released from the Devil's Courtyard.

Doris is a grand dame now, who along with her daughter Koko, shares the home with Cordell and myself. Mimi and Ken have the other two from that first litter, who they have named Taffy and Sassy.

I had Doris and Koko spayed as soon as possible, because otherwise I knew I would be looking for homes to place kittens in all the time. Mimi learned that lesson when she had to find homes for ten kittens when Taffy and Sassy had their first litter, most of the Clearys now having at least one cat.

Ken, or I should say Doctor Ken, will soon be completing his residency, and will be going into OBY or OBG as a specialty (I could never get that part straight). Ken's siblings will either be graduating high school soon, or are already enrolled in college. Mimi says Ken is considering moving to California to open a practice here once his residency is completed, but I know he'll do well where ever he goes - the women will be lined up to have their babies delivered by Doctor Ken.

The escorts, limo and modeling agency businesses are doing extremely well, with branches up and down at the east and west coasts. Not that I am much involved in any of it, being just the figurehead/chairperson of the board. Jo is the chief executive officer, and has a good management team working with her to run the business, as does Mr. C. with the real estate developments and investments.

I bought the condo where I lived for the first year, then leased it to the Escort service PKM. Ltd. when I bought my first home and had the home renovated, as Mr. C. got me a good deal on the house. I now have homes and apartments in several cities: L.A., San Francisco, San Diego, and one overlooking the ocean in Malibu. Most of which are leased out, as we mostly stay in L.A. or the house in Malibu.

After six months at Chef M's restaurants, I opened my own bakery which had contracts with many of the area's finest restaurants for breads, deserts and pastries. Chef M. Arranged an exclusive contract for the Double Chocolate Devil's Food cake and other favorites, his restaurants carrying these as their signature desserts.

I also have a side business of providing special orders for birthday and wedding cakes delivered the day before the event, which is sometimes a task as I get orders from both coasts. The cakes are personalized for the person they are being prepared for, refusing to do traditional birthday or wedding cakes, beyond some of the decorations.

Before making the cakes, I find out which tastes (fruits and candies) are preferred by the recipient, and with wedding cakes, I try to blend and meld those of the bride and groom's together. My cakes are traditional in the sense that they are tiered, but that's where I do away with tradition; birthday and wedding cakes should be celebrations, not bland sweet concoctions.

Some of the employees at the bakery "Poison's Delights" are chefs in their own right, looking to perfect the pastry, bread and dessert aspect of their craft by working and learning from me. I never thought I would be a teacher, but here I am.

The problem with most is they are bound by the traditional way of doing things, crippling their creative spirit. They forget that traditional is just the baseline (the canvas if you will), to which we apply the paint of creativity. I encourage them to never be afraid to experiment or try something new, explaining that while good chefs go by tradition, great chefs are the cutting edge of culinary arts, leading where others follow, becoming the new tradition and baseline.

I visit with the Clearys during the holiday with Doris and Koko, and for the last couple of years with Cordell. Doris and Koko are always welcomed by Taffy and Sassy, and have their own family reunion. My de facto residence, the guest house, is always kept available for me.

I did get Jo the 63 Plymouth Sport Fury, which wasn't as easy as I had first thought it would be, as the aluminium engine block in those models had tendency to crack, resulting in many of the vehicles being disposed of. I eventually found one in fairly decent shape, sans the original engine.

I took both the cars (including mine) to an auto shop specializing in customizing cars, and told them to replicate the modifications Mimi had incorporated into mine onto the other. The paint scheme for Jo's however, was a baby blue metal flake with tan leather interior and seats. It cost quite a bit to have it done up like that, but it was worth it to show Jo my appreciation for her friendship and loyalty. The car was delivered to Jo at the escort service with a big ribbon and bow around it on her birthday, and she loves and takes special care of it, calling it "Honey catcher".

Over the past years, I have maintained contacts with Koju and Frank T. Koju got another life sentence added for Michael's killing, while the state dropped charges against Frank T for his failed attempt on Sonny's life. Both were transferred from the East Unit within eighteen months of my departure.

I ensure Frank has subscriptions to the culinary arts publications. He is always assigned as cook in the staff kitchen and/or diet cook at the prison he's at, and I send him money for extras. I also send money to Koju, plus packages of smoke delivered where he wants them. He insists on repaying me from the procedures of the sales, asserting his maleness. I don't argue the point, figuring men will be me.

Unfortunately, Koju also had a kidney failure and is on dialysis three times a week. He has to be housed at whatever prison providing the dialysis and its equipment (the prison contracts out the service, so the contractor and prison which houses and services the prisoners on dialysis changes). I do get in to visit him from time to time, which is usually when I'm in Florida on business or the holidays.

The intake procedures for the visitors at the prisons are sometimes tiresome, as my appearance befuddles the officers processing visitors. It takes them forever to figure out whom to have search me for contraband, male or female. There's nothing in their rule book to cover it. They get it done, but there's always a delay for the process while they scratch their heads and figure out what to do. I had to have an attorney talk to some people in central office about taking legal action, and the problem got resolved.

Surprisingly, Sonny was able to track me down, or rather his sister in Pensacola did. Jo called one day from the escort service, telling me, "Some lady out of Pensacola, Florida keeps calling here for you. She says to tell you it's for Sonny." I got her information from Jo, figuring they had used the escort service to track me down (Sonny knew about the escort service in L.A. and that I would be returning to California). I called the number Jo had given me, and was connected with Sonny's sister Mary.

I was curious as to what Sonny wanted, but I should have known… money and smoke, wanting to put the arm on me for both. After thinking it over, I said "Why not?" as we were still friends, his killing Boss not having changed that. However, what I had learned since about the killing did alter the nature of that friendship.

If Sonny hadn't tracked me down, I probably would never have gotten in touch with him, and still don't. All my dealings are with his sister, sending Mary $1,000 every six months along with a pound of smoke. I had people who do that kind of thing for living handle the delivery of smoke, as I did with Koju, as I didn't want to have anything to do with the packages themselves.

Florida had held me twice in the Devil's Courtyard, and I was not about to give them a third bite at the people. I learned you can't escape your past entirely; that you can run from it, but eventually it or its effects will catch up, and trip you at your vulnerable moments. It's far better to face it head on, learn from it, and go on. To avoid or deny it just leads to problems and grief later on down the line.

Unlike Koju, Sonny doesn't attempt to repay me; this was about what I had expected from him, knowing him like I do now. I believe it takes the load off Sonny's sister of having to look out for him, while also thinking if he can't survive off two pounds of smoke and $2,000 a year in prison, something is most definitely wrong. I let Mary know he would have to make it, as that would be it from me.

I once sat down and calculated that during the time I spent at the Unit the second time, there had been between forty five and fifty killings. At first you would think that so many killings in a three year period isn't so bad, until you recall this was among a prisoner population of a little over twelve hundred, with over four hundred of them locked in solitary confinement cells.

The experiences within the streets and prisons are a bile acid which erodes holes in your spirit, and if you are not very careful all your humanity will leak out like sand from a torn bag until you no longer recognize what you've become. Even if those holes are mended, the scars remain; the only things which will heal the wounded spirit are love, patience and time.

It wasn't until Cordell came along that I had the realization of how lonely and hurting I had been. I had filled my life with many positive things and yet beyond my few friendships like with Mimi, Ken, Chef M, the Cleary's and Jo, I had avoided relationships by thinking that love was for other people and not for someone like me. Nor I had been looking to get involved; I was too busy with work and school as I was attending college for veterinary science. I also volunteered a few days out of the week at the animal shelter, as I knew very well what it was like to be abused, cast away and left astray. I had satisfied myself with sex and the brief flings.

I met Cordell while attending college, taking courses in veterinary science while auditing other classes I found interesting. I didn't expect I would be able to get a license to be a veterinarian, not with my felony record. However, that couldn't prevent me from obtaining the knowledge required of one, or from putting it to use.

Cordell was a history professor at the university campus I attended, and I would sit in and audit his classes mainly because I loved to hear the sound of his voice. He has one of those rich rolling voices which carry you along on its tones, and it sent shivers down my spine and through me just listening him to teach.

I was leaving his class one evening when he called me back, "Ms. Marks could I speak with you a second before you leave?"

"Sure, Professor Hunt," I replied, while wondering how he had learned my name as it wasn't listed on his student roster. Sometimes the professor can be such prima-donnas about people who audit their classes.

He was putting his papers into a briefcase as the rest of the students left, some throwing curious glances my way. "I'll be with you in a sec. I just want to be certain I've gotten everything," before asking, "I certainly could use a cup of coffee and a bite to eat, would you care to join me at the study hall?" This was the name of the university's snack shop, where you could get juices, fresh coffee, pastries, sandwiches, burgers and fries. While eating you could also study for your next class as they didn't rush you.

"Okay," I said, curious as to where all this was leading to.

"How do you like the class so far?" he asked, as we walked out of the building, heading across the campus to the study hall.

"Fine, you're really an effective teacher," I said, not wanting to tell him it was his voice and not the lesson I came to class for.

"I've been noticing you in class for quite some time now and I was wondering if you would care to go out to eat and take in a movie with me sometime… like this weekend?" he asked tentatively.

I stopped walking, which caused him to stop as well. God, this was the awkward part of being a man and living as a woman; you didn't want things get off on the wrong foot by having them believe you to be a woman when you weren't, at least physically. You want to be upfront with them, yet wondering why it should matter at all to accept me as I am. The situation becomes even more difficult when you find yourself attracted to the person, as I was to Professor Hunt.

I looked down, not wanting to see his reaction when I told him, "Look, Professor Hunt... I'm not... I mean... you should know," stopping because I was flustered. He saved me, saying, "That you're not really a woman, but a transsexual? Yes, I was aware of that. A friend of mine is an acquaintance of Chef M, and when my friend was out here a few weeks back, he saw you in class and told me of you. Nor is it a problem for me. Is it a problem for you?"

Looking up at his face, I could see he was serious, I said, "Yes... I mean no... certainly I would be glad to go out with you this weekend. But I insist on preparing the dinner."

"I wouldn't miss it for the world. Shall we continue on to the study hall?" he said, smiling and offering me his hand, which I took.

Over iced lattes and sandwiches, I kept calling him 'Professor Hunt' which caused him to tell me, "We can't keep using surnames and titles with each other. You can call me by my first name, Cordell, or Cord if you prefer.

I laughed, saying "Cordell... Excuse me for laughing, but you're not what I picture when I hear the name Cordell."

"Oh, and what is this Cordell supposed to look like?" he asked.

"Tall, rangy, with aristocratic features, wind-blown hair and wearing one of those coats with leather patches at the elbows."

"I certainly miss the boat there...," he chuckled.

Cordell was short at 5'9", and stocky, and if you were in a generous mood, could be called ruggedly handsome, with brown hair and eyes. He looked like the longshoreman he had been as he worked his way through the college.

"And what do they call you, other than Chef P or Ms. Marks?" he asked.

"They call me Poison, or at least my friends do," I replied.

"Well I intend on being one of those. However, you don't look at all poisonous to me. Just how did you come by that name?" he asked.

"Actually, it's a nickname, and how I got is a long story. I'll save it for when we both know each other better," I replied.

"I'm looking forward to both," he replied.

"Both what?" I asked.

This man kept off balance. We talked for some time before he walked me to my car, which he admired as I gave him my address and phone numbers.

"What time should I be there on Saturday? I wouldn't want to be late for dinner on our first date," he said.

"Say about seven… wait a minute, what time does the movie start?" I asked.

"We can catch the late feature which starts about nine," he said.

"That should give us enough time for dinner then."

"I look forward to seeing you then at your place at seven."

"Me too… do you know where it is?" I asked.

"Born and raised in L.A. Only time I've been away is in the service and while attending college in 'Frisco."

"Then I'll see you at seven on Saturday," I said, and started the car up, yet still reluctant to go.

"Count on it…," he replied, as he turned and headed for his car parked in the section reserved for teachers.

While driving home I was strangely elated, but still leery of it all. I did not trust it to be what I hoped it would be, and was uncertain about it all. For the next couple of days I was on edge and distracted. On Saturday I got home early, took a long bubble bath. I had already prepped the meal: filet mignon cuts wrapped in rashers of bacon, whole baked potatoes with a sour cream (chives and green onion diced and mixed into it), rolls, corn and green beans.

And for the dessert was what I called a Flan Pie, flan being a Filipino desert, rich sugary thick egg custard which looked like yellow fudge, served chilled. I would bake the pie crust separately, and then pour the flan into the crust, sprinkling the top with cinnamon and brown sugar, putting it in the cooler to set. All in all, a light dinner that would leave us plenty of time to catch the movie.

Cordell showed up a little before seven, and I opened the door when he rang the doorbell, after putting the finishing touches on the dinner table. He was dressed casually. I had primped a little, as I couldn't decide what to wear, before settling on slacks and a blouse.

Looking around the house, he remarked, "This must cost a pretty penny to rent, how many bedrooms?"

"Five bedrooms, four bathrooms, two half baths, the requisite California pool and hot tub spa. I imagine it would cost a pretty penny to rent… come on in," I said.

"Don't tell me you own this?" he said, coming in and closing the door.

"Lock, stock and cats…," I replied, as Doris and Koko came to investigate the stranger in their territory.

"Maybe I should have become a cook myself instead of a teacher," he said.

"Go have a seat in the living room, while I get everything ready," I said. I just had to get everything on the table from the kitchen.

Cordell went into the living room and sat on the couch, followed by Doris and Koko, who were still curious about the stranger in their midst. Doris jumped up on the couch, checked Cordell out, and decided he was acceptable, plopping herself in his lap. Seeing that from kitchen where I was opening a bottle of wine, I said, "You'll have to pet her or she'll never go away."

"Oh, I don't mind, I like cats," he said, "they were always around the docks when I worked there."

We ate, talked and never did get to the movie, as Cordell spent the night. We dated steady for six months before Cordell's lease was up on his apartment. I had him movie in with me, as he spent more time and nights there than at his place.

During the holidays, I brought him to the Clearys. I had told Mimi about him during our phone conversations and she had talked with him a few times on the phone, yet this was her first time meeting him. She later asked me, "Where in the world did you find him? And a professor at that."

"I didn't... he found me... he's my keeper. This is what schooling will get you," I replied. Mimi was happy for me, and the Clearys approval of him, saying it was about time I found someone to settle down with.

Cordell turned out to be a fitness fanatic, working out with weights, jogging and doing laps in the pool. I had never been much for exercise, thinking I got enough exercise every day at work, although I swam in the pool every day and was still a trim 125 pounds.

We have been living together for over two years now. Sometimes at counseling sessions, the other trannies (transsexuals) would talk about sex change operations and ask me, "When are you going for it?" However, I'm a little bit afraid of the knife, thinking something might go wrong, having heard so many stories about the problems before and after. If I could do it and give birth to a child afterwards, I'd do it in a heartbeat, but that's not going to happen. I would like to, but I'm put off by all the complications.

Cordell loves me as I am, and the pressures haven't gotten to the point where I just have to have it done in order to become complete. When and if the time does come, then I will just have to take the plunge and get it done. But for right now, I'll keep on like I am, taking hormones and living as a woman.

Cordell and I did look into adopting a child, but in the States it's so difficult for a couple like us to be approved as adoptive parents. So, we took alternative routes, adopting a baby girl from China, and are just waiting on the paperwork to clear to bring her here to the United States.

Plus, since adoption in the States was such a problem, Mimi and Ken came up with the idea of using surrogate mothers. Mimi's sisters said they will donate the eggs, Ken and Cordell the sperm. Once impregnated, the surrogate mothers will live with the Clearys and us until they come to term, and turn the babies over to us when they are born.

It will cost some money, but it would be well worth it and still cheaper than trying to fight the system of bureaucracy, and less than our daughter cost us in China, as it required several trips and other expenses before we were approved, and there remained the paperwork to have the child brought here to America. Sometimes I think they should line up all the bureaucrats and run them off a cliff like lemmings.

Cordell and I figure on three children, and I am already interviewing nannies who will live with us. I intend being a hands-on mom, but I am also a business person with a business to run. I also have a part in running "Safe Harbors", which is a non-profit I started to provide a refuge for runaways and street kids to stay a night or however long they want to. It was currently housed in an old apartment complex Mr. C found for us, that we refurnished and remolded into efficiency units.

Mr. C is also on the Safe Harbors board, as is Jo, Chef M and Mimi. The kids know they can come there and stay without being hassled, and we have staff and counselors on hand. The idea is to provide them with a place of safety so they have the opportunity to find themselves and resolve their issues.

Some we are able to reconcile with their parents, and some we have attorneys who will submit emancipation papers pro bono with the courts for them, with Safe Harbors as guardian ad litem. There are also those we try to keep out of the system long enough for them to find a sense of direction and be given a chance of life.

The kids can stay a night or as long as they like, and we help them to find jobs, and enroll in regular schools, vocational trades and G.E.D. classes. I even give classes in culinary arts so they know how to prepare food for themselves, and I've also given scholarships to a few who have shown a penchant for it. What's money for if you don't do some good with it? We don't use state or federal monies or grants, so we don't have the bureaucratic hoopla to go through or them looking over our shoulders at everything we do.

Our attorneys and the ones who do pro bono work for the kids also ensure that we are doing everything legally and in keeping with the child welfare laws and labor laws. We have even started getting referrals from children's services and the courts.

Cordell asked me why I keep the picture of the escorts and myself standing in front of East Unit on the day of my release framed in the library. I told him, "To remind myself where I came from, and where I still might be if someone hadn't cared enough about me by providing me with the opportunity to be something other than that."

The Devil's Courtyard will always be there, only we don't have to be in it. Even with those the rest of society had given up on, I had lived with the debris of their humanity, and in spite of their wounds, pain and scars, they were still human beings - with all the foibles, potentials and failings of their inherent humanity.

I can't take away the fact that there were some who were beyond salvaging, too far gone into themselves or the system to ever find the road out. I can't do anything for those, but I will do all I can to keep the children from falling prey and finding themselves in the Devil's Courtyard, with no way out and no hand to reach out to them.

I am by no means perfect and I never will be, as my humanity will keep me away from it. However, I will do the best I can with what I have, to be as good as I can be. Which is all any of us can do...

THE END

About the Author

I've spent the majority of my life, from childhood to the present, either on the streets or locked up in jails and prison. This life and these experiences granted me the unique vision and keen insight into the disenfranchised outcasts of society-sparing neither the system nor the individual.

Becoming a writer by default, since it was the only means to succor the shredded, tattered remnants of humanity and ever-present lure into despondency, I resisted temptation to surrender into desolation and despair and bring the readers a sense into what it is to be one such as I.

The state raised me but did not bury me so that I would live and tell the stories that need to be told. And until the day when we all shall meet, I pray you find what it is inside that you are seeking.

Printed in the United States
By Bookmasters